A MAN AND HIS HOBBY

The man hummed "Whistle While You Work" as he dug. Every so often, he'd stop and spare a glance at the body in the basement. Its eyes bulged out like Ping-Pong balls.

After he completed his preparations, the man stepped over to the body and took a wallet from its back pocket. If you killed someone, he thought, you ought to know who he was for your records.

He knew that if any shrinks ever got hold of him, they'd say he was crazy. No. Mentally ill, that's what they'd say. Or they'd lay some jawbreaker technical name on him. No one was just plain crazy anymore.

Cops, on the other hand, would say he was just a cold-blooded killer who got his rocks off watching people die at his hands. That wouldn't be right, though. He felt good afterward, but pleasure wasn't what drove him. He didn't like to think about the real reason. What he liked to think about was never getting caught. . . .

THE CONCRETE INQUISITION

Sometimes a cop's job is pure murder. Other times, it's a lot more twisted than that.

THE CONCRETE INQUISITION

Joseph Flynn

A SIGNET BOOK

SIGNET
Published by the Penguin Group
Penguin Books USA Inc., 375 Hudson Street,
New York, New York 10014, U.S.A.
Penguin Books Ltd, 27 Wrights Lane,
London W8 5TZ, England
Penguin Books Australia Ltd, Ringwood,
Victoria, Australia
Penguin Books Canada Ltd, 10 Alcorn Avenue,
Toronto, Ontario, Canada M4V 3B2
Penguin Books (N.Z.) Ltd, 182–190 Wairau Road,
Auckland 10, New Zealand

Penguin Books Ltd, Registered Offices:
Harmondsworth, Middlesex, England

First published by Signet, an imprint of New American Library,
a division of Penguin Books USA Inc.

First Printing, June, 1993
10 9 8 7 6 5 4 3 2 1

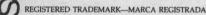
PUBLISHER'S NOTE
This is a work of fiction. Names, characters, places, and incidents either are the product of the author's imagination or are used fictitiously, and any resemblance to actual persons, living or dead, events, or locales is entirely coincidental.

This book is dedicated
with love and affection to
Catherine, Caitie, Mom, Dad,
Mary, Ellen, Steve,
and
Marie Stone.

ACKNOWLEDGMENTS

One of the great joys of writing this book was to discover how many people were so generously willing to share their time and expertise with me. My heartfelt thanks go to Judee Zydowsky, CPD; Steven Kastenbaum, D.O., Ph.D.; Renee Cohen, Ph.D.; Patricia I. Meagher, American Academy of Opthalmology; William R. Nunery, M.D.; C. W. Cox, Jr., B.C.O., F.A.S.O.; Laura Hammond, R.N.; J. T. Flynn; Frank Witt; and the staff of the Beverly Hills Public Library.

Author's note: Two of the Chicago neighborhoods mentioned in this book, The Wedge and Hardrock Park, are as fictional as the characters who inhabit them.

1

Michael "Doc" Kildare's new glass eye was really plastic. Acrylic, to be precise. The same stuff they use for airplane windshields and storm doors. That didn't matter. He would have hated the fucking thing if it were a diamond.

He pushed it into his vacant left eye socket.

Doc's real left eye, so deep-dark blue, so wonderfully sharp it practically had X-ray vision, had gotten shot out when he was still Sergeant-of-Detectives Kildare of the Chicago Police Department. Now he was just an ex-cop, and he sat alone in the office of Gunther Dietz, ocularist, practicing how to put his prosthesis in and take it back out again.

He felt no better with the thing in than if the surgeons had just closed the wound and sewn a button on, like goddamn Little Orphan Annie.

He popped the prosthesis from the enucleated socket. Doc looked at his disfigured reflection in Gunther's mirror, and he wanted to kill somebody. Maybe himself.

The thought brought a bitter smile. What was the point of suicide when there was nobody left to care? Moving his scarred eyelids apart, he worked the prosthesis back into place again.

His shrink had told him not to dwell on it, but as he stared at the reflection of the plastic marble in his head he thought for the millionth time about the raid that had cost him his eye and his job.

The whole thing had started when one of his snitches, Bobby Ro, came to him with a new idea in law enforcement.

"Confidential Informant Credit," Bobby said. "What do you think?"

"What's that? A layaway plan for snitches?"

"Hey, Doc. Have a little respect. Lookit where I brought you."

The two men were having drinks at Fullwell's. It was the priciest new bar on Rush Street. They clipped you six bucks for a beer, but threw in all the atmosphere you could stand. Then after you walked out the door, depending on how your expensive buzz had left you feeling, you could stroll a few short Gold Coast blocks to either the city's most elegant brothel or Holy Name Cathedral.

Wherever Bobby Ro planned to go next, he didn't intend to get there on foot. His new black Jaguar XJS gleamed in the crisp autumn night outside the window where they sat. Bobby saw Doc looking at the car.

"Nice, huh?"

"You hit the Lotto, Bobby? I'm surprised I didn't see your name in the paper."

"Bought me a house out in Barrington Hills, too."

"Yeah? You pay for it with some of that Confidential Informant Credit?"

"Paid cash."

Doc drank his six-dollar beer straight out of its imported bottle. He looked at Bobby, all five-foot-five, hundred and twenty-three pounds of him. He was a Chicago-born Puerto Rican, twenty-two years old, and he ran small errands for a Colombian named German Aldena. The only reason he'd gotten the job was because the Colombian had married Bobby's knockout teenage sister, Maria Rosario.

Doc had caught Bobby delivering half a key of coke to a party thrown by a trader from the Mercantile Exchange. He'd been Doc's snitch ever since.

Now, he was buying British cars and suburban mansions.

Doc said, "Okay, let's hear about this idea of yours."

"I got it reading *The Wall Street Journal*."

"Come on, Bobby."

"Yeah, really. It was this story on the sale of intractables."

"What?"

"You know, things you can't put your hands on. Like ideas—or information."

"The word is 'intangible.' "

"Like I said. Anyway, they was talking about one company runs a clean business can sell another company a credit to run its business twice as dirty. I mean, for pollution and shit like that. Or two guys're are putting up skyscrapers, see, and one doesn't build as high as the law allows, so he sells his air credit to the other guy so he can go above the law. You get all this?"

Doc rolled his eyes and ordered another beer on Bobby's tab.

"Just explain what it has to do with you."

"Well, I got some information you really oughta know."

"So tell me."

"I mean, this is big-time."

"How much?"

"Not money, man. Credit."

"For what?"

"For something I ain't been caught for yet, but still might be."

Doc glanced at the car again.

"See," Bobby said, "my problem is, what I got to tell is only good for a little while, and then it's too late. So if I wait to see if I get caught to tell you, I might have nothin' left to trade. So what I thought was, I tell you now and if I need it get credit later."

"Confidential Informant Credit."

"Yeah, why not? The *Journal* says we're livin' in the Information Age."

"And if you don't get caught, I get a freebie."

"That, plus knowin' you helped me retire honest."

"You're gonna retire? At your age? Must be some ripoff you pulled. You sure you got something big enough to trade for that?"

Bobby smiled. "Put you on the front page of the *Trib*, man. Politicians be linin' up to shake your hand."

"Maybe put a bad guy away just to ice the cake?"

"The baddest, man."

Doc stared at him, and Bobby's smile only got wider.

"Okay, Bobby. Your credit application's on the table. Let's see how you fill it in."

The planning session had to be fast. Doc had wanted to limit the information to the fewest people possible: him, the eight guys on his team, and his boss, Lieutenant Vince DiGiuseppe. Vince overruled him and said the Captain had to know. The Captain included a token fed from DEA, for reasons that actually made sense. Even with all that, they still got the whole thing laid out in twenty-four hours.

Armando Guzman himself was coming to town, and nobody wanted to miss him.

Guzman was a Medellin big boy, one of the famous "extraditables." According to Bobby, though, he'd fallen into deep shit with his fellow *coqueros* and had to make some fast vacation plans. He was on his way to Spain, but he had to stop in the States first to pack a few bags.

With money. As Bobby had put it, he wasn't coming to Chicago to shop for socks at Sears. Guzman was cleaning out his pipeline so no one could rip off his cash.

Bobby'd given Doc the location of a *caleta*, a stash house, and the time Guzman would be there. Bobby had reminded Doc that Guzman wasn't the type you took alive. He'd also added that his brother-in-law, German, would be on hand, and don't spare any bullets on his account, either.

The treachery among in-laws had been what convinced Doc that Bobby Ro wasn't just jerking him around. And if everything worked out right, Doc was determined that Bobby would receive a get-out-of-jail pass for anything short of murder. Even then, it'd depend on who he'd killed.

The *caleta* was a rundown cinderblock house sitting alone on an open, weed-filled lot between two factories on Ogden Avenue. Behind the house was an alley. Along the far side of the alley ran a block-long fence that enclosed a giant scrapyard, which held a mountain range of discarded car and truck tires.

Doc and Detectives Junior Little, Steve Petrovsky, and Frank Wallis waited in a '65 Chevy with heavily tinted windows, parked around the corner at one end of the block. They were the guys who'd be going inside.

Vince, DEA Special Agent Starling, and three other detectives from Doc's team were parked in two cars around the far corner of the block. They'd take the perimeter of the house.

The junior members of the team, Detectives Janet Foxx and Burt Levitt, were hiding in the scrapyard opposite the rear door of the *caleta*, in case anyone climbed over the fence.

Eight squad cars of uniforms would pull up to block off the street and the alley; all they'd been told was to be ready for anything.

Everybody's radio was set to channel 5, the car-to-car frequency. They weren't going to communicate through an operator and let the whole world in on the raid. When everyone was in place, they sat and waited for Guzman.

"You know," Wallis said, "just once I wish we'd go charging into one of these things and have the assholes outgunned."

He held a pump-action shotgun between his legs. Junior Little smiled and shook his head.

"Frank, I wanna be outta town the day they turn your ass loose with an Uzi."

The argument revolved around a standard cop gripe. Everyone from dopers to drag queens was arming for World War III, and the department still limited them to handguns and shotguns.

"Least they give us raid hats," Junior said, twirling a baseball cap with CPD on the front, "so we won't shoot each other."

They talked to keep from getting too cranked up, and to pass the time. The next topic was how much money Guzman was coming to get. Everybody figured it'd be enough that he'd have to bring a step-van to hold it.

When the Colombian rolled past at three A.M. he was in a two-ton truck. *If Guzman planned to fill that thing with money,* Doc thought, *this was going to be a motherfucker.* The truck turned into the alley that would take it behind the house.

The plan was to hit fast and hard, but the timing had to be just right. Doc started his engine and wheeled around the corner onto Clybourn. He did twenty miles per hour. He wove back and forth over the double yellow line. If any lookout was going to spot them, he'd see a drunk who forgot to turn his lights on.

Doc had Junior radio the contact to Vince. Then he had him talk to Foxx in the scrapyard. She whispered back that the truck had stopped in back of the house and three men had gotten out of it. Two other men had opened the steel-covered back door of the house and were now looking around, checking things out. Four of the men had automatic weapons. At the back of the truck, two of the ones who'd just arrived were having trouble getting its doors open; the third was cursing them. No one was going into the house yet.

Doc wanted them all in one place. He didn't want to rush the ones outside and get caught in a crossfire if anybody else was still in the house.

He pulled the Chevy over to the curb. Wallis got out and, maintaining their cover as drunks, peed noisily in the doorway of the building across the street from the *caleta*. He zipped up fast when Foxx reported that the men had opened the truck doors and were walking toward the house.

Doc keyed his handset and whispered, "We're going in."

Wearing Kevlar body armor and carrying their

weapons openly, the four detectives raced silently across the front yard of the house. Doc whipped around the rear corner of the structure just in time to throw his shoulder into the back door before it closed.

His momentum carried both him and the man on the other side of the door to the floor. A split-second later a hail of bullets scorched the air over his head. A return shotgun blast roared from behind him. Despite all the explosive racket, Doc heard someone groan—practically right in his ear. The man he'd knocked down was regaining his senses, and he had a machine pistol in his hand.

The guy never got a chance to use it. A fusillade of automatic weapons fire cleaved his head open, and a round grazed Doc's left shoulder. Doc rolled to his right and took cover behind a packing crate.

Somebody wanted him bad, because they fired right through the crate. He backed up as fast as he could, until he bumped into a wall. Bullets, jagged pieces of wood, and bits of green confetti exploded all around him.

He got a moment's reprieve when the sonofabitch who was shooting at him had to change his clip. Doc bounced to his feet, firing as fast as he could to give himself cover. There were only two Colombians left alive, Guzman and German Aldena. They crouched on opposite sides of another crate kitty-corner from him, out of the line of fire from the doorway.

Doc cut Aldena down as the Colombian was trying to seat a magazine in his AK-47.

Then, before Doc could swing the barrel of his Walther, he saw Guzman's gun—a pistol—pointed at him, and he knew he'd shot the wrong guy first. He tried to turn and duck.

Guzman's first round missed, but the bullet fragmented against the cinderblock wall next to Doc's head and he felt a red-hot lance of pain as a ricochet shredded his left eye into a leaking bag of jelly. Guzman fired again, and the round hit Doc in the middle of his Kevlar vest.

As he fell, losing consciousness, he noticed that the top of the crate he'd sheltered behind had been blown off. It was filled with money.

"Look over here."

Doc jumped at the sound of the voice. Gunther Dietz had entered the room with an eyeglass case in his hand. He saw that Doc had the prosthesis in. Doc turned his face. It didn't help a bit that Dietz's own eyes—brown—were bright and clear, and looked like they could see through a bank vault.

"Look up," Dietz said.

Doc looked up.

"Look down . . . and follow my finger."

Doc tracked the finger. Dietz was experienced enough to know when his finger would go out of Doc's limited field of vision, and it skated just along the boundary.

Dietz and all the doctors had told Doc that only a small rim of the visual field on his left side was lost to him, but it sure as hell seemed that his "blind spot" was everything to the left of his nose.

"Good motility," Dietz said. "The prosthesis is tracking well. I think we've got the right one this time. How does it feel?"

"Like a cue ball."

Dietz laughed.

"A distinct improvement. Last time it was a pine cone, I believe."

"Can I see the glasses, Gunther?"

The ocularist handed the case to Doc. He took out a pair of tinted sunglasses and put them on. In the fluorescent light of the office the tint on the lenses was a light gray. The color didn't stop Doc from seeing clearly, but the reflection in the mirror showed it was enough to disguise the goddamn marble.

The only way you could tell was to get nose-to-nose, and Doc wasn't going to let anyone get that close.

"The lenses'll get darker outside, right?"

Dietz nodded. "Yes, they'll polarize. Are the frames comfortable?"

"Yeah, they're fine."

"Okay, that's it then. I'll see you next Monday for your checkup."

Doc got up to leave, still looking at himself in the mirror. The sunglasses had a nice style. *He* might know he was a cyclops, but no one else had to be the wiser.

"Mr. Kildare."

Doc looked at Dietz.

"The best way to adjust is to just let it happen, let the body make its accommodations. You can help that along if you find something else to focus your time on."

"Easy for you to say, Gunther."

There *was* one thing for Doc to think about. Getting his hands on fifteen of the forty-five million bucks they'd taken away from Armando Guzman.

2

"My boy's missing," Glenna Handee said.

The cop looked up from the report he was writing and saw a thin woman with a lined face. She sat down at his desk.

"Scuse me," he said.

"You've got to help me find Jerry."

The cop heard a touch of country in her voice, and despite her hard-looking eyes, he could see she was scared. Scared, but keeping it under control.

"I'm not the guy you want, lady."

"You're Detective Bourne?"

"Yeah."

"The sergeant up front told me to see you."

Bourne was a vice cop. It wasn't his business to take a report on a missing person, much less find one. But he didn't even have to look around to know he was the only schmoe in plainclothes still hanging around the station house.

"You got a picture of your boy?"

Glenna had a photo ready and she handed it over to Bourne, thinking he looked more like a crook than a cop. He was fat, too. He looked like he couldn't even button his coat over his belly.

The cop glanced at Jerry's picture and frowned.

"How old is he?"

"Jerry's seventeen."

21

"How long's he been gone?"

"He never come home from work tonight."

"He's got a job?"

"He makes deliveries for Szell's drugstore, but he's home by six-thirty, regular as a clock."

Bourne looked at the station clock. Eight-forty. The kid, husky from the looks of him, hadn't been gone three hours yet.

Glenna saw the expression on the fat face change, and now he was handing her picture back.

"Jerry's retarded."

"What?"

"It happened when he was a baby. His air got shut off too long when I was birthin' him. 'An-ox-i-a,' they called it."

Bourne looked at the picture again. The kid's face looked back at him, and it did seem too innocent for a teenager's. There wasn't any smirk or smart-ass to it.

"Jerry's got the mind of an eight-year-old. That's all he'll ever have."

"But he's smart enough to hold a job?"

"He only delivers right in the neighborhood."

"Can he read?"

Glenna nodded. "Some. If the words aren't too big. He knows his street signs."

Bourne scratched the stubble on his jaw. He thought this made him look pensive. His ex-wife had said he scratched when he was itchy to be somewhere else.

He asked, "Does the kid deliver any drugs somebody might want to take from him?"

"No. Mr. Szell makes people come in for those."

"What about money?"

Glenna was puzzled. "What about it?"

"Does he collect it when he makes a delivery? If someone knew he was retarded and carrying money . . ." Bourne let Glenna fill in the thought. Then he went on to another. "Or Jerry might've had a few bucks in his pocket and decided to have a good time."

Glenna had looked worried, but now her eyes narrowed.

"I raised my boy honest. And everybody that knows Jerry likes him."

Bourne sighed. "I raised my kid honest, too, and if I wasn't a cop he'd be doin' time by now."

He studied Jerry's picture again. Seventeen on the outside, eight on the inside. He lifted his face to Glenna.

"He works to help make ends meet?"

Glenna flinched at the personal question, but only momentarily.

"That, and to give him his self-confidence."

"Does the boy have a father?"

"No."

"You have a boyfriend?"

Glenna's mouth tightened. She hadn't wanted to come to the police. Admitting that she needed help only twisted the knot of fear in her chest.

"You got a boyfriend, maybe he's got the kid."

"I ain't got no boyfriend."

Bourne scratched his jaw again. "Lady, I'll make some calls. See what I can do."

"Calls to where?"

"To the hospitals. If I can't find him there . . . then I call the morgue."

Glenna's face hardened so much she could only get a whisper out of it.

"That's how the police find a poor boy in this city?"

Bourne saw the contempt in her face. He

couldn't miss it. Her attitude pissed him off. He didn't have to do squat for her. He was going out of his way as it was.

"Listen, lady. You know how many Missing Persons reports are filed in this town every year? Twen-tee thousand!"

Bourne knew he had the number right. He'd read it in his newspaper just last week.

"Another thing," he said. "A kid gets to be seventeen in his state, he's no longer a juvenile, he's a minor. He's legally entitled to take off if he wants. Now, you say Jerry thinks like a little boy, but I see he looks like a big boy. And if he's got a job and can read street signs, he's two notches up on most of the creeps we arrest around here every day."

The cop tossed Jerry's picture down on the desk in front of him.

"You want me to make the calls or not?"

Glenna Handee picked up her son's photo and left without a word.

3

The first thing Doc did when he stepped outside of Dietz's building was to look in a store window. The reflection showed that his glasses had turned darker, even though it was almost evening and the early spring sky was overcast. He couldn't see his real eye or the marble—and if he couldn't no one else could, either.

He started off down the street for the long walk home. He was now in the Loop, and his neighborhood, The Wedge, was on the North Side, miles away. He had to walk because he couldn't drive, he refused to take the CTA, and cabs were for yuppies. That left the old shank's mare. Maybe losing his eye'd be good for his heart.

He stopped for a red light and took another peek at himself in another window. It was stupid, he thought, to worry about his looks before he considered other things.

A horn honked and he jumped back as a *Sun-Times* truck raced around the corner in front of him, its rear wheel climbing the curb.

Doc never saw it coming. *To hell with looks*, he thought. He damn well better pay attention to what was going on around him. Whatever anyone else said, he was sure he saw only half as much as he had before. Which meant his chances were twice as good the next reckless fucking driver would nail him.

The light turned green and he carefully stepped out into the intersection. With a bitter grin, he told himself he really should keep an eye out.

His warped sense of humor made him shiver. It was as if he had to needle himself, put himself down for being less than he used to be. Part of it, he knew, was self-pity. That was something he'd never let himself feel before.

His shrink had told him it was a form of mourning. He was grieving for his loss. Doc didn't joke about that.

The thing that worried him the most—and he couldn't help it—was that the goddamn marble would fall right out of his head.

He thought of all the ways it could happen. He might be jogging up the front stairs of his house, land a little hard on the top step, and, bang, out it'd come. He could see it. The marble would go bouncing down the steps, always looking back at him. It would roll along the sidewalk, and just before it disappeared into the gutter it would give him a big wink.

But it didn't have to be that involved. He might just be sitting in his kitchen one night blowing on a cup of tea to cool it down. Next thing he knew, *plop*, eyeball soup.

He'd told the shrink about both of these ideas. She didn't laugh. She offered him the comfort of her warmest smile and said that while it wasn't impossible to displace a prosthesis, it wasn't all that easy, either.

Gunther had told him the same thing, with a lot of technical reasons why.

Doc had told neither of them his worst-case scenario: having it fall out while he was making love.

He'd kill himself if that ever happened. But since he didn't know any woman he'd trust going to bed with, maybe he'd never get laid again.

Of course, for a thirty-six-year-old guy, that wasn't a bad reason for killing yourself, either.

When he thought about suicide, he thought about Harry. Maybe she'd come back and save him. From himself, if nothing else. Maybe he was a jerk-off kidding himself, too. Harry hadn't called once since the divorce. Not even after he'd been shot. Not in all the time he'd been recovering.

If recovering was what the hell he was doing.

"Michael."

Doc stopped and looked up. He saw the familiar frame houses and brick two-flats of his neighborhood. He was almost home, and he had no idea how he'd gotten there or how long it had taken him. Glenna Handee was standing in front of him. She was the only person he could think of who still called him by his given name.

He didn't need more than one eye to see the worry written into Glenna's face.

"Michael, can I talk to you?"

He knew he should say yes, but he was surprised that she was speaking to him at all. All of his neighbors had been tiptoeing around him for months, ever since he got out of the hospital, not saying more than a hurried "Hello!" or a nervous "Good to have you back!"

"I need your help."

That was even more surprising. Glenna was fiercely self-reliant. He wouldn't have expected her to ask for help unless she was bleeding freely.

"With what?" The question came out flat and hard. He hadn't intended it that way, but he didn't know how to tell Glenna that without sounding stupid.

"I was by your house just now. Michael, I'm sorry for your troubles, but . . ."

He tried again, taking a little of the edge off.

"Glenna, what's wrong?"

"Jerry's missing."

"How could he be missing? He never goes anywhere."

"He didn't come home from work tonight."

Glenna had kept her voice steady and her back straight, but that was when it hit him. She was bleeding freely. *Inside*.

"Glenna, are you and Jerry having any trouble?"

"What do you mean?"

"I mean, every kid has days when he gets mad at his mother and feels like taking off."

Glenna shook her head.

"Michael, Jerry didn't run away."

Doc had known Jerry literally from the day he was born. Glenna had been his friend, and one of the truest, from that same day. Suddenly, the cold fear that Glenna was feeling wrapped itself around his heart.

He said, "Come on. I'll walk you over to the station house."

"I been to the police already."

"So they're looking for Jerry."

She shook her head and told him what had happened. Doc knew Detective Eddie Bourne.

"Glenna, a guy like that . . ."

He saw her face harden. It was easy to imagine her giving Bourne the same look. Hell, he could see any frightened parent reacting the same way. A cop would have to go charging out of the station with his gun in his hand and blood in his eye to get any other response.

He tried to explain.

"Detective Bourne is a pretty decent cop."

"Decent enough to make phone calls," Glenna said harshly.

"Glenna, he's been on the job for years. He deals with pimps, pedophiles, and pornographers day in and day out. He can't afford to have a lot of empathy. To Bourne, making a few phone calls would be like donating a kidney."

He saw that *she* didn't have a lot of empathy right now, either.

"I know some other cops over there," he said.

"He was the only one to talk to. I asked the desk sergeant after I got done with him."

Goddamn cutbacks, Doc thought.

"Michael, I've been huntin' around and callin' out Jerry's name ever since I left the police. I can't find him anywhere. Please help me. Help me find my boy."

He watched flashes of horror flicker across her eyes like a nervous tic. He could practically see her imagination suggesting and then repressing explanations of what had kept her son from returning home.

But fear wasn't the only emotion he saw in her eyes. A raw red flame of rage burned there, too. Glenna suspected someone was responsible for Jerry's disappearance, and she wanted to strike out. She wanted to make someone pay.

The desire for vengeance quickly seized Doc's wounded soul. He, too, might have a chance to hit back at someone here. Not for what had been done to him, but for what might have been done to Glenna.

At the moment, that was good enough.

"Let's start looking," Doc said.

4

The Wedge was nothing special, just a lower-middle-class slice of the city. As a neighborhood, it fell somewhere between gentrified Wrigleyville and desolated Uptown. Its houses, two-flats, and courtyard buildings had grown tired. Aging facades and drooping gutters waited for the day when money could be spared to meet their needs.

Doc and Glenna walked along, looking for any crack in the concrete that might hide a boy.

"I'm scared, Michael."

"I know."

"I'm angry, too. Nothin' bad should happen to a boy like Jerry."

"We don't know that anything has. He's only been gone a few hours."

"Something's happened. He wouldn't be out this late of his own mind."

Doc had no answer for that.

A smile formed unexpectedly on Glenna's lips. It came so clearly from the heart that it grafted a surprising loveliness onto her tired face, and reminded Doc that she was a year younger than him.

"Jerry buys me presents. Did you know that, Michael?"

Doc did, but he didn't say anything.

"Usually, it's a candy bar from Mr. Szell's store. But once," she marveled, "once it was roses."

"He's a good kid."

Doc had helped Jerry buy the flowers, as a favor. Jerry had promised to keep Doc's help a secret. Crossed his heart and hoped to die.

"People think I have it hard with him."

"Don't you?"

"Jerry's the easiest, happiest part of my life."

Doc nodded. "Let's look in there."

They stepped down into a pitch-black gangway between two apartment buildings. Doc went first, brushing his fingers along a brick wall and poking around with a foot before taking each step.

"Jerry?" Glenna called out. Her voice filled the confined space. There was no answer.

They continued to the end of the passage, looked into the empty yard behind the building, and retraced their steps to the street.

Doc and Glenna pushed on in silence.

A lot of families who lived in The Wedge had been in the same places for generations. They were people who were getting by, but not ahead. So, they stayed put. Favored sons and daughters assumed low-interest mortgages on tiny principals, and took care of Mom and Pop. Grandma, too, as often as not.

As a rule they kept their property clean, but their gardens were never going to make the Sunday paper and their buildings weren't going to attract the rehabbers any time soon. There was a working-class stasis to the place.

Urban amber.

Doc thought he, himself, was typical. He lived in his parents' house, and every day he saw faces he'd known all his life.

It made him wonder. If he had to, could he

stop looking at these people as a neighbor, and start seeing them as a cop?

Because every instinct he had told him that Glenna was right. This wasn't just a kid goofing off. Something had happened to Jerry. More to the point, someone had *made* it happen. Maybe someone who lived in The Wedge.

"What are you thinking, Michael?"

Doc realized that Glenna had stopped walking, and he turned to face her.

"Just trying to recall the places I hid out when I was a kid," Doc lied.

"Think of any?"

Now that she mentioned it, he did.

"Yeah."

"Well, let's go then."

They turned a corner and headed for a lumber-yard he'd just remembered. But Doc didn't expect to find Jerry there. Or drinking beer in the cemetery with the guys. Or making out in a dark corner of the neighborhood park.

He expected he'd wind up doing exactly what Detective Eddie Bourne had offered to do several hours ago.

Calling hospitals and the morgue.

5

Harriet Wilkerson was booking a second-honeymoon trip to Seattle for a periodontist and his wife, when that bitch Shirley passed by with a smirk on her puss and dropped the morning's *Trib* on the corner of Harry's desk.

Harry ignored what she was sure had to be a taunt, until she got her work done. Dr. and Mrs. Kirpak were flying first-class to the Great Northwest and spending exactly one night in the Honeymoon Suite of the Seattle Hyatt. Then it was load the little lady and the rented camping gear into the rented Bronco for a week of fishing in the Cascade Mountains. This would recreate their first honeymoon.

A month earlier, Harry had booked this rustic romantic and his mistress into a "convention" at the Mauna Kea Hotel on the Big Island of Hawaii.

Harry had to smile at her disapproval—her hypocrisy. She'd had more than one episode of flyaway nookie herself when she'd been married. And her flights and hotel suites had been on the house.

"Harriet," Shirley cooed.

The bitch never called her Harry, even though she'd been asked a million times.

"I believe there's something in this morning's

paper that might interest you. Right on the front page, too."

Harry looked over at her tormentor, who sat at a desk three feet away. Shirley was smiling at her. Shirley's smile was as phony as her singsong voice, her red hair, and her tits. But she was the daughter of the travel agency's owner.

Harry knew if she didn't look at the paper Shirley would pick it up and read it to her. She decided to save herself from that. A moment later she thought that Shirley's idiotic voice might have taken away some of the impact of the headline: EX-COP FILES CLAIM ON DRUG MILLIONS.

Doc's picture ran right under the headline. It was the photo that had earned him his nickname, and she felt a lump in her throat as she gazed at it.

Years ago, the department had wanted Officer Michael Kildare to do a recruitment poster. They'd even brought in some hotshot photographer to take his picture. But the department's ad consultant took one look and said no way. He'd said this guy looks more like Dr. Kildare than Officer Kildare. No one would believe he wasn't a model they had hired.

Another career shot to hell, but the story got out and Michael became "Doc" Kildare forevermore.

Harry reluctantly shifted her gaze from the picture to the story. Doc's lawyer had filed a claim on his behalf for one-third of the money that had been recovered in the drug raid where he'd lost his eye. One-third came to fifteen million dollars.

For a moment, Harry felt dizzy.

The story added that forfeited drug money was usually divided among the law-enforcement agencies involved in its confiscation. But Attorney Rudd Wetherby had claimed to have found citations in the U.S. Code that entitled Michael "Doc" Kildare to file for compensation for the loss of his eye and his livelihood.

Harry couldn't get over it. Doc was going to be a millionaire less than a year after she'd divorced him! She was too stunned even to object when Shirley sat down on the corner of her desk. She just kept reading.

A spokesman for the CPD noted that Kildare was receiving a seventy-five percent disability pension of thirty-three thousand dollars per year, and that was all to which he was legally entitled.

The DEA, which was said to have assisted in the raid and therefore was the only other agency entitled to a share of the forfeited money, had declined to comment.

"You ask me," Shirley said, "I wouldn't mind jumping a guy who looked like that, even if he was broke."

Shirley's smile lasted only until Harry shoved her off her desk.

"Nobody asked you," she said.

Doc was sleeping like the dead, and dreaming that somebody was barbecuing his feet. Then his mind registered that the pain he was feeling was real.

"Goddamn," he said, waking up and kicking off the covers.

He pulled up one foot and then the other for a look. There were blisters everywhere. He remembered last night, and early this morning, too. He and Glenna hadn't given up until two-thirty A.M. When they'd both gotten too tired to do any good, Doc had insisted they go home.

All that walking—and the hike home from Gunther's office before that—had taken their toll on feet that were still used to riding around for a living.

Doc hobbled into the bathroom on the sides of his feet and lowered himself into the empty old clawfoot tub. He put the cork in the drain and turned the water on as hot as he could stand it. The heat and the pressure of the flow from the tap hurt like hell, but his mind was already elsewhere.

He'd lived in this house for all but a few months of his life. During their "honeymoon months," he and Harry'd had an apartment of their own. As the water rose over his throbbing feet, Doc wondered if it would have made a difference to Harry if they'd sold the place years ago and started fresh in a house of their own.

It was a useless line of thought. He hadn't been ready to leave then, and didn't know if he could even now.

He looked around the room, at the old-fashioned fixtures, the huge medicine chest with the mirror his father had reglazed, the walls with the tile pattern so dated it was sure to be back in again any day now.

People in The Wedge never had much to leave to their kids. The usual legacy was advice to keep your nose clean, get as much education as you had brains for, and work hard. When someone was the lucky recipient of a house or two-flat, he knew he was receiving a family treasure earned by long years of double-shifts and side jobs. It wasn't real estate that you peddled on a whim.

At least, Doc felt that way.

This had been his parents' bathroom when they'd been alive, and the place had been Big John Kildare's house. Big John had been a fireman who moonlighted as an electrician. Marie had been his wife, and she'd been more than happy to raise the kids, keep the house, and manage the family budget. Patricia, Michael, and Richard had been the three kids, smart as whips and one better-looking than the next.

For some reason Doc thought of his family more, and missed them worse, in here than in any other room in the house. He remembered his mother bathing him and Richie in here, when they were very young. Big John lathered his sons' faces with shaving cream in here, then let them stroke it off with a safety razor that didn't have a blade in it. Mom helped Pat primp for her big dates. All the cuts and scratches and bruises that everyone had suffered were brought here to be healed. Years later, he and Harry had taken showers together, making love giddily while trying not to drown or break their necks.

When he reached forward and turned off the water so the tub wouldn't overflow, Doc remembered that he was here all alone now.

He looked at his feet again. He'd let them soak a few minutes, then see if he couldn't use his head to find Jerry Handee.

6

Anton Szell, R.Ph. and owner of Szell's Drugstore, was a methodical man. He arrived at his store on Tuesday morning at eight-thirty, as usual. He smiled when he saw Artie Fuentes, R.Ph. and junior partner, out front waiting for him. Tony'd had his worries about the *mañana* mentality when he'd taken the younger man on, but Artie observed a punctuality that pleased Tony down to the bottom of his German soul.

"*Buenos días*, Arturo," Tony said, unlocking the front door.

"G'morning, Tony," the younger man replied. "How was Gerta's schnitzel last night?"

Tony beamed, locking the door behind them.

"Magnificent, Artie. It was . . . It made me think again of how right my father was. He told me, 'Tony, after the first year of marriage you will make love to your wife two or three times a week at most. But you will have to eat her cooking two or three times a day for the rest of your life. Remember this when you choose your bride.' "

Tony smiled and patted his ample stomach, as if to show the reward of being a dutiful son.

Artie had heard the story a hundred times before, but he liked the joy Tony brought to it with each telling. It also made him feel good that after eight years of marriage and two kids, he and Denise still made love every morning and most nights, too.

The two men got ready for the start of business. The store didn't open for thirty minutes yet and, as always, they'd left it spotlessly clean and ready to go the night before. They were there early, anyway.

Because Tony had a routine for the store, too.

"Arturo, whose name is on this store?"

"Yours, Tony."

"That's right. 'Szell's Drugstore,' it says. My store, my building. No *scheisskopf* landlords for me. You know what *scheisskopf* means?"

"Cabeza de mierda."

"That's right. Shithead. Which is what I'd be if I took any chances with this place. What if one night a pipe should burst, or some cockroach has the nerve to crawl in through a crack we don't know about?"

"That'd be terrible, Tony."

Artie always made sure he said that with a straight face.

"Damn right, it would. And one-third of that terrible would be yours, since that's your share of the profits."

Artie thought the old man had a point about that. So, while Artie loved to squeeze his wife's warm round body to his every morning, he always let go in time to beat Tony to work.

As usual, their precautions were just that and nothing more. So, at nine on the dot, Tony unlocked the front door for another day of business.

Doc Kildare was waiting for him when he did.

"Good morning, Doc," Tony said.

The pharmacist put a little extra into his smile. Like everyone else in the neighborhood, he knew about Doc's eye. But this was the first time since it happened that Doc had come into the store. Tony noticed the sunglasses Doc was wearing and was grateful for them. He dealt with internal miseries; external disfigurement made him uneasy.

"Hey, Doc!" Artie called. "Good to see you again!"

Doc nodded to Artie and took Tony aside.

"Jerry Handee's missing," he said quietly.

He didn't know why he was whispering. Tony was one of the neighborhood's more accomplished gossips. He'd spread the word to everyone he saw. Still, Doc felt he had the tone of voice right.

It had an effect on Tony. His mouth fell open.

Doc went on, "Glenna said he never came home from work yesterday, and we were out most of the night looking for him."

"I don't understand," Tony said. "He left at five o'clock to make his last batch of deliveries. Every one was a credit account, no money to handle. I told him, 'Don't bother coming back, I'll put the trash out for you.' "

"That was the last time you saw him?"

"Yes."

Doc thought a moment.

"Did anything seem different about Jerry yesterday?"

"No, what could be different? He did his work. He smiled. He thought I was Santa Claus when I gave him a Baby Ruth for the nice job he did cleaning the bathroom."

"Did anybody you didn't know come in and talk to him?"

"No, not while I was here." Tony called out to his partner. "Artie, when I was at lunch yesterday, did any stranger come in and talk to Jerry?"

Artie looked up from a prescription he was filling, ran the question through his mind, shook his head, and went back to work.

"That's the only ninety minutes I'm out of the store all day. You think something bad's happened?"

Tony looked genuinely worried. Like everybody else who knew the boy, the pharmacist had a real affection for him.

"It's getting hard to think anything else," Doc said with a grimace. "You got a list of Jerry's deliveries for yesterday?"

"Absolutely," Tony said.

7

The man hummed "Whistle While You Work" as he dug the grave. Every so often he'd stop and spare a glance at the body on the basement floor next to the excavation. Its eyes bulged out like ping-pong balls, and the nose was smashed flat. The man had caught the stiff a good one with his lug wrench.

You forgot to duck, buddy, the man thought.

He stopped digging at a depth of four feet and climbed out of the hole. He went over to a metal trough to mix cement. He'd use some of it to line the bottom and the sides of the grave. That way he'd have a neat box, and the body wouldn't pollute the soil as it turned to pus.

Then he'd cover the body with cement, and no one would ever smell anything, either.

After he completed his preparations, the man stepped over to the body and took a wallet from its back pocket. *If you kill someone*, he thought, *you at least ought to know who he was for your records.* He noted the name carefully and then rolled the body into the hole. He tossed the wallet in, too. Without taking the money out of it.

He knew that if any shrinks ever got hold of him they'd say he was definitely crazy. No. "Mentally ill," that's what they'd say. Or they'd lay some jawbreaker technical name on him. No one was just plain crazy anymore. They'd ask him if he heard voices, and if he wanted to be truthful he'd say there was one. *Only* one.

Cops, on the other hand, would say he was just a cold-blooded killer who got his rocks off watching people die at his hands. They wouldn't be right, though. While he had to admit that he felt good afterward, pleasure wasn't the force that drove him.

He didn't like to think about the real reason.

What he *liked* to think about was never getting caught. And with the way he looked, there was no reason why he should. Medium height, medium weight, medium-brown hair, medium-blue eyes. At a glance he disappeared into a crowd; in a moment he faded from memory. He was always around, but never noticed. The only possible thing that could give him away was when he heard the voice—he might look like he was tuned into some kind of invisible Walkman.

The man poured the remainder of the cement over the body. Next he graded the surface of the grave until it was smooth, then waited for it to dry. He checked the new surface with his level, and the air bubble was perfectly centered. Anyone who wanted to find the body now would need a jackhammer.

Of course, he didn't expect anyone to find the body. This one, or any of the rest. He knew that there had been others who'd felt the same way, and a lot of those clucks were on Death Row right now.

But they really were crazy.

They'd buried bodies in their *own* basements.

8

Doc was back pounding the pavement, but this time a pair of Dr. Scholl's Air-Pillo Insoles came between his feet and the street. They were a gift from Tony and Artie. They'd refused to let him pay. They'd been equally adamant that he use their private line to make his calls to check up on Jerry.

Why should he use the pay phone? They were all neighbors. Doc had been touched by the sentiment—after he'd seen that their morning *Tribs* and *Sun-Times* hadn't been delivered yet.

Rudd Wetherby had called him that morning just before he'd stepped out the door, to tell him that his story would be front-page news. Since Tony and Artie had yet to find out he might be coming into money, they'd been nice out of friendship. It had been enough to make him feel halfway human again.

According to the list Tony provided, Jerry had been supposed to make seven deliveries after leaving the store at five o'clock yesterday. Doc knew all the people on the list, at least by appearance.

Three of them, Martha Perkins, Mary Ann Walsh, and Jim Squiers, had received their orders. None had noticed anything unusual about Jerry. Each of them could provide an approximate time of delivery. All of them were bright enough to guess that something was wrong.

One customer, Karen Zatekas, hadn't received her prescription, and three others, Desmond Riley, Otille Coultier, and Yolanda Gonsalves, didn't answer their phones.

Tony had given Doc one of the store's handout maps, which showed a delivery area of roughly one square mile. Tony'd written down the addresses of all seven names on the delivery list, and Doc had marked them on the map.

Neither Tony nor Artie knew if Jerry followed any set pattern when making his deliveries. The kid just got the job done. Or had, Artie said, before he could bite his tongue.

Taking the times of delivery he'd been given, Doc was able to work out the direction Jerry had been heading when he left the store. The boy had been traveling due south, then turned right to the west. Continuing in an arc to the northwest would have brought him to Desmond Riley's house. The last three, Gonsalves, Coultier, and Zatekas, were in a line on the same street moving back east. When Doc had finished drawing his diagram it looked like a ragged semicircle.

The route seemed logical to him. Probably too logical for someone with the mind of an eight-year-old.

But that was the way he started walking.

Doc found Jerry's delivery bike chained to a light pole two doors down from Otille Coultier's house. It was the next-to-last address he had to check. Insoles or no, his feet were hurting again. If he wound up scoring with this claim on Armando Guzman's money, Doc decided he'd buy a goddamn limo and hire a chauffeur.

He looked at the red bike with the delivery basket, but didn't touch it. He saw no blood, hair, or other tissue remnant on it, but he was no forensic scientist. He glanced up at the sky. It was still cloudy, and the air felt like rain. He wondered if it would do more harm than good to find something to cover the bike.

He stepped back and looked up and down the street. There was no one in sight on the block of sturdy brick bungalows. When people were at work and school was in session, there wasn't a lot of idle pedestrian traffic in The Wedge.

Doc wondered if Jerry had been delivering in a straight line—one, two, three—and locking the bike up at each stop. Or had he locked it up once in the middle, near Otille Coultier, and walked back to Yolanda Gonsalves and ahead to Karen Zatekas? A kid bopping back and forth would attract more attention than one moving in a straight line.

He didn't see anyone he could ask—until he spotted Old Lady Coultier sitting in her window behind all her bars. He remembered the old busybody from when he was a kid. Now she sat in her window like she was staking out the block for the FBI. She was on the delivery list, too.

If anyone had seen Jerry, it had to be her. He figured that she must've been on the crapper when he'd called earlier.

Doc waved to the woman but she didn't wave back. He searched his memory about Otille Coultier as he approached her house. What he remembered was two words: old bag. The kind who'd scare the hell out of any kid who chased an errant baseball onto her property.

He even recalled some of his friends telling of times she'd actually rattled her bars at them. Like she was Jimmy Cagney in some prison movie.

The bars were on all the basement and first-floor windows. The rate of burglaries had been going up in The Wedge for a long time, but those bars had been there even longer. Otille was either paranoid, or twenty years ahead of her time.

The smell hit Doc as he mounted the stairs next to Otille's perch. The window had been left open a crack, and he was surprised he hadn't noticed the familiar odor sooner. It was the stench of decomposition.

Otille Coultier was dead.

Doc glanced back at Jerry's unattended bike. He hoped the old bag was the only one to die around here lately.

9

Doc knew the uniformed cops who answered his call, a couple of young guys, Brian Mularkey and Braxton Williams. They had time to talk while the locksmith Doc had told them to bring opened the three deadbolt locks Otille had on her front door.

The back door was similarly guarded.

In the old days, when Doc had been a patrol officer and cops had to get into a place where there was a stiff, they would "effect their own entrance." The City Attorney put an end to that when he got tired of fighting suits for broken-down doors. For the next year or so, the Fire Department provided access. The City Council stopped that practice when they saw how much it was costing. Now the department used contract locksmiths.

"Fifteen mill, huh?" Williams asked. He thought about it for a moment. "Wonder if I'd trade one of my eyes for that much scratch."

"I wouldn't," Mularkey said.

"Yeah, but you'd want it like Doc here, after the fact."

"That's a different story. Then, hell yes. I'd want it."

Doc withheld comment.

"Word is, you got the Superintendent shitting red-hot rivets," Williams said.

Doc stared out from behind his glasses. The marble, which he'd somehow forgotten about for almost half a day, felt like it was pressing into his brain.

"I'll recommend a proctologist," he said.

The cops laughed.

Mularkey said, "Yeah, the brass is pissin' and moanin', but every street cop I talk to is behind you a hundred percent."

"Hey," the locksmith called out. "If you gentlemen are done with your quilting bee, the premises are now open."

Maggots writhed at the corners of Otille Coultier's slack mouth. Teach her to die in front of an open window. Flies buzzed right in, and when they saw the cranky old lady wasn't up to shooing them away they used her for a breeding ground. Drop a batch of eggs, wait a little while, and presto change-o, maggots on parade. One of Nature's wonders.

Doc thought societies that immediately cremated their dead had the right idea.

"How'd you find this biddy, anyway?" Mularkey asked.

Doc told them about looking for Jerry, how the boy'd been missing since last night. He didn't like the look he saw the two cops exchange.

"What?" he asked.

They looked at each other again, and then Williams answered.

"Nothin' really. Just that there's been talk between some of the guys in the basketball league. After games, you know."

Doc snorted. He did know. Cops in this town formed sports leagues—softball, bowling, basketball—to relieve themselves of the pressure of their work. Then as soon as the game was over, the job was all they talked about.

Mularkey picked up where Williams had left off.

"One of the things we've noticed is almost a pattern of missing males, juvenile to young adult. It's been goin' on for a while, and it seems to be happening more often lately."

"The department has a crazy out there?"

Williams shook his head.

"Ain't the department at all. Just cops comparin' notes, same as always. You ain't been gone that long."

Sure as hell felt like it.

"Listen," Doc said, "Jerry's bike is locked up to that light pole out front. Call the lab boys to come get, will you?"

"Add it to our list," Williams said.

"What was your kid supposed to deliver?" Mularkey asked.

Doc checked his notes. The ever-efficient Tony had provided this information, too.

"Nitroglycerin pills."

Williams said, "Let's see if we can find a new 'scrip around here."

"Easy does it," Mularkey cautioned. "We don't want to mess anything up, in case we gotta call the detectives out."

There were three levels to the place. Mularkey went upstairs, Williams down, and Doc searched the first floor. The place was neat as a pin, with doilies and fussy old lady touches everywhere. The newest piece of furniture had to be thirty years old.

Williams came up out of the basement after just a minute and started helping Doc. Doc nudged open a cabinet under the kitchen sink and saw an empty bottle from Szell's Drugstore marked NITROGLYCERIN in a plastic garbage can.

Williams saw it over Doc's shoulder.

"Musta thrown that out. Expected the new one to be on its way."

Mularkey entered the room, saw what they were looking at, and picked up on his partner's train of thought.

"Expected the kid to deliver it," he said.

"When it didn't come—good-bye, Charlie."

"Heart failure."

Williams finished the sequence.

"Which means if someone fucked with the kid, that someone could be charged with the biddy's death."

To Doc, it also said that Jerry hadn't been in Otille Coultier's house. If he had, she'd have gotten her new bottle of pills and would be alive and as nasty as ever. But with Otille gone to her reward, no medicine to be found, and six locks bolted against the outside world when he'd arrived, there was no way Jerry could have entered.

Doc knew there was no more for him to do there, and that he should get out of Williams and Mularkey's way. But then he thought of one more thing.

"Say, who's the Youth Division officer for this neighborhood? The guy who handles missing kids."

Mularkey gave him the name.

Williams gave him a piece of advice.

"Keep lookin' your ownself, too. Case you forgot, even without a crazy, people on these streets keep dyin' younger all the time."

10

"What do you mean, some cop's trying to steal 'my money'?" Armando Guzman asked.

He was speaking to his cousin Hector, who was also his lawyer, at the federal lockup downtown.

Besides being the biggest Colombian fish the federal government had ever netted, Armando was also the centerpiece of a landmark case destined to be studied by generations of legal scholars.

What made *U.S. v. Guzman* so noteworthy was that the defendant's right to a *speedy* and public trial as provided for under Article Six of the Constitution had been guarded zealously. On the other hand his expectation of a protracted legal circus, where judgment might be put off and bargains made, had been dashed utterly. Armando had been arrested, arraigned, indicted, tried, convicted, and sentenced all in six months.

By the usual standards of the justice system, this was only slightly less breathtaking than if he'd been sent straight to a firing squad.

The feds had two good reasons for moving so fast. One, they wanted to show that they could mete out swift punishment for big-shot drug bosses—and score political points with the voting public. Two, there were rumors that Armando was a token sacrifice by the cartel, and the feds wanted to get all the mileage they could out of Armando while he still had some PR value.

The government's sense of urgency was aided and abetted by a judge who had publicly declared to the city bar association that he didn't believe in wasting his time and the taxpayers' dollars on drug scumbags.

The feds had hoped that by confiscating Armando's money they'd make him rely on a public defender. They were shocked when Cousin Hector came out of the woodwork, a U.S. citizen and a goddamn Beverly Hills lawyer. But it didn't really matter. Clarence Darrow couldn't have gotten Armando Guzman off.

People *wanted* to see him in front of a firing squad.

"*What* money?" Armando demanded.

"You remember your forty-five million?"

Armando nodded vigorously.

Two inches of Lexan separated him from his cousin, and they had to talk through telephones. Both men figured that the line was bugged, so they spoke *indio* laced with Spanish slang.

"Well, the cop wants a third of it." Hector did the arithmetic for Armando. "Fifteen million."

"*What* cop?"

"The one you shot. The one who testified against you." Hector smiled. "He wants the money for the eye you took from him."

"And you think that's funny?"

"I was just thinking, if he wants a third for one of his eyes, he'd want all of it if you'd shot off one of his *cojones*."

Armando got up and banged his fist against the divider. A guard who stood in the far corner started toward him, then stopped when he saw Armando sit back down.

Hector waited until his cousin had composed himself. He wished he could get up and just leave this mad dog to rot in prison. He'd hated Armando from the moment they'd met.

"Lawyer," Armando finally hissed. "I sent you here, paid for your universities, made you an American, made you rich. But I see the meaning of what this one-eyed bastard is trying to do, and you don't."

Hector put on a properly submissive front.

"What does it mean, cousin?"

"It means if the cops can steal from us like this and get away with it, they won't let us buy them. Think of it. Honest cops will break down our doors and not be afraid to be shot. Why? Because that would only make them rich."

Hector stared at Armando. He wondered what good all the money in the world would do a cop if he ran into somebody who could shoot straight.

"So you intend to have him killed?"

Armando shook his head.

"Killing him is not enough. I must make him an example. Find out all you can about this greedy cop. What I do to him must truly be remembered, passed from mouth to mouth until it becomes legend."

Hector shuddered.

"But first you must get me out of here, cousin. Have you made the arrangements?"

Hector had indeed come up with a plan. He'd seen as clearly as anyone that the feds had made a political example of Armando. Filing appeals on the conviction would just be going through the motions. No judge or jury in the whole country would set Armando free. His fate was on greased rails. The only concession the government made at all was to let Armando rot in Chicago for the time being, rather than ship him to the federal pen in Marion, Illinois.

Escape was Armando's only way out.

The reason Hector had to help his cousin was because he was afraid not to. If he just walked away and Armando found another way to escape, he'd make *him* another example. Hector hadn't gone to law school and passed the bar in four states just to die young—and horribly.

"I've had five million dollars transferred to a local bank for expenses," Hector said.

"Is that enough? These *cabrones* want to see me die in here."

"If it's not, I'll get more."

Hector thought that was the one good reason to help Armando get out. The cops might have grabbed forty-five million from him, but there was a billion more in accounts around the world. If Armando got out, he'd be a fugitive. Hector would have to be the one to deal with all the bankers. Then, perhaps, once Hector had been given the power of attorney for those funds, an accident might befall Armando.

Armando interrupted this pleasant conjecture.

"While you are doing your work, I will think of what to do with this cop. And with the traitor."

The "traitor" was the informant who'd passed the word from Colombia to Chicago that Armando was coming for his money.

He was also Hector's younger brother, Fidel.

11

Doc spent the rest of the afternoon in Ray's, sitting at a corner table near the phone. Ray's was a neighborhood institution: part street-corner hangout, part itsy-bitsy grocery store, part soda fountain and grill, and, when Ray's wife Dottie had been alive, part bookie joint. About the only thing you couldn't get at Ray's was a drink.

For that you went to the neighborhood institution directly across the street, Nat's Tap.

Over the last three hours Doc had been resting his feet, revving his brain, and wearing out his phone-calling finger. Officer Schumann of Youth Division was either a very busy cop or he didn't believe in returning his calls.

People came and went while Doc lingered. Red Penwell came in from a day at the track and knocked down a double Alka-Seltzer for his hangover, then went home to yell at his wife. Ben Haskins and Sy Wasserman came in but, before they even ordered, started arguing about the location of a building that had been torn down in '39. They left to determine who had the right spot. Various kids came in for Cokes and candy bars and left with their sugary treasures.

A rattle of dishes coming his way made Doc look up. Ray set a burger, fries, and a chocolate shake down on the table in front of him.

"Eat," Ray said.

Doc hadn't asked for the food, but seeing it and smelling it brought back memories of all the times he'd ordered just these things, a teenager's idea of a well-balanced meal.

One of his earliest memories, in fact, was of Big John bringing him into Ray's for the first time. He was so small his father had to help him get up on the stool at the soda fountain. He'd had a nickel Coke, and Big John got ten bucks down on a Notre Dame game.

Doc took a bite of the burger and wondered why he never found one anywhere else that tasted half as good.

Ray sat down across the table from Doc and started reading the paper. Doc looked around. There was a kid reading at the comic book rack near the front of the store. Otherwise, they had the place to themselves.

Doc spoke up.

"Ray, you know of any empty buildings around here?"

"Why," Ray asked, putting his paper down, "you lookin' to buy a place?"

"No. Jerry Handee's missing."

Doc saw Ray's face cloud over. He hadn't heard. Doc was mildly surprised the news hadn't made it from Tony Szell to Ray by now.

"I've been looking for him since last night, but I can't find him. I thought he might be playing hooky from Glenna in some abandoned building."

Ray said, "I don't think Jerry'd do something like that to his mother."

Doc sighed.

"I don't either, but it's a possibility. So, how about it? You know any place he might hide out?"

"Let me think."

Ray preferred to pace while he thought. He also took a minute to chase the kid out of the store before he could read his third comic book for free. When Ray turned back toward Doc, he was smiling.

"You got something?" Doc asked.

"I got someone. Have you noticed that cute widow they hired at Babson Realty?"

"No."

"Well, I have. Who'd know better about buildings in a neighborhood than a real-estate lady? I've been looking for an excuse to talk to her, anyway."

"Go to it, Ray." Doc handed him his copy of the Szell delivery-area map. "It'd have to be somewhere in here."

Ray went into his phone booth. It was the old-fashioned kind, with the door you could close behind you. Doc couldn't hear what kind of line Ray was using on the widow, so he turned his attention to his food.

As he ate, Doc thought of something else. He'd just popped his last fry into his mouth when Ray finished his call.

"Ray, you know of any kids I should talk to about Jerry?"

Ray stopped to consider the new question.

"No, I don't. The kids around here go pretty easy on Jerry, because they know they'd catch hell if they didn't. They let him hang around when they aren't doing anything special, but that's about it. I don't think he's got any close friends his own age, if that's what you mean."

"That's what I meant." Poor fucking kid. "What'd your new girlfriend tell you?"

Ray brightened.

"She's going to check her listings for me, and

she knows someone in the assessor's office who'll check the tax records."

"That's great, Ray."

"Yeah," he smiled, "and she said she'd have dinner with me, too."

Doc grinned.

"Way to go, Ray."

That was when Glenna Handee, home from work, walked in and found them looking so pleased with themselves.

"Have you found Jerry?"

12

"What an asshole I am," Doc muttered. Glenna had just closed the door to her apartment over Nat's Tap behind him.

He'd spent the past three hours conning her, feeding her tons of bull while she ate the steak and hash-browns Ray had insisted she take home with her.

The only reason she'd gone to work at all that day was that he'd persuaded her he could look for Jerry better than she could. Once she'd bought that, she had to concede that she couldn't afford to miss a day's pay.

He'd told her all the things he'd done today. He said that finding Jerry's bike was a good sign. It had to mean he was still somewhere in the neighborhood. He told her he'd be out there looking again tomorrow.

Everything he said was meant to reassure her, and every word he spoke was another he felt sure he'd regret.

He'd saved the worst for last.

"I'll find out what happened. I promise you that."

Shit. He'd given away his fears right at the end.

Even worse, he was far from sure he could deliver on that feeble promise. If Jerry's luck had gone to hell, then he was dead. If his body wasn't found soon, it just as likely never would be. And if there was no body, there'd be no explanation.

He pushed open the stairwell door and stepped out onto the street. Whatever the reason he'd opened his big mouth, he had to try to follow through. He might as well start with a beer. Maybe pickling his brain would improve the way it worked.

It wasn't more than twenty feet to the entrance of Nat's Tap, but Doc had covered only half that distance when the Mercedes came idling around the corner. One of the big models, four doors, tinted windows. Doc stopped to look.

The guy behind the wheel had the dome light on. Combined with the tinted glass it created a chiaroscuro effect. But, as shadowy as it was, Doc could still tell the driver thought he was some kind of dude.

He wore one of those foreign correspondent trench coats with the collar turned up. Had a hat on with the brim down. Big old hat, right out of a Bogart movie. Wrong car for the outfit. *Definitely* wrong car for The Wedge.

Mr. Dude looked at a piece of paper in his right hand and then glanced out his windshield at the other side of the street.

He was looking for an address. He didn't notice Doc. But he stopped the Mercedes four houses down the street from Ray's—directly in front of Doc's place. Mr. Dude looked at the number on the door and then at his piece of paper.

Doc started toward the big car. A moment ago he'd been wishing he had someone to strangle. Maybe Fate delivered the goods on fancy German wheels.

He didn't make a run at the Mercedes or try to be sneaky. He strolled like someone out to walk off his dinner. Mr. Dude must have caught him in one of his mirrors, because he dropped the piece of paper and hit the gas.

Doc cut between two parked cars to get a look at the license plate. The next thing he knew something whacked him the hell across the left knee. He went twisting and stumbling into the street, got his feet tangled, and landed sprawled out on his back.

It took him a minute, staring up into the spinning streetlight, to figure things out. What had happened was, he'd sprinted between the two parked cars and run his blind-side knee into the bumper of the blind-side car.

And Mr. Dude in his phantom Mercedes was long gone.

Unless he'd seen Doc's clown act, and decided to circle the block and run him over.

The whole fucking thing was infuriating. But it told him Gunther Dietz had been right. He could do a header into the asphalt and the goddamn marble wouldn't come out.

Because he had, and it hadn't.

13

Superintendent of Police William Malloy chewed his way through a mouthful of steak tartare and paid no mind to the blood that ran from the corners of his mouth. His dinner companion, DEA Agent-in-Charge Warner Carswell, tried to concentrate on his filet of sole and not Malloy's table manners.

"We've got to get this sonofabitch," Malloy said.

"Sergeant Kildare?"

"No, Nelson Fucking Mandela."

When Malloy finally noticed that the twin streams of blood had reached his chin, he dragged his napkin across the bottom half of his face. Carswell thought the moment opportune to reach for his glass of sparkling mineral water.

The DEA man paid no mind to Malloy's attempt at sarcasm.

"Might a vigorous investigation of the sergeant's background turn up something . . . unfortunate? Something that would make him seem an opportunist in the public eye?"

"Eye, huh?" Malloy snorted. "That's a good one. You know what this is all about, don't you?"

"Just what I read in my files."

Carswell had taken over the DEA's Chicago office after the capture of Armando Guzman and the seizure of his money.

"Well, I'll tell you what the real story is. After Kildare got shot, while he's still in the hospital, my office gets a call from him. I don't speak to him personally, but the message is, he wants to stay on the job."

"Not working the streets?"

"No, he knows that's out. But he wants to stay a cop."

Carswell sipped his water.

"Couldn't you have worked something out?"

"I didn't want to," the Superintendent said, shaking his head. "You asked just now, couldn't we get some dirt on Kildare?"

"Not in those exact words."

"Yeah, but that was what you meant."

"Close enough."

"Well, I doubt we could."

Carswell had to smile.

"Diogenes couldn't find an honest man. You mean we've found an honest *cop*?"

The Superintendent of Police wasn't amused.

"Like all you feds're pure as snow."

"Touché."

"What?"

"Your point is taken."

"Okay. You're new in town, so let me explain about Kildare. Back when he was first assigned to narcotics, his team and another team were in on a big bust. Lotsa dope, lotsa money. Only not as much of either as the dealer who took the fall said there should've been. The department investigated everybody involved, including Kildare. He was one of four guys completely cleared. Twelve others get their mail in Joliet now."

"Perhaps the others just didn't want to split the take with a new man," Carswell suggested.

Malloy popped another piece of steak into his mouth. The DEA man forced himself to maintain eye contact.

"Uh-uh," the Superintendent said with his mouth full. "The fucker was smart. He'd almost been burned once, he wasn't going to let it happen again. The first time he led a raid of his own, he decided he'd need a witness. He wanted someone who'd say his men kept their hands off the goodies."

Malloy's narrative was interrupted by the act of swallowing. Carswell watched the lump of cow crawl down his throat.

"You know who he brought on the raid?"

"No."

"The goddamn police chaplain, that's who. You think anyone is going to make accusations about a raid when Monsignor O'Dowell gives it his blessing?"

"The Sergeant is obviously a smart man."

"He's a fucking hot dog. On a couple of other raids, he brought a Congressman and a goddamn newspaper columnist along even after I sent out memos against including civilians in dangerous police activities. Kildare claimed he didn't see them. So he brings these jerks along and has them watch his guys like hawks. Nobody takes nothing. They all get this big media reputation as the cops with nothing to hide. Me, I got to smile and go along, because the public is eating it up— they're actually on the department's side for a change. I don't know how the hell you missed it, even if you *are* new here."

Carswell said, "I was in the jungle a few years."

Malloy grinned and wondered what jungle that was, Safariland? Carswell saw the lout's look of disbelief and ignored it.

"Anyway," Malloy continued, "Kildare stuck it to me once. I wasn't going to give him a chance to do it again, sitting in some desk job with a lotta time to think."

"Which brings us to our present situation."

"Right. Now, he's mad at us. He loses one lousy eye and he tries to hold us up for fifteen mill."

"It's the precedent that's more important than the money. If I thought we could buy him and his lawyer off for a million or even two, I'd recommend it."

"*No*, goddammit!" Malloy roared. "He's not getting a cent of my money!"

The men were eating at the Superintendent's club, in a dining room designed for privacy, but the outburst still drew attention. Malloy glared at the audience he'd acquired, until one head after another turned away.

"*Our* money," Carswell quietly corrected.

Malloy dropped his voice, too, but there was iron in his whisper.

"That's right, our money. And you know the only reason DEA was cut in at all. Just to babysit Guzman at your lockup, because Cook County Jail has more revolving doors than Marshall Fucking Field's. Nine million bucks you got for turning a key. You expect any more sweet deals from this department, you better hold the line on this fucker Kildare."

Carswell drained his water glass.

"We'll have to give the matter some more thought then, won't we?"

"That's right, we will," the Superintendent said. "Dinner again tomorrow?"

The DEA man shook his head.

"Let's make it drinks."

14

Doc watched the skin around the ice bag on his left knee turn blue, and he shivered. He was pretty sure he'd stemmed any swelling, but didn't want to take any chances. He couldn't afford to be a gimp as well as a cyclops.

The thought that he could fuck himself up worse than he already had made him shiver harder.

He remembered lying in the street out front after he'd fallen. What if another car had come whipping around the corner? He'd have been run over, sure as hell. Thinking about it, he was surprised a garbage truck hadn't come barreling along. Could've run him over, and the driver could've tossed him in with the other trash.

The only reason he could see that it hadn't happened that way was the family curse must've been out for a beer.

The phone rang, and he decided he'd had all the cold he could take. He lifted the ice bag off and limped from his bed over to the phone, having a hard time with his knee. He didn't know if it was stiff, or frozen.

"Yeah, what?" Doc said into the phone.

"Well fuck you, too."

Doc knew the voice at once.

"I've never been desperate enough to fuck a guinea."

Lieutenant Vince DiGiuseppe said, "You've never been lucky enough, you shanty Irish bastard."

If things had been normal, the vulgarity would have been part of an ordinary exchange between Doc and his old boss. Since nothing was normal anymore, it was one more thing Doc missed about his old life.

"What's up, Vince?"

"What, I can't call you to see how you're doin'?"

"Did you?"

"Yeah, among other things."

Actually, Vince had been the one person that Doc's abuse hadn't been able to drive off. Vince had come to Doc's hospital room day after day. Doc had cursed him, yelled at him, pleaded with him to get out and leave him alone. Husky, gray-haired Vince cursed him right back. When he didn't just light his cigar and stink up the room.

"What other things?" Doc asked.

"You still eat at that dump on the corner of your block?"

"Ray's isn't a dump."

"Says you. Meet me there for breakfast tomorrow. We'll chat."

"You can't tell me on the fucking phone?"

"I'll tell you to your fucking face. Tomorrow at eight."

That should've called for a comeback, but Doc thought of two things. He should tell Vince about Mr. Dude, and ask him to apply some heat to Officer Schumann of Youth Division.

Doc said, "Listen, Vince, as long as I've got you . . ."

"You ain't got me. I'm hanging up. You want to talk, I'll listen tomorrow. Good-bye."

"Asshole."

"Nice talking to you, too."

The phone rang again before Doc could get back in bed. Vince must've reconsidered.

"You got me out of fucking bed again," Doc lied.

"This is the first time I called, Doc."

Jesus. It was Harry. She finally called. The euphoria lasted only until he figured out the reason why.

"I haven't got a penny yet," he said coldly.

There was silence, and for a moment he thought she'd eased her phone back onto its hook. For some reason, even though he knew there was no way she could see him, he put his tinted glasses on.

"I didn't call about the money," Harry finally said. "I was wondering how you are."

Doc laughed.

"Sure. That's why you visited me in the hospital all those times. And you didn't just happen to see a newspaper today."

"I saw it. I had someone rub my nose in it."

"Good."

There was another pause.

"But that's really not why I'm calling. I'm sorry I didn't come to the hospital. I was feeling too guilty. It happened too soon after . . . I felt like I was responsible."

He wanted to say "Good" to that, too, but he didn't. When Harry continued, there was a tremor in her voice.

"After letting so much time go by . . . Well, it got harder and harder to make contact. But this morning after I saw that old picture of you, I had to call—even though this is the hardest time of all."

"It was the picture, huh?"

"Yes."

"Not the money?"

"No."

A lone tear fell from Doc's right eye. He'd lost the tear duct on the left.

"I don't believe you, Harry."

She was crying now, too. He could hear her.

"I'm sorry, Doc."

"The settlement was final, Harry. Not another cent."

He hung up on her.

15

"I cut that fuckhead rat!" the woman screamed.

She stumbled onto the sidewalk outside the Up-town apartment building wearing a torn house-dress and a shiner under each eye. Still staggering, she looked back over her shoulder as if someone might be following her.

Mike Kildare, eighteen months on the job, had to slam on the brakes of his patrol car to keep from running her over. The woman brought her-self to a shaky stop and looked at him through his windshield. Then she banged her fist on the hood of his unit and restated her claim.

Since Mike's partner was out sick he requested backup, and Terry and Billy Conn responded. The woman repeated to them what she'd told Mike.

"I cut that fuckhead rat!"

None of the cops doubted her for a minute.

It was four-thirty A.M., the dregs of a hot, sticky night in the middle of July. People lounged on fire escapes and slumped on stoops to escape their steambath apartments. They watched the woman and the cops, grateful for the prospect of a little entertainment.

"Is he dead?" Mike asked.

The woman shook her head. "I don't know. I'm not sure I got him good enough."

"What's this guy's name?"

"Reuben Fuckhead Gadoy."

Billy Conn took the woman back to his car. Mike and Terry went inside. Since Mike was the first one on the scene, Terry generously let him take the lead. Mike cautiously poked his head through the open apartment door.

"Reuben, you okay?"

He jumped when Terry nudged him.

"Take out your weapon," he hissed. Terry's gun was already in his hand. Mike knew that the Conn brothers had fifteen months on the job.

Working Uptown, though, was liable to make any cop jumpy. You never knew how people there would react. Some days you could reenact Pearl Harbor, and they'd just turn up their TVs so they wouldn't be bothered. Other times, a traffic stop was reason enough for a gunfight.

In heat like this, Mike felt "easy does it" was the right attitude.

He left his .38 in its holster and took out his billy club. He stepped inside.

"Reuben, you need a doctor?"

No answer. The only light burning was at the back of the place. Made sense that the guy was back there, but Mike and Terry took it slow, turning on lights as they went. They found their man in the bathroom.

Reuben Fuckhead Gadoy—all three hundred pounds of him—was sitting in the bathtub drinking a beer. With a pair of orange-handled shears sticking out of his huge belly.

Looking over Mike's shoulder, Terry muttered, "Talk about Moby Fucking Dick. Harpooned even."

Mike elbowed him in the ribs and asked from the doorway, "How you feeling, Reuben?"

Reuben frowned. Looked at Terry.

"What'd he say? Something about my dick?"

"Yeah," Terry said. "Lucky she didn't snip."

Mike turned to his partner and whispered harshly. "I'll handle this, okay?"

"He some kinda fag cop, or somethin'?" Reuben asked.

Mike put a forestalling hand on Terry's chest, then turned back to the fat man.

"He didn't say anything, Reuben, but it's not a real good idea to call a cop names."

"You're right, man. It's this fuckin' heat. Makes everyone cranky." He casually scratched his stomach, working around the shears. "You guys want a beer?"

Three cans remaining from a six-pack sat on the floor next to the tub.

"Reuben," Mike said reasonably, "you've been stuck a good one. You sure you want to sit there drinking beer?"

Mike didn't see any blood; with all the guy's fat he couldn't even see the *wound*. But he had to be bleeding inside.

"Yeah, I feel better than I have all night."

"This is bullshit," Terry said.

Reuben shook his head and peeled a finger off his can of beer to point at the cops.

"No, that's not bullshit. You know what's bullshit?" he asked indignantly. "It's when you try to do a little good, and this is what you get."

He nodded to his belly, then continued.

"I work an extra shift to have a little more money around here, and when I come home the old lady says I'm out whorin' with my no-good buddies. I say, 'Baby, I was *workin'*. But now that you mention pussy . . .' She says it's too hot. So bein' real nice, I run a bath and say let's do it in the water. That'll be nice and cool. She says get the fuck away from me. After that, you know, well, one thing led to the other."

Reuben took a long drink of beer and smiled peacefully. Then he burped a gout of blood onto his belly, the stream dividing at the shears.

"Reuben," Mike said, "let's get you to a hospital."

"When I'm done with my beer, man."

Mike wasn't going to argue, but Terry got impatient.

"You're goin' now, buddy," he said over Mike's shoulder.

"Fuck you, man," Reuben said and took a swallow of beer.

"You're also under arrest, asshole."

Mike looked around at his backup man.

"Will you shut the fuck up? Just let him finish this one goddamn beer."

"Yeah, motherfucker," Reuben added.

Terry glared at the fat man but spoke to Mike.

"You know what happens if this PR dies on us?"

"Hey, shit-for-brains, I'm Cuban!"

Terry rephrased his question.

"You know what happens if this *spic* dies on us?"

"Let him be," Mike insisted.

"Ain't nobody calls me spic in my own house," Reuben said behind the two arguing cops.

"He dies because we didn't render assistance, the broad can sue and we'll all be goin' to court and fillin' out papers until we—"

An obscene sucking noise cut Terry Conn off. Both cops turned to look. Reuben's massive body was rising from the water. Moby Dick wasn't a bad comparison at all, Mike thought.

The two cops saw blood now. There was plenty

of it on the shears Reuben had just pulled out of his stomach.

"Outta the way, man," Reuben said to Mike, stepping out of the tub. "I'm gonna cut that fucker."

Mike held out his billy club. "Put it down, Reuben."

Behind him, Terry shouted, "Get outta the way! Gimme a clear shot!"

"Don't shoot!" Mike yelled.

Reuben, who obviously didn't back down from anything, kept coming. He held the shears high, as if he were going to plunge them into a pumpkin.

"I'll cut you, too, you don't get outta my way."

Mike surprised Reuben by stepping toward him rather than away. He used the superior reach of the billy club to deliver a sharp crack to the back of the fat man's wrist. Even with all the guy's padding, Mike could hear the bones break. The shears fell to the floor, and that was when Reuben noticed the blood he was trailing across the ceramic tile floor. Then he glanced at his dangling hand.

He looked up at Mike, disappointed. "Aw, shit, man. You didn't have to do that."

Reuben deflated like a three-hundred-pound balloon, smacking the floor with a fleshy thud. Terry insisted that the fucker would die on them if they waited for an ambulance. It took Mike and both of the Conn brothers to load the unconscious naked body into the back of Mike's car and get him to the hospital.

Reuben made it, but the three cops didn't get out of the hospital until eight-fifteen, and they were filling out paperwork until noon.

Mike and Terry were pissed at each other. Each

of them thought the other had handled things badly. So Billy played the peacemaker.

Like the good Bridgeport lad with political connections that he was, Billy pulled box-seat tickets to the White Sox game out of his pocket. He said an afternoon of drinking beer at the ballpark was on him. If that didn't smooth over any hard feelings, fuck them both.

Mike Kildare fell in love when he saw the girl selling beer at the concession stand in Comiskey Park. She had auburn hair, blue eyes, and full lips that he wanted to kiss right away. She also looked too young to be selling beer.

"How old are you?" he asked.

"Old enough to know what that goofy look means."

"Yeah, what's that?"

"That you've been drinking, and now you're thinking."

She was right. The game was in the bottom of the third, he'd guzzled four beers already, and he definitely had ideas about her. She smiled at him. The name tag on her shirt said HARRY.

"So what'll it be?" she asked.

Mike flashed his badge.

"Schlitz, if you're old enough to sell it."

A pained voice called out from behind him.

"Jesus Christ, buddy, if you're gonna bust her, let her work another five minutes first."

He turned and saw a line of men behind him waiting for beer. The guy who'd complained had a big red nose and was standing right next to him.

"Sure, but if she's under-age, I'll have to bust *you* for contributing to the delinquency of a minor."

The beer drinkers grumbled but moved to another window. He looked back at the girl.

"Show me some ID."

"Show me that badge again. You look kinda young to be a cop."

He saw she wasn't going to take any crap, even if she was still smiling. She took a good, long look at his badge before deciding it was real.

"You want to see my gun, too?"

"Ooh, right here in public?"

He had to laugh. She dug her driver's license out of a purse she had under the counter. Harriet Wilkerson. Five-seven, one twenty-two. Far South Side address. She'd turned twenty-one last week.

He committed the address to memory before he handed the license back.

"Schlitz, right?"

"Three. I'm with friends."

She tapped the beers into paper cups.

"Yeah? You show *them* your gun, too?"

"They've got their own."

"Wow. All the cops around here, a girl sure feels safe."

She gave him his beers and made change from a ten.

"You'd feel even safer if I knew your phone number," he said, giving her his best smile.

"You're cute, and you know it, too. But no one's as cute as you think you are."

"No phone number, huh?"

"Uh-uh."

"Not even if I tell you how I disarmed a wifebeater waving a pair of bloody scissors this morning?"

That caught her interest. Everyone loved a good cop story.

"Guy was big as an ox. Had these eight-inch shears."

She was trying to decide if he was bullshitting her.

"That's not the good part. You should hear what he pulled them out of."

He was sure he had her, but an old bat who must've been her boss came over and gave them both the evil eye.

"Look," Harry said, "if you're not going to arrest me or anything, I've got a job to do." She turned toward the crone. "He didn't believe I was twenty-one."

"Beat it, sonny," the old broad said, "or I'll introduce you to some *serious* cops."

That was the thing about Chicago, you never knew who had clout. Doc left. But he did get Harry's phone number. It was in the book.

They went out on their first date two nights later.

Within a week, they knew they were made for each other. Not only couldn't they get enough of each other's body but they had great conversations before, after, and sometimes during sex.

Unless someone had a mouthful.

Which Mike didn't when he noticed that Harry wasn't just looking down as she straddled him; she was staring.

He said, "I know you're looking at me, but what are you looking at?"

"Trying to see signs."

"Of what?"

"Whether you'll be a drunk."

"I won't."

"Lots of cops are."

"Not me."

Harry nodded. They were in the bedroom of her apartment. The shades were pulled against the late-afternoon sun.

"I don't think you will, either. You're too vain."

"Too smart, too. Anything else you want to check out?"

She stared some more.

"I wonder if you'll cheat. The way you look, it wouldn't be hard. Of course, if you did . . ."

There was a sudden, startling contraction in the wet warmth around him. He jackknifed into a sitting position before sinking back against the pillows.

"God . . . How did you do that?"

"Practice," she smiled.

"Do it again. I'm ready for it now."

"Tell me what you see first."

A shit-eating grin spread across Mike's face.

"I don't just mean my tits."

"You won't mind a little corn?"

"Try me."

"I see the girl I'm taking home to meet Mom and—God!" He rolled them over so he was on top. She didn't allow them to come apart for a second. "Mom and Dad'll have to wait a while," he said.

Doc looked at the phone a minute, and almost wished Harry would call back.

Then he crossed to the high mahogany dresser that he'd climbed as a kid. The trick was to stagger the drawers. Pull the bottom one out farthest, the next one a little less, and so on. What you made was a staircase up to the top—where Mom and Big John dumped their spare change.

The money was easy pickings for him and Richie, and Ray had a storeful of Hershey bars, Batman comics, and Cokes only a furtive scurry away. The trick worked time and again.

Then he and Richie had gotten the shock of their young lives when one climbing expedition netted not any purloined silver but a one-word note: *Gotcha!*

They'd turned and found their father standing in the doorway. Caught red-handed. Big John hadn't punished them, hadn't even said a word. He'd just left them standing on that open drawer, pinned fast by undeniable guilt.

They'd learned their lesson.

As Doc opened the top drawer now, he half expected to see his father in the doorway behind him again. Big John, or the Internal Affairs Unit, or someone. He reached under a pile of T-shirts and pulled out an envelope. He opened the flap and withdrew a stack of Polaroids. They were of Harry. Nude.

Doc had taken them early in their marriage; he still remembered the night. The poses were meant to be as humorous as they were erotic, but any time he saw Harry without her clothes on other sentiments took second place to the way his pulse pounded.

When he and Harry had divided their belongings for the divorce, Doc made sure these pictures were hidden away. He took the precaution even though he doubted she remembered them.

Shuffling through the yellowed images, getting excited, he recalled something his shrink had told him. She'd said everyone has a subconscious fixed age, usually between eighteen and twenty-five. So no matter how old you got, you thought of yourself at your fixed age.

The age you chose had to do with how you liked to see yourself: your looks, your personality, your intelligence. When something happened to you—like getting your eye shot out—it fucked up that self-image and made you doubt yourself.

Looking at Harry's pictures helped Doc restore himself. He'd been a young cop, and Harry'd been his new wife, and most of his family had still been alive.

So now he was going into the bathroom to have sex with his wife. As he had on several other nights. But then he got caught again.

He looked out his bedroom window and saw Glenna Handee come out her door across the street, to go looking for Jerry.

He put the pictures back in the envelope, hid the envelope under the T-shirts. He got an elastic bandage out of the same drawer, wrapped his knee, got dressed, and went out to help look for the missing boy.

16

Doc limped into Ray's after another futile night of roaming the neighborhood and saw that Vince DiGiuseppe had staked out the table at the back of the store.

The usual breakfast crowd filled the place and was keeping Ray hopping, but there was an invisible moat around Vince. He had the table and four chairs to himself. People kept their voices down so even their conversations wouldn't intrude. Maybe it was because you took one look at Vince and you thought: cop.

The kind who made you feel guilty even if you weren't.

Doc made his way over, pausing to give false reassurance to Monie Watkins about his well-being, and to shake hands with Bill Springer, who told him if anybody deserved that bastard Guzman's blood money it was him.

Without being asked, Ray brought Doc a cup of coffee and refilled Vince's cup.

"The regular, Doc?" Ray asked.

He nodded.

"Get you something, Lieutenant?"

Vince shook his head. "Coffee's all I need."

Ray shrugged and went away.

"Ray still run that backroom book?" Vince asked.

"No. It died with Dottie."

"You knew about it all along, didn't you?"

"Sure."

"But you never busted it even after you joined the force."

"My dad would've killed me if I busted his bookie. Yours would've killed you, too."

Vince snorted. "My father never bet on horse races."

"No," Doc said and sipped his coffee. "He fixed them."

Before Vince could respond, Ray was back with a plate of ham and eggs for Doc. He refilled both coffee cups and was gone again without a word.

Vince smiled.

"Old guy really moves, you gotta give him that. Why doesn't he get some help?"

"He says you don't know who you can trust these days."

"He's got that right."

Doc started on his eggs. He was so tired his head was getting heavy. If it fell, he wanted it to be on a clean plate.

"The Superintendent and the new DEA boss, Carswell, had dinner last night," Vince said. "You were the sole topic of discussion."

Doc didn't need to ask how he knew this; Vince had more spies than the CIA.

"What'd they have to say, not that I give a fuck."

"Basically, Malloy wouldn't give you a dime if you lost both eyes, your balls, and your ass. Mr. DEA doesn't mind you getting some money as much as he does having other wounded cops get the idea they can cash in, too."

"This isn't exactly surprising, Vince."

"I know. But that's all they said last night. I

thought I'd hear more. That's why I wanted to wait until this morning to talk to you. They're supposed to get together again tonight. They're lookin' for some way to screw you."

He leaned forward and whispered, "If you got anything you need to keep hid, now's the time to bury it."

Doc shook his head.

"They won't find anything because there *isn't* anything. They try to make something up, and Wetherby'll crucify them."

Vince lit a cigar. "Okay, but I'll keep my ears open, anyway."

Doc nodded his appreciation. "Listen, I need your help with a couple of things."

"What?"

"There was some guy in a Mercedes checking my house last night."

Vince frowned. "You get a license?"

"No," Doc said, rubbing his knee. It was still sore. "I didn't see his face clearly, either. He had a hat on and the collar on his coat was up, like he was some yo-yo playing secret agent. Thinking about it, I come up with only one guy who fits."

Vince said, "Cousin Hector, Armando Guzman's Hollywood lawyer."

"Beverly Hills," Doc corrected.

"Excuse the hell outta me."

"What I wonder is, why is he casing my house when he should be working on his cousin's appeal?"

"I don't know, but I'll find out."

Doc said, "There's one other thing."

He explained about Jerry Handee being missing and how his calls to the Youth Division cop, Schumann, hadn't been returned.

"You like this kid, huh?"

"Yeah, but what the hell does that matter? He's a handicapped kid and he's missing."

"What I meant was, you sound emotionally involved here. Probably that's the reason you didn't use your head."

"What's that supposed to mean?" Doc asked.

"I mean you've made yourself a political issue in the department. Working cops love your angle; the brass hate it. So even if a cop, this Schumann say, wanted to help you, he'd still be taking a big chance. One of his enemies could rat on him to a higher-up."

Vince was right, and Doc should've seen it. All cops had enemies on the force. They came from politics, envy, or simple dislike. Let it get around that you helped a persona non grata like him and your enemies could make you pay—and have a good time doing it.

He couldn't blame anyone for ignoring him, and he couldn't see Glenna going back to the department and asking for help again. The whole thing sucked.

"So Jerry's left hanging, is that it?"

Vince shook his head.

"No. He's got you. You got me. I got enough ammunition to protect the guys on your old team. They'll see what the Guzmans are up to for you. Now I gotta go."

Vince stood up, puffed on his cigar, and looked down at Doc.

"Hey, those're those changeable sunglasses you got on, aren't they? The lenses get lighter and darker?"

"Yeah," Doc said.

"You know where I could get some?" Vince asked.

*   *   *

Doc struggled to stay awake after Vince left. He understood now that he'd get no help from the department. He'd have to find Jerry on his own, but he didn't think he could do it. By himself, he was getting nowhere fast.

Ray came by to refill his cup again, but Doc covered it with his hand. He didn't need to be both tired and wired. He looked around and saw that most of the morning regulars were still in place.

He decided it was time to go public.

Doc got up and asked Ray to turn the TV off. No one had really been watching the thing, but everyone stopped what they were doing as soon as it went off.

Doc said, "I'm sorry to interrupt, but I need to talk with you. In case anyone hasn't heard, Jerry Handee is missing and I'm looking for him."

Most of them hadn't heard, and they babbled about it for a minute before Doc broke in.

"Glenna is very worried, and I'm getting nervous myself. This is the second day he's been gone, and the longer he's missing the worse his chances are. I need your help."

Help was offered. Eagerly. But to Doc's ear it sounded like they were discussing a missing puppy.

"What I'd like you to do is keep your eyes open. If you see Jerry somewhere, bring him home and call me at my house or leave a message for me here."

There was a chorus of agreement.

"For all we know he might just be visiting with someone in the neighborhood. If you see him in the house next door or something, call me. I'm going to be knocking on doors around here looking for him. I hope you'll understand."

They did, but their enthusiasm dropped off a cliff. Doc could see it in their faces: *What the hell, did he suspect* them *of something?*

Doc concluded, "Please spread the word. I imagine I'll be talking with all of you."

After I get some frigging sleep, he thought. He left the money for his breakfast and Vince's coffee, nodded to his neighbors, and walked home.

It didn't make him happy to plant seeds of suspicion among people he'd known for years, if not all his life. But suspicious people would be doubly watchful. Nosy even. They'd tattle every little thing to him, and he needed that.

Because after two nights of searching, he was pretty sure Jerry wasn't anywhere outdoors in the neighborhood. That left indoors, he hoped.

Doc just prayed Jerry wasn't anywhere *under* the neighborhood.

17

Sixteen-year-old Fred Welles came out of the Lakeside Country Day School just in time for a CTA bus to whip past and leave him gagging in a cloud of exhaust fumes. The boy cursed and raced after the bus to the street corner, where it was supposed to stop. But the light was green, nobody was waiting, and the bus kept going.

"Asshole!" Fred yelled.

He heard people laughing and looked around. A carload of seniors who'd seen his futile dash passed him honking and jeering.

Fred gave them the finger—once they were out of sight. He wasn't a jock, so he didn't go in for physical confrontation. He wasn't a brain, either. He didn't worry about these shortcomings, because what he *was* more than made up for them. He was rich.

His mother had family money, and the amount his old man made every year should have been criminal.

That was why it pissed him off that the old man said he couldn't have his own car until he was a senior. Even then, he'd been told, the *kind* of car he got would depend on his grades. The old man called this "the incentive system."

Fred called it a crock.

There wasn't another bus in sight, but he saw

a cab. He hailed it, thinking maybe if he spent enough money on taxis the old man would get pissed and buy him a car as a means of saving money.

The cab pulled obediently to a stop in front of him and he got in. Fred gave the driver his Astor Street address. He wasn't sure if the guy could hear him through the bulletproof partition, but the cabbie nodded and pulled away.

As soon as school had been left a block behind, Fred took a joint out of his pocket and lit it. The driver saw him in his mirror.

"What's that?" he said.

Fred realized that the driver's voice had come through a speaker.

"Clove cigarette," he said.

"Clove?"

"Yeah, it's a plant. Comes from the tropics."

"I know what kind of plant that is. Put it out."

"Hey, man, I don't see any 'No Smoking' sign."

To emphasize his point, Fred took a deep drag on the joint. It was good stuff, and ragging the driver already seemed like a pretty funny game.

"Kid, you don't want to argue with me."

Fred could see the guy was getting tense. He thought maybe he should personalize the discussion. He leaned forward to look at the chauffeur license for the guy's name. What he saw made him giggle. And exhale his smoke.

"Hey, your name."

"What about it?"

"It's French, right?"

"Yeah, so?"

"You know how it translates?"

"What do you mean, 'translates'?"

"The English equivalent. If your name was English, it'd be . . ." He took another hit off the joint. "Andy Slick!"

Fred burst out laughing. Until a finger of paranoia touched the back of his neck. Then he clammed up fast and looked to see if he'd pissed the guy off too much.

But the driver was smiling.

"Andy Slick, huh?"

"Yeah." Fred tried to stifle another giggle attack.

"I never knew that." Actually he *was* called Andy, but never slick.

That's when the voice whispered to Andy. Told him what he had to do. Which surprised the hell out of him. Usually, he could feel it coming.

This one? he asked the voice, wanting to be positive. He used his mirror to look at the kid in the backseat. Sure he was a rich punk, you could tell by lookin' at him, and he just came outta that stuck-up private school, and—

Fred saw Andy looking at him, and he didn't like the way the driver suddenly went all glassy-eyed. Like somebody had changed his channel by remote control. Maybe turned his set off altogether. The damn guy wasn't even watching the road. Fred's paranoia soared. He was about to say something when Andy snapped out of it.

"No offense," Fred said, thinking an apology might be wise. "That's just the way your name translates."

To his surprise, Andy smiled.

"That's okay. I kind of like it."

Fred couldn't help giggling about that.

The driver said, "Look, we both know that's grass you're smoking, and the reason I got ticked just now is because I got a record."

"For crime?" That knocked Fred back in his seat.

"I used to deal that stuff in your hand. Still have some connections. So if the cops stop us, what are they going to think?"

The idea that a cab driver could be a dope dealer had never entered Fred's mind. It blew him away. He could see why the guy would get pissed. They were getting close to home anyway, and his building employed Deacon Ezra Fobb, the world's snoopiest doorman. Fred stubbed out the joint on his sneaker and stuck the roach into his pants.

"Sorry, man, I didn't know."

"No problem," Andy told him. "You ever want some really great stuff, I'll introduce you to some people."

Fred thought of the mileage he could get at school from having a heavy dope connection.

"How'm I going to find you if I do?"

"I work this area a lot. Just flag me down."

The cab pulled into the driveway of Fred's high-rise. There were twenty-two luxury apartments, one per floor. Fred lived on top.

"Or," Andy said, "you need some right away, I'll pick you up here tonight at ten."

"Good stuff?"

"Great stuff."

Fred knew that neither of his parents would be home that night. Getting out would be easy. He saw the Deacon walking this way to help him out of the cab.

"Ten o'clock," the boy said. "But not here, on the corner."

Andy nodded and Fred got out.

The cab pulled away before the Deacon could lay a hand on it. Andy smiled to himself as he turned onto Lake Shore Drive and cruised toward Michigan Avenue. He had the little bastard hooked.

The voice had been right. But then, it always was.

18

Rudd Wetherby was ready to give his second press conference in two days. Since the pencil press had gotten such a good reaction from yesterday's story, the boys and girls from the TV stations showed up for this one.

A ghost of a smile crossed the attorney's lips. Things were building just the way he had hoped. The hotel meeting room he'd booked was just big enough for the crowd.

The television camera lights came on and Wetherby got the signal that everyone was ready to proceed.

"When I spoke to you ladies and gentlemen yesterday," he began, "I was asked what the legal justification was for my client's claim. I'm prepared to discuss that with you this afternoon."

Wetherby paused to allow the slow note-takers plenty of time. He wanted them all ready for what came next.

"By way of preparing you to understand the legal underpinnings of the claim, I'd first like to show you just what kind of agonizing ordeal Michael 'Doc' Kildare endured. I must warn you, though, the exhibits I have for you are nothing less than gruesome."

The media people nodded soberly, but Wetherby could almost see them calculate the number of column inches and minutes of air time they'd be getting out of him. He had them right where he wanted them.

"First, however, we'll begin with what Doc Kildare looked like before he was shot by Armando Guzman, the convicted drug trafficker."

Wetherby had set up Doc's recruitment poster photo and his other visuals on an easel. The print media had the picture from the day before, but the lawyer made sure the TV people had a chance to take their shots.

"Now, please brace yourselves. This is what happened to Mr. Kildare after he was shot."

Harry had stayed home from work that day. She had the noontime news on the TV on for company, and she gagged when she saw what had happend to Doc. He looked like something out of a nightmare. His left eye socket was a bloody hole, and strips of white—part of his eye?—hung down his cheek.

Harry ran to the bathroom so she wouldn't throw up all over the living room rug.

Wetherby himself was still disturbed by the photo. It had been taken at the hospital before Doc's surgery had been done. But he'd seen it enough times to keep a deadpan expression.

Seeing it for the first time, the media people were having trouble keeping their collective cookies from snapping.

Wetherby didn't know what medical purpose these pictures served, but they were a lawyer's wet dream.

Hector Guzman loosened his silk tie in his hotel suite as he looked at the horrific mess his legal colleague was showing. He decided he wouldn't want to live if such a thing had happened to him.

He knew, of course, that Armando had done far worse things to other victims. In fact, if Armando was watching right now, Hector was sure he was laughing.

Laughing, and planning on how to improve his work.

Wetherby gave his audience a compassionate look.

"I understand how disturbing it is to see such a terrifying wound, but try to imagine what it must have been like to suffer through it. And this was just the beginning."

He went on to show them photos detailing the enucleation and repair of Doc's eye socket. Wetherby estimated that by the time he had finished the only people not feeling queasy would be surgeons and sadists.

Now, saving the best for last, it was time for his final photo.

He asked, "After all he went through, what was left for Doc Kildare? This."

Wetherby displayed a picture of a single prosthetic eye. It floated against a seamless gray background. The blue pupil staring out at the cameras seemed to have an alien awareness all its own. After what had gone before, it was the most obscene image of all.

"This is what they put into my client's head."

While his audience was still hypnotized, the lawyer let the photo fall facedown and quickly changed gears.

"The United States Code, Title 21, Chapter 13, Subchapter 1, Section 853 (h), concerning the disposition of forfeited property, says in part, quote,

'Following the seizure of property ordered forfeited under this section, the Attorney General
shall direct the disposition of property . . . making due provisions for the right of any innocent
persons,' close quote."

Wetherby gave the cameras his most earnest
look.

"I ask you, what person could be more innocent, what person should be more duly provided
for than my client?"

That appeal made, he quickly got back to
business.

"The U.S. Code, same heading, Section 853 (i)
says in part, quote, 'The Attorney General is au-
thorized to . . . protect the rights of any innocent
person which is in the interest of justice . . . and
to award compensation to persons providing information resulting in forfeiture under this
section. . . .' "

Superintendent Malloy and DEA Agent-in-
Charge Carswell were having drinks in front of
Malloy's office television. They listened to Rudd
Wetherby's continued appeal.

"If making this claim for my client isn't a cry
for justice," the attorney said, "I don't know what
is. I don't know what else it could be called."

"It's called a *fucking ripoff*, that's what!" Malloy
shouted. Carswell gave him an unnoticed side-
long glance.

Wetherby went on. "Even were we to reduce
our considerations to the most pragmatic level, it
was information developed by Doc Kildare that
led to the arrest, conviction, and life imprisonment of one of the most heinous monsters ever
to threaten the welfare of the American people."

"That was his *job*, goddammit!" Malloy roared. "He was a fucking *cop*!"

"*Was* is the operative word," Carswell said, adding dryly, "thanks to you."

Wetherby paused to survey his audience. They still followed along nicely.

"Let me just say, in conclusion, that Mr. Kildare's claim is on funds which now belong to the United States Government. And as we all know, in our great country the *people* are the government. I'm sure that the people would want one of their own, after all he's suffered on their behalf, to be rightfully compensated. Thank you."

He quickly packed up his materials and left the room. The media were on his heels, of course, and he promised, without answering any questions specifically, to keep them apprised of any further developments.

They let him get into the elevator alone, and once the door was closed he slumped back against the wall and smiled. He thought he'd given quite a performance. Legally, it was a lot of mumbo-jumbo. Ethically, it was questionable. But theatrically, it was socko.

Doc was now a public hero. That left the government two choices. It could choose to look appropriately generous, or choose to look ungratefully tightfisted.

Wetherby had just given the feds what the feds had given Armando Guzman. The political shaft.

19

Fred Welles felt pretty sure he'd made a big mistake the minute Andy Slick's cab took off with him in back.

He'd been on the corner at ten sharp. Five seconds later, Andy pulled up and popped open the passenger-side door with some kind of automatic gizmo. That part had been cool, like they were doing a spy caper or something. It was only when the door *closed* by itself behind him that Fred's stomach sank.

He thought it would probably be bad manners to ask for details of how everything was going to work. He didn't intend to question the quality or the amount of the dope he got for his money, either. All the thoughts of how cool this would sound at school had vanished.

He saw Andy watching him in the mirror.

"You nervous?"

"Nah," the boy said, but his throat was so dry he sounded like a frog croaking.

"It's okay. Sometimes being nervous is a reasonable thing." Andy smiled.

Tonight, after dark, it spooked Fred that Andy's voice was coming through a speaker. And it looked like Andy *hoped* he was nervous.

"I'm fine," Fred lied.

"You're not carrying, are ya?"

"Carrying what?"

"You know. A gun or a knife or something."

"No!"

"Take it easy. I only mention it because some people get dramatic when they go to score some weed or a little blow."

Fred sat back in the seat. That surprised him, because he wasn't aware that he'd moved forward.

He looked out the window and saw they were in a part of the city he'd never seen. The tall buildings that looked like they were held together by graffiti had to be housing projects. Cabrini-Green, maybe. So they were west of Old Town. Andy made a right. They were going somewhere on the North Side.

"Hey, I got a question," Andy said.

"What?"

"How come that school where you go is called 'Country Day' when it's right in the middle of town?"

"They call it 'Country Day' because 'City Day' sounds shitty."

Fred saw Andy's eyes in the mirror, and could tell he didn't think that was funny. His eyes seemed a little glazed again, too, and he nodded, as if agreeing with a point somebody'd just made. Somebody Fred couldn't see or hear.

The boy decided right then he wasn't going to smart-off to this guy anymore.

"The school's over a hundred years old," he said. "It was out in the country when it was built."

Andy's eyes cleared, but he was pissed. "You got a mouth on you."

"Yeah, I'm sorry."

"Didn't your parents teach you manners?"

"My parents didn't take the time to teach me

anything," Fred said bitterly. For a moment the boy thought he saw Andy's hard eyes soften, until Fred added, almost by force of habit, "Those fuckers."

Andy turned into an alley that ran alongside of the "L" tracks. Most of the lights in the alley were out. When the cab bounced unexpectedly through a pothole, Fred almost screamed.

"Hey, where're we going?"

"Relax. You think you make a buy at Woodfield Mall?"

"Look, I just want to get this over with."

"Me, too."

"I lied before; I am scared."

"I know."

"Your door started it."

"What?"

"The way it closed all by itself. That scared me."

Andy smiled.

"That's something I got from Japan. All the cabs over there have automatic doors. You know why I put it in?"

"Why?"

"Because of this one guy. I picked him up almost in Evanston. He wants to go all the way across town. We got so far on the South Side we're halfway to Alabama. The meter up here sounds like a slot machine paying a jackpot. Two blocks before we get to the address the guy gave me I stop for a red light, and he's out of the cab like a shot."

A train roared by on the tracks overhead.

"You know how I felt?"

"How?"

Andy glanced over his shoulder at Fred. "I wanted to kill the guy."

The boy started to shake.

"Now there was no way I'd catch this guy on foot, and since he ducked between a couple of houses I couldn't follow him in the cab. But then I thought maybe, just maybe, I have a lamebrain here who gave me his right address. So, I drive over there doing sixty. And what do you know?"

"You got him?"

"Sure did."

Andy pulled the cab into a space under the tracks, between the huge supporting structures of the elevated line. He shut the engine off and turned sideways on his seat to face Fred through the protective partition. There was just enough light for the boy to make out his face. It looked crazy.

Fred hoped Andy couldn't see his hand reaching for the door handle. He'd taken all of this he could.

"So, you made him pay?" Fred asked, trying not to give himself away.

"No. I killed him."

Fred yanked the handle and threw himself against the door. It didn't budge. He jumped across the seat and tried the other door. It was locked, too.

Andy said, "I went the Japanese one better: automatic locks. That way nobody leaves until they pay. Neat, huh? You should have expected it. After all, you call me Andy Slick."

Fred shrank back into the far corner of the seat.

"I lied, too," Andy said. "I don't really have any dope connections." That's when Fred saw the gun in his hand.

Fred screamed. But now Andy was trembling as much as the boy was.

"Shut up, you little bastard!" Andy's voice

cracked. Fred sat frozen, unable to do more than tremble. When Andy continued it was in a high-pitched whine, his throat choked with rage. "You could have ruined everything for me, smoking your goddamn grass in my taxi. You could have spoiled all my secrets." The gun in Andy's hand was shaking. "And I didn't even realize how much danger I was in, until I was warned." Tears fell from Andy's eyes. "So now you have to pay."

Andy pressed a button and the bullet-proof partition started to go down. Fred screamed again.

But not much sound carried beyond the cab, and the little that did was drowned out by the train roaring past overhead.

Andy carried the canvas-covered body from the garage to the house. All the old-fart neighbors were asleep, and the yard was dark. It was no problem. He went in through the back door and relocked it behind him.

He took the boy down to the basement.

There were two large rooms down there, and he put the body in the second. Both rooms were very neat, no junk or clutter lying around like most basements. In fact, the only thing that took up any floor space at all was a gas furnace in the first room.

Andy pulled a clipboard from a space in the back of the cement pedestal on which the furnace rested. Clipped to the board was his floor plan. He consulted it. Just as he remembered, the first room was full. He'd have to open up the other.

He'd put this new boy in the far corner of the second room. When more came along, he'd work his way across and then down, going in rows, just as he had in the first room.

He went back into the second room, looked at

the boy, and then at the space available to him. He was pretty sure that it wouldn't take him as long to fill up this room as the first one. Not that he was in a hurry. He didn't go out looking to kill just anyone.

He only killed people who pissed him off, he told himself. But a hot wave of shame rose through Andy, and because he was alone and in this very special place he could admit the truth to himself.

He only killed people who scared him.

And he needed the voice to tell him who to be afraid of.

The thing was, more people seemed to scare him every day. Lately, it was like they came looking for him. The wise-ass kid at his feet was just one example. *If the little jerk gets in my cab and minds his own business, he's home with no fuss and I pocket another fare. Everybody's happy. But the punk has to start smoking his goddamn dope. Goddamn rich kid. Probably thinks he can get away with anything.*

At first Andy was just annoyed. Then the voice wised him up: *What if the cops see the kid and pull you over? What if the kid tries to lay off the blame on you?* Who would the cops believe then, him or some rich brat? He knew goddamn well who. Didn't even need the voice to tell him that one. Then the cops have him, and they're gonna find out about his taxi first thing. From there, it wouldn't be hard to figure out what else he'd been up to.

He pulled the canvas away from the body and gave it several hard kicks. In a way, he did kill people who pissed him off. Because people who scared him pissed him off.

When he had calmed down he pulled a wallet from the back of the boy's bloodstained jeans. A bus pass said the little prick's name had been Fred Welles. He dropped the wallet onto the body.

"Now you'll disappear and nobody'll find ya," Andy said aloud. "Is that slick enough for ya?"

He sat down tailor-fashion and rested his clipboard against his legs. Actually, he liked the name Andy Slick. Knowing it was a version—a hidden version—of his real name made it even better. Like he was a superhero with a secret identity.

He started to hum the theme music from the old *Superman* TV show. He flipped the pad on the clipboard over to a blank page and drew a grid chart of the second room. To scale. He reached over and consulted the bus pass again, to make sure there was no mistake about the name.

Then in the top left box of the new chart he neatly lettered: BAD FRED.

The ritual pleased him. If he ever did talk to a shrink about it, he would say, sure, he got a charge killing someone who pissed him off—he wouldn't tell that he'd been scared—but that the lasting satisfaction came in looking back at how neatly you followed through.

Well, he *had* been slick. He *was* slick. (He really liked that new name.) Not only was he able to take care of any asshole who gave him grief, but each time he did he could look back at all the others.

From Bad Fred all the way back to the first name in the very first box on his chart: BAD DADDY.

Technically, he couldn't claim his old man.

But who didn't learn by example?

20

Millie Bogarde, Ray's real-estate widow, had seen Doc's story on the TV news and was sure he was going to wind up with a lot of money. So she was happy to show him the seven empty buildings that were for sale in The Wedge.

There were two others she didn't care about, since they were tied up in probate and wouldn't come on the market until the heirs had settled their squabbles. But he'd demanded to see these, too.

Doc was willing to put up with the sales spiels, for the pleasure of riding around in Millie's powder-blue Cadillac.

"You have my deepest sympathies for your suffering," Millie said. "Did I mention that?"

"Yes, you did."

She'd mentioned it after four of the first five places she'd shown him. A rat ran through the kitchen of number three, momentarily throwing her off form. Now she was back in stride.

"You say the poor boy you're looking for is retarded?"

"Yes, he is."

They'd been over this a number of times, too. Doc thought it was time to introduce a variation on the theme.

He said, "You know, it might be helpful if the

local merchants put a photo of Jerry in their windows. Keep his face in front of the public."

A look of consternation surfaced on Millie's face, and her corseted bottom squirmed in its plush seat.

"He's not . . . I mean, he isn't . . ."

"Mongoloid?"

"Well, yes."

"No, he isn't."

Millie smiled, relieved.

"This is what he looks like."

Doc showed her the photo he'd gotten from Glenna. She took a quick peek.

"Why, he's very handsome. How did he . . ."

The real-estate lady was hung up on another awkward question, and Doc knew what it was.

"He was nearly garroted with his umbilical cord."

Millie's panicked stop put the Caddy's bumper into a nose dive that scraped the pavement. Their seatbelts were the only things that kept her and Doc from going through the windshield. Millie looked at him for confirmation of what she thought she'd just heard. He nodded.

"The family thought they'd save some money and use a midwife for the delivery. It didn't work out so well."

"Oh, dear."

Doc waited until the woman was able to get under way again. When he saw she wasn't going to run down any inattentive pedestrian, he said, "You won't mind putting Jerry's photo up? I'll have copies made."

"No, no. It will be perfectly all right."

"Good."

At least he'd accomplished *something* worthwhile that morning. He'd seen no trace of Jerry at any of the places they'd visited, and he doubted the remaining ones would yield any information.

"Mr. Kildare, I hope you don't mind, but I'll just let you look around the remaining buildings by yourself. I'm not feeling well all of a sudden."

"No problem," Doc said.

He'd take any break he could get.

Officer Dolph Schumann was supposed to be out looking for six-year-old Rogelio Rios. At the moment, his search was confined to the premises of Danny's Donuts. He was working on his third eclair and his second coffee with extra cream and four sugars.

He thought that if his goddamn cousin Frank didn't get here pretty soon, his teeth were going to rot right out of his head or he'd come down with diabetes or something. But he also figured that, as the only child of parents who owned a German bakery, there was no way to stop his craving. His sweet tooth had to be genetic.

For a moment his thoughts strayed back to his job. The mother who had filed the report on the Rios kid thought her ex-boyfriend, Rogelio's father, had taken him. Schumann figured she was probably right, too. The problem was he had checked the guy's apartment and the janitor said he hadn't seen him around lately; the guy's employer said he no longer had a job, since he'd missed three days without calling in.

The boyfriend and the kid were both probably on a banana boat back to Central America. If so, that was a kidnap and the FBI's worry. Of course, the boyfriend might've gone off the deep end and killed the kid. But then the case belonged to Homicide.

Schumann stirred his cooling coffee to get the sugar off the bottom. A horn honked and he looked up. Fucking Frank, finally.

Sergeant Frank Pankraz came in and plopped down at the window counter next to Schumann.

"Sorry I'm late, something came up."

"Your dick came up."

"What?"

"You think I don't know about your lonely housewife? The one who gives you meals and other little treats."

"How'd you know about that?"

"You called me to pick you up the last time your car was in the shop. I drive all the fucking way out to 35th and Normal to get you, and I see you driving off with some broad."

Frank Pankraz looked pained.

"I forgot all about callin' you. Listen, not a word of this to Ilse."

"Yeah, sure."

The Pakistani guy who worked mornings at Danny's brought Frank a cup of coffee and a donut. He bowed slightly and went back behind the counter. Frank smiled.

"I like that little bow he does. Be nice if more people took that attitude."

"He probably thinks you'll shoot him if he don't."

"Be nice if more people took that attitude, too. So, what's up?"

"You still tuned in to things over at the gym?"

"Tuned in? I own the fucking broadcast tower."

"Yeah? Your antenna reach to the second floor?"

The second floor of the police gym, for reasons that Frank had never understood, housed the offices of the Narcotics Unit. Frank's domain, first as a fitness instructor and now as a pencil-pusher, was the gym. Still, even narcs exercised some-times, and where there's a locker room there's talk.

"Yeah, it does," he said.

"Then you remember Doc Kildare?"

"Sure, I know him. Some balls on that guy, wanting fifteen mill."

"Yeah, well, the Superintendent wants those balls."

He told Frank that he'd ratted to Malloy about Doc wanting some help finding a missing kid, and what the reply had been. The word would be whispered in every cop's ear before the end of the day, but Frank was getting it first.

Any cop who helped Doc Kildare was cutting his own throat.

"Now, I'm not going to help him find this kid," Schumann said.

Frank said, "No fucking kidding."

"But what if he goes to some of his narc bud-dies for an unofficial favor or two? They might take the risk."

Frank chewed on the idea along with his donut.

"Yeah, they might."

"So if you pick up something interesting on that tower of yours, who knows how the Superin-tendent might feel if the word was passed along? Someone might score a point or two."

"Make an enemy or two, too. I'd have to be damn careful."

Schumann shrugged.

"I'm just telling you something. You decide if it's worth it. If it is, remember where you got it."

Frank got up.

"Yeah. I got it at Danny's Donuts."

Dorothy Welles sat at her desk, vetting the list

of those who'd be lucky enough to receive an invitation to the gala at the Art Institute. She was interrupted when her private phone rang. She hoped it would be her husband, Walter, calling, but somehow she knew it wasn't.

"Hello."

"Good morning. This is Lakeside Country Day calling. Please hold for the headmaster."

Dorothy hated to hold when someone called her. On the other hand, she was in no hurry to hear of Frederick's latest excess.

A deep, commanding voice came on the line.

"Mrs. Welles, this is Roger St. John. How are you this morning?"

"Quite well, Roger. And you?"

"I'm a bit concerned, actually."

Dorothy could see her beautifully planned schedule going right out the window.

"Is Fred ill?" the headmaster asked.

"No. I don't believe so."

"Then is there some other reason for his absence from school?"

"He's not at school?"

"No, he is not."

A chill passed through Dorothy Welles.

"Could you hold for just a minute, Roger?"

"Certainly."

Dorothy got up from her work and ran to Frederick's bedroom at the far end of the apartment. It was empty, but his schoolbooks were on his desk. The bed hadn't been slept in, and the room was still neat from Carmela's cleaning of it yesterday.

She knew something was wrong. Fred wasn't home and he wasn't at school, and disappearing wasn't his style. Humiliating his parents in public was.

Dorothy was out of breath by the time she hurried back to her private line.

"He's not here, Roger. Do you think he could be hiding somewhere in school? Playing some sort of prank?"

There was an uneasy pause on the line.

"I had our custodial staff check for him before I called. He's not here. Perhaps you'd better call the police."

"Yes, of course. After I talk to Walter."

She knew it. Her day was ruined.

Walter Welles was the chairman of First Citywide, the fastest-growing bank in town. He wielded the sharpest knife in a cutthroat business, and he intended to show the Japanese a thing or two about building giant banks.

He didn't have time for any crap about his son.

Welles barked at his wife through his speakerphone. "Does the boy have any friends? He could be malingering with them."

"I could think of only two."

"Call them."

"I have, dear. Their housekeepers say they're at school. When I called Lakeside back, Roger summoned the boys to his office. They said they hadn't seen Frederick since yesterday in class."

"Shit."

"Really, dear, I tried everything I could think of before calling you."

"I hate this." Walter Welles hated any problem he couldn't solve by bluff or intimidation.

"What do you suggest?" he asked.

"I think we should do as Roger advised. Call the police."

"Won't that fill the little bastard with glee?"

"Please, dear. I'm afraid. I don't think he's acting out this time."

" 'Acting out,' " Welles sneered. "Psychiatrist's crap. The boy simply hates us because we're successful and he's not."

"Walter!"

"It's the truth."

"He doesn't hate *me*."

Welles ground his teeth. He really didn't have time for this garbage.

"Very well. Our beloved son is missing. I'll call the police."

"Thank you. Whom do we know with the police, dear?"

Welles' exasperation returned to full boil.

"Who else? The Superintendent, of course!"

21

Harry waited on the front porch of Doc's house, imagining that all the ghosts inside were peering out at her. They weren't the kind of ghosts that terrified you. They were the kind that haunted your heart and broke it again each time you thought you were finally healed. In the thirteen years she'd lived in this house with Doc, she'd never once thought of it as her own.

Being there was even harder for her than making the phone call had been last night. But she had to do it. She'd told Doc that it wasn't the money that mattered, and she meant for him to know it.

He sure as hell hadn't been rich when she married him.

He hadn't been a madman undercover narc, either.

Doc wasn't home, but Harry intended to wait for him all night if that's what it took. She was going to tell him again, this time without the screaming and the insults, why she'd had to leave him. She'd tell him she still missed not having him in her bed. She would even explain, somehow, why she'd fooled around on him.

She would do all that and he wouldn't be able to hang up on her, ignore her.

Then, if he didn't believe her, she'd tell him to go fuck himself.

Doc sat on Glenna Handee's sleeper sofa with her, and couldn't decide which of them looked worse.

"Are you going out again tonight?" he asked.

"Yes."

Glenna had put in another full day at work, and now she was looking through a photo album. She smiled at a shot of Jerry as a little boy, eating cotton candy and craning his neck to look at a giraffe.

"Do you remember this day, Michael?"

"Sure. It was the time I took you and Jerry to the Lincoln Park Zoo."

Glenna nodded.

"He sure loved those animals."

"Except for the snakes."

Glenna turned the page.

"He got that from his mama. I hate snakes, too."

"Glenna."

"Yes."

"I don't think it'll do any good to go out tonight. I don't think you'll find him."

She was looking at another picture. Jerry was holding a baseball. Handicapped or not, the kid'd always had a good arm.

"Why not?"

"I don't think he's outside."

She didn't look up, but he told her about checking the empty buildings in the neighborhood without finding a sign of the boy. He told her how he'd had Jerry's picture blown up and duplicated, how he'd taken them around to all the stores to put in their windows.

More goddamn walking, but he didn't complain to Glenna.

"Where is he, Michael? What's happened to my boy?"

Doc wanted to put his arm around her, but he knew it would only make her uncomfortable.

"If he's still in the neighborhood and he isn't outside, then he has to be inside. Someone has to have him."

Glenna finally looked up, and her eyes were stony.

"What would someone want with Jerry in their house? What would they be doing with him?"

"I don't know."

"Then I'll start going around."

"Glenna, let me do it. I've had some experience knocking on doors, and a lot of experience being lied to. I'll know if someone's seen him. Or grabbed him."

"You'll go out right now?"

"I'll start tomorrow."

"Why can't we go tonight?"

Doc had to get some sleep.

"Because I'm about to collapse, and so are you."

"I feel fi—"

"Goddammit, Glenna! I have one fucking eye, and *I* can see you're ready to fall over!"

She looked like he'd hit her.

"I'm sorry, I'm really sorry. I wouldn't have said that if I wasn't so tired."

"You wouldn't have said it if it weren't true, neither."

Her voice was small and quiet. She'd dropped all pretense that she wasn't exhausted.

"Please, Glenna, stay home. Get some sleep. I'll start looking again in the morning."

Glenna laid the album down and opened a drawer in an end table. She took out a Bible and began to read.

Doc didn't say good night. There was nothing good about it. He left as silently as he could.

Tonight it was a Maserati, not a Mercedes, rounding the corner as Doc stepped out of Glenna's doorway. Doc had a sudden, fervent wish that he was carrying his gun and was still able to hit a target.

He stepped back into the shadow of the hallway, but it was too late. He'd been spotted.

The driver honked at him.

The driver's side window eased itself down electrically, and Doc saw Steve Petrovsky behind the wheel. Junior Little sat in the passenger seat. They'd both come to visit him in the hospital. Once. He'd told them not to come back.

"Hey, baby," Junior said, "sorry if we scared you."

Doc walked over to the car. The two detectives were as lean and stylish as ever. They reminded Doc of a pair of switchblades.

He was glad to see them. Petrovsky reached a hand out the window and shook with Doc. Junior smiled and waved.

"How they hangin', baby?"

"They're dragging, not hanging."

"No luck finding the kid?" Petrovsky asked.

Doc shook his head.

Junior said, "Damn. Anybody take my baby, I'd blow his head off all the way to Wisconsin."

"Got to find the guy first."

"That's a definite point you got there."

Petrovsky changed the subject.

"Vince had us keep tabs on Cousin Hector today."

"And?"

Junior picked up the baton. "And for an up-standin', licensed-in-four-states lawyer, a no-drinkin', no-smokin', don't-even-mention-dope-to-me naturalized citizen, he started hangin' out today at Mr. Teach's. What do you think of that?"

Mr. Teach's was a bar just off North Michigan Avenue where you could find any drug dealer in town who liked his clothes hand-tailored and his liquor unadulterated. The place was named for Edward Teach, aka Blackbeard the Pirate. Every law enforcement agency that owned a camera kept track of who came and went at Mr. Teach's.

For someone like Cousin Hector, who kept his hands clean and his fingernails polished, going there definitely meant that something was up.

Petrovsky could see the thought clearly on Doc's tired face.

"We're wonderin' what he's doin', too. We'll find out for you."

Junior added, "Even if you are number one on Malloy's shit list. He's got a verbal ban out on givin' you any kind of assistance."

"Vince thinks he has enough ammunition to buck that?"

The black detective smiled.

"Yeah. We think he's got pictures of the Supe fuckin' poodles, or votin' Republican. Somethin' awful like that."

Tired as he was, Doc laughed. Even Petrovsky cracked a smile.

"Good. Then Vince won't mind one more favor."

He told the detectives he wanted a computer search of any convicted sex offenders living in

The Wedge. As an afterthought, he asked for a list of Missing Person reports for any males, thirteen to twenty-one, that had been filed in the last three months.

Junior shook his head. "We better hope Malloy's fuckin' *black* poodles. Get a little miscegenation in there with our bestiality."

"Thanks, guys. Tell Vince thanks, too." Doc stifled a yawn. "I gotta get home before I pass out."

"Good to see you on your feet again, Doc," Petrovsky said.

"Ditto over here."

Doc nodded. He started to leave, but Petrovsky stopped him.

"One more thing. We went around the block once before we spotted you. You got someone waiting on your front porch."

"Who?"

Junior smiled his brightest smile.

"Harry."

Harry was sleeping on the old glider that Big John had put up the year before they invented sin. Doc sneaked right past her. He got the lock turned without the bolt clicking and the door open without the hinge creaking.

Then two thoughts hit him: If women were so afraid of aging, how come Harry kept getting better-looking? And why the fuck should he have to sneak into his own house?

He slammed the door without going in, and Harry almost rolled off the glider. She stopped herself by reaching out her left arm. She looked up and saw Doc from what wasn't a very dignified position.

"Jesus, you look fierce in those glasses."

She eased herself around until she was sitting

upright. Doc didn't respond. She knew he was going to make her do the talking.

"I wanted to see you."

He stood there looking at her, silent as the Sphinx.

"Come on, Doc, say something."

He pushed the door open and went inside. He didn't slam the door; he closed it firmly and quietly behind him.

She heard the *click* as he locked her out.

22

Harry still had a key.

She stormed in spitting mad. "I came to talk, and you're going to listen, damn you."

Doc refused to let her bait him. He just shook his head.

"Get out, Harry."

"No. Not until we talk."

Doc turned and started up the stairs to his bedroom.

"I won't leave," Harry said. "I'll be here in the morning."

He kept going.

"All right, goddammit! I can't make you listen to me. But there's no way I'll ever believe that this is *all* my fault. And if you do, you're lying to yourself."

Harry was about to throw the house key at him when he turned. She was stopped by a horrible thought: What if she hit him in the eye, his one good eye? She quickly jammed her hand in her pocket. As mad as she was, she hoped he couldn't tell what she'd intended to do.

Doc sat down on the stairs and looked at her.

He said, "Who cares whose fault it was, Harry? There's enough blame for both of us. The problem is I can't trust you, and maybe you shouldn't trust me."

Harry thought he looked like some grim judge staring down at her.

"You never fooled around, did you, Doc?"

"No."

"You never felt the need."

"I had you."

"You had me, but you got off on your job."

He couldn't deny that.

"I didn't start sleeping with other guys until you stopped coming home nights."

"You knew you were marrying a cop."

"I knew the cop part, I didn't know the narc part. I didn't know everything else that was going to happen, either."

They both felt the ghosts nearby.

"Neither did I," Doc said.

"I did the best I could. For as long as I could."

"Me, too."

Harry slumped down and sat at the foot of the stairs.

"Does it hurt?"

"What?"

"Your eye."

He laughed. "Only when I think about it."

"I really am sorry, Doc."

"I believe you're sorry about the eye."

"I'm sorry about us, too. I could almost reach out and touch you, but I'm afraid you'd pull away. I'm scared that this is as close as we'll ever be."

"I don't trust you, Harry."

"Because of the money?"

He nodded.

"We were married a long time, Doc. I never cared about money then."

"We didn't have enough to be tempting—and

you never had reason to feel you'd been cheated out of what we did have."

Harry smiled, thinking of her reaction to the newspaper story. "I did feel cheated, and angry. Now, I just feel sad that we have one more thing between us."

She looked up across the half-dozen steps that separated them and shook her head forlornly.

"Why are you so sure of me?" he asked.

"What do you mean?"

"How do you know I wouldn't let you down again?"

"You're not a cop anymore. Your goddamn job was the problem for me."

"Maybe I'd find some other way to fail you."

She hadn't thought of that.

"Would you?"

"I couldn't make any promises."

Harry bided her thoughts in silence for a moment.

"Do you miss me, Doc?"

He nodded.

"I miss you, too. There hasn't been anyone else since the divorce. Have you . . ." She couldn't finish the question.

"There's not much of a singles' market for a cyclops."

For a second, Harry's temper flared up. Doc was still the best-looking man she'd ever known and she hated the note of self-pity in his voice, but she remembered those awful photos of him she'd seen on television. She hadn't suffered as he had. She put her anger aside.

"May I see your eye?" she asked.

He hesitated and then nodded. Harry moved up the staircase without standing fully upright. She sat beside him and very gently removed his glasses. The prosthesis was really good, but Harry wasn't able to keep the heartbreak off her face. That left her only one thing to do.

She kissed Doc.

She took his face in her hands and delicately worked her way around his cheek, nose, and brow. There were tiny scars all around the eye socket. She kissed each one of them. Doc trembled under her touch. When she felt tears flow from his right eye, she caught them with her tongue.

Harry took his hand and put it on her breast. He shuddered and pulled back. She asked what was wrong. He was reluctant to tell her, but finally did. Harry smiled with great compassion and told him to leave everything to her.

She undressed for him right there on the staircase. Doc had always liked to look at her, and she'd always liked the way it made her feel. It wasn't just the excitement, as wonderful as that was, but the power she seemed to draw from his gaze.

Tonight, she'd use that power to make him forget his pain. When her clothes were off she reached down and unbuckled his belt.

"How much will this change, Harry?" Doc asked.

She slid his pants down, straddled him, and lowered herself until they were one.

"We'll just have to see."

23

Glenna Handee feared evil, even though the Bible that lay on her chest was opened to the 23rd Psalm. She feared for Jerry until her heart ached.

Of all the things she remembered the doctors and social workers telling her from the time Jerry was a baby, it was not to overprotect him. They'd said she would find it easier to bathe, dress, and feed him than to teach him to do these things for himself, but that would serve him ill. Jerry had to learn to do for himself.

Now, despite her years of effort, she doubted that she'd even taught him enough to survive.

She wondered for the millionth time how things might have been different if Billy had lived.

Billy and Glenna Handee had moved to Chicago from West Virginia so Billy could work with his army buddy, Dom, at the garage Dom's uncle owned. The plan was that Uncle Sal would sell the boys his business when he retired in a couple of years and they could save the money to buy it from the wages he paid them.

Billy said the whole thing was like a Christmas present. He'd work hard, they'd save every penny they could, and before long Billy and Dom would be businessmen, not just grease monkeys. It was a powerful dream.

They took the apartment over Nat's Tap be-

cause it was cheap and only two miles from Billy's
work. For entertainment they took long walks
through the neighborhood and around the city to
see the sights. Glenna loved sitting with Billy on
the lakefront at North Avenue. They'd look at all
the tall buildings on Lake Shore Drive that
seemed to grow right out of the water, and find
it hard to believe that they lived in such a place.
Billy told her that there were opportunities here
that they'd never have back home. All their
scrimping and saving would be well worth it one
day.

After paydays, they'd go over to Ray's for ice
cream sundaes and to say hello to all the new
friends they were making. That was their one ex-
travagance. Everything else above the necessities
went into savings.

It was a happy time for Glenna, and it got better when Billy said he thought they should have
their first baby right when Uncle Sal retired and
he and Dom took over. He and Glenna would be
ready to start a family then. Their baby would
have a mama and daddy who were someone in
this world.

The plan seemed to be perfect, because Glenna
got pregnant practically the first time Billy left his
rubber off. They were even lucky enough to meet
a midwife, Mrs. Turello, who lived right up the
street. Neither Billy nor Glenna had ever considered a doctor a necessity. Back home, midwives
did all the birthing and babies were born at home.

No one could afford doctors. Medical expenses
certainly didn't fit in with the Handees' savings
plan. Maybe for their second child they'd do
things fancier.

Everything went well until one night late in
Glenna's term. She had been sleeping lightly

when she felt the baby shift violently inside her. This wasn't the kicking and poking that had been getting more and more common lately. This woke her with a terrific fright, and she waited in dread of what would happen next. When nothing did, she lay back down, glad she hadn't had to wake Billy.

The next morning Glenna saw Mrs. Turello at Ray's and told her of the pain. The old woman said it was probably false labor, but to call her if it happened again.

The pain hit again shortly after six o'clock that evening. This time it dropped Glenna to her knees. After all these months, after everything had been so easy, Glenna feared she was going to lose the baby. She had to get help, but she had no phone. Both she and Billy had agreed it was an unnecessary expense, a luxury they couldn't yet afford.

Glenna dragged herself to the open living room window and screamed into the early summer evening. She saw a boy across the street who'd just come out of Ray's. She remembered hearing someone calling him Mike. He looked up and saw her just before she collapsed, slumping down against the wall.

A contraction wracked her body, and she knew somehow that if she delivered her baby now it would die. Almost gagging from the pain, she fought against the urge to push and be free of the monstrous pressure inside her.

After a moment, she realized someone was rattling her door. It was locked. Glenna called for help but she didn't know if her voice was loud enough to be heard. The door crashed open. Splinters of wood flew everywhere. The boy stumbled into the room, caught his balance, and stared at her.

At that moment, Glenna's water broke and gushed out onto the living room floor.

"My baby!" she gasped. She had to bend her knees and open her legs.

The boy ran to the window and yelled for someone to call an ambulance. The anxiety in his voice heightened her own fear. She thought her heart would burst. The boy knelt down next to her and took her hand.

"Is my baby coming?"

He nodded.

"I think I see the top of its head."

Glenna moaned from the pain and fear and humiliation. She wore only an old housedress, and the boy had seen her with her legs open and her baby poking out. He was trying to calm her, but all they were doing was being afraid together.

Then Billy rushed in.

He ordered the boy to fetch Mrs. Turello quick, but Glenna cried that something was terribly wrong. She pleaded to be taken to the hospital. Billy, tears falling like rain, took her legs and told the boy to take her under the arms. They carried her headfirst down the stairs.

They laid her across the seat of the tow truck Billy had driven home from work, and with her head on Billy's lap the young couple raced off for the hospital. Billy cried freely, ran red lights, cursed traffic, and leaned on his horn.

Glenna screamed. The baby was coming. She saw Billy wasn't looking at the road; his eyes were on the baby. She raised herself up enough to look.

The baby was face-up, and the cord was

wrapped around its neck. The baby was turning blue!

Billy stomped on the gas pedal. He was sobbing that this was all his fault. He should've come straight home from work, but Dom had wanted to have a few beers to offer his congratulations. Glenna was too weak to respond, and all she could think about was her baby. It was suffocating.

She felt Billy reach over and hold her onto the seat as the truck screeched to a halt. She heard him yell for help, but his voice sounded far away. She was losing consciousness. Somebody lifted her. She was rolling away. Voices were yelling things, but she couldn't tell what.

From a great distance she heard Billy's voice say, "Oh, Lord, please forgive me."

Then there was a sharp crack, and she blacked out.

They told her when she woke up that she'd been sedated for two days. They told her she had a son, but he'd suffered brain damage. They told her she'd have no more children. They told her she was a widow.

Billy, under the influence of alcohol and the assumption he'd lost both his wife and his child, had shot himself.

Glenna was eighteen. Billy would have been twenty-three on his next birthday.

Now, as she lay on her bed staring sightlessly at the ceiling, Glenna feared that she'd lost her son as well as her husband.

And her faith was no comfort.

Armando Guzman looked out the slitty little window of his cell at the federal lockup downtown. He had a view of the Loop three inches wide and fifteen stories high. It was enough to see the *chica* who always worked so late in the office building down the block. Since he had no one else to talk to, he talked to her.

He said, "I got this cop, I'm gonna eat his brain."

Unimpressed, the woman continued to labor at her computer.

"I ate a guy's heart once," Armando said. "It was my *muerto de prueba*. The test killing to show my employer I had the *cojones* to do the job when he wanted someone to die. You understand?"

The woman yawned and drank from a styrofoam cup. She got up from her desk and stretched. She tossed the cup in her wastebasket and walked out of Armando's view.

He cursed her for interrupting his story, but he knew she was just going to the *lavabo*. She peed a lot, but she worked long and hard.

"Do you use cocaine, *chica*, to work so late?" he asked when the woman returned. "Or do you stay to keep me company? Tell me, *querida*, do you think a man must kill his enemies to survive? I do. He must kill them with such savagery that others will run before they will let his shadow fall on them.

"When I get out of here my enemies will think to come after me. They will think Armando Guzman is on the run. But what will they think when they hear I have eaten a cop's brain? They might think me mad; they will certainly know I am evil. Will they pursue me so eagerly then?

"Would you, *querida*?"

As if in response to the question, the woman abruptly threw down a file she'd been holding, turned off her machine and the lights, and left.

"I didn't think so," Armando said with a smile.

*   *   *

Harry could feel Pat's presence in the bedroom. Pat was Harry's favorite ghost. She'd been Doc's sister, and she'd died one month after Doc first brought Harry to meet his family.

Harry let her eyes drift around the room. Gaps in the curtains allowed in enough illumination from the sodium streetlight out front for her to see how little the room had changed. The curtains were the ones she'd bought years ago. Their bed was the only piece of furniture that hadn't belonged to Doc's parents. The wallpaper had been hung by Big John shortly after he and Marie were married.

With the old furnishings and the soft yellow glow sneaking in from outside, this was a good room for ghosts.

After all these years, Harry still had a hard time believing how quickly Doc's family had died. Four people within two years. In one of his darkest moments, Doc had suggested that someone or something had cursed them. They'd been in bed in this same room when he'd voiced that horrible thought. The only comfort she'd been able to give was to cling to him until he fell asleep.

Technically, Pat had died of a stroke. She'd been twenty-eight. What really killed her, everyone had said, was a broken heart over the death of her husband of eleven months in Vietnam.

Big John had gone six months later. He'd been moonlighting on his electrician's job the day after his engine company had answered two false alarms and fought a three-alarm fire. He had to have been exhausted when he accidentally touched the live wire. No one mentioned the depression he'd been feeling over the death of his first child.

Harry and Doc had married a month later. They'd been ready for it, and Mom and Rich had needed something to pick them up. After the honeymoon, they'd moved into the Kildare house. Marie had moved out of her bedroom for them. Doc had said the family needed to be together, and Harry hadn't argued.

Doc twitched in his sleep and rolled over, lying on his back. Harry looked down at him. She saw his right eyelid flutter as the eye beneath it danced through a dream. She wondered if it was a nightmare, and pulled the covers up over him.

A year after Big John's death, Rich had stepped out of the office building where he worked and been struck by a runaway car whose driver had suffered a heart attack. The driver had lived, Rich hadn't.

The grief had been crushing. For Harry the fear had been, too. She'd worried about Doc every time he went to work. He was young, strong, and healthy, and he carried a gun. And he could die as easily as any of the others.

But he hadn't. Marie had. After six months of mourning during which she'd rarely set foot from her house, and never without Doc or Harry hovering over her, Marie had insisted on rejoining the world. To mark her renewal, she'd decided to go to Carson's and buy a dress. Coming home, Marie had fallen on the stairs leading down from the "L" platform and broken her neck.

That had been it for Harry. She wanted out of that house. Maybe the curse was on people who lived there. Doc said he couldn't go. Memories were all he had left of his family now, and they were all tied into the house.

The only reason Harry had failed to force the issue had been because she'd seen how deeply

Doc was suffering already. She hadn't been tough enough or mean enough to hurt him further. But she'd made sure she was out of the house as much as possible.

Harry got a job with a travel agency. She worked as many hours as she could, even throwing in free overtime when necessary. She was compensated for her effort with travel perks. She and Doc went places every chance they got; they made love all over the world.

They stayed the hell away from the house and its ghosts as much as Harry could humanly manage.

Then Doc got a slot in the Narcotics Unit. It was the result of that goddamn picture for the recruitment poster. The public had never seen it, but Vince DiGiuseppe had. He figured it the same way as the ad people: Nobody would ever believe this guy was a cop. In other words, he was perfect for undercover work. When Vince checked Doc's record and liked what he saw, he recruited him.

Vince didn't have to do a hard sell, either. Doc jumped at the offer and loved the job.

He'd be gone for days at a time without a word. Harry didn't know where he was or what he was doing. The only way she could reach him was through his beeper, and Doc had told her to do that only if it was *really* important.

Harry was sure Doc would get killed on this job, and it scared the hell out of her. But what pissed her off was when he started missing the trips she'd planned for them, ones he'd agreed to. He worked so much that practically the only time they made love anymore was when they left town.

The third time Doc canceled out on her, he'd

struck out as far as she was concerned. She went by herself. And fucked the first decent-looking guy she found.

After that, she took all the trips and had all the men she could manage. When Doc hadn't noticed, or pretended not to notice, what was going on, she left him little clues. Harry never knew whether he was too tired to see them or was just plain ignoring them.

Eventually, she started worrying about AIDS and thinking of herself as a whore. That was when she knew she'd reached the end. She told Doc she wanted a divorce. He could live in the house forever or die tomorrow. She didn't care. She was going, and she left.

A month after the divorce became final, Doc got shot. Harry's heart, to her surprise, broke once again.

She looked over at Doc. He was sleeping quietly now. She hoped that she could fall off soon.

The ghosts gathered over her. They knew all Harry's secrets. They understood her pain, accepted her contrition, forgave her sins, and let her sleep.

Back in his own apartment, Andy Slick had been drifting off, pleased with the neat job he'd done burying Bad Fred, relieved that the boy was no longer a threat to him, when the phone rang. And rang and rang.

It was the Coroner's Office.

They'd had a hard time locating him.

They wanted him to claim a body.

Doc heard the soft buzz of Harry's breathing in his ear and felt her warm body against his. He'd never expected this to happen again. He would have bet they'd done each other too much harm.

He knew about her trips. She'd come home practically flaunting it: *Look at me, I've spent seven days in the sun and six nights with some guy I'd never seen before.*

Occasionally she'd had the problem that when she came home he wouldn't be there, and her tan had faded and her glee had turned to bitterness by the time he did show up. After a few of those, he started finding little trinkets around that didn't belong to him: cuff links earlier on, packs of condoms toward the end.

He tried to blame her, to get mad, maybe even work himself up to belt her one, but he couldn't. How many women would have stuck around as long as she had, with people dying all the time and a husband who was never home?

He knew it was the job, more than anything else, that made Harry crazy. He knew, but he couldn't do anything about it. The job was the only thing that gave him a sense of control.

Most undercover cops, if they're honest, would admit that they did their jobs because they got off on it. The stalk, the chase, the capture: the thrill of the goddamn hunt.

When it wasn't thrilling, it was mysterious and suspenseful. You matched wits with bad guys who thought they could waltz tons of dope right by under your nose. And sometimes they did. But sometimes you strolled right into their hotel rooms and homes like you were one of them, knowing you were going to bust them, and knowing they'd kill you in a second if they found out the truth.

Wasn't that a crotch-tingler?

So, despite all the dangers undercover cops

faced, the hours they put in, the broken marriages they suffered, the political wars they fought, there were certain personalities who were obsessed by the job.

Have gun, will travel. Secret agent man. Able to leap tall buildings at a single bound.

The job itself was a fucking narcotic.

Beyond all that, Doc Kildare did it because it gave him control. By busting the bad guys, he controlled them. By staying alive in the face of danger, he controlled himself. He faced up to the family curse and spit in its eye.

If he'd told Harry all that, she'd have left him sooner rather than later. She would have told him, "Tempting your fate is the surest way to meet it," and she would have been right. Because after spitting in the curse's eye for years, the curse had finally spit back into his.

With Armando Guzman's bullet.

Doc snuggled closer to Harry's warmth.

She had solved his worry about the goddamn marble coming out, though. Maybe in the morning he'd take a chance with him being on top.

Now if he could just find out what had happened to Jerry Handee.

And get his share of Armando Guzman's money.

24

"Frederick Welles is missing, and Superintendent of Police Malloy is looking for him," Conrad Walters said.

The city's most-watched morning news show had just come on, and the story of Frederick Welles' disappearance was the lead item.

"Good morning," Walters said. "We start the day with an exclusive story of personal drama and political intrigue. This reporter learned last night from a confidential informant that Frederick Welles . . ."

A photo of the boy was inserted into the shot.

". . . the only child of banker Walter Welles and heiress Dorothy Cotter Welles . . ."

The boy disappeared for a stacked insert of his parents.

". . . is missing. As of yet, no ransom demands have been made. Instead of filing a Missing Persons report with their local police district, contacting the FBI, or even hiring the services of a private investigator, Mr. and Mrs. Welles took the situation directly to the Superintendent of Police."

Malloy's picture appeared. It wasn't one of his best.

"Perhaps not surprisingly in the case of two such influential people, the Superintendent responded personally to the Welles' plea, heading his own investigation and raising questions of whether such special treatment is available to everyone or only the elite few."

A close-up of Conrad's face showed what he thought the answer to that one was.

He continued, "As you can see, the principals in this matter have refused to comment."

A videotape rolled showing the doorman of the Welles apartment building refusing Conrad admittance, and the newsman and his crew being escorted from Malloy's outer office.

"However, the facts remain: Frederick Welles is missing; no one is saying a word about it; and political favoritism is alive and well in Chicago."

Conrad paused to favor the camera with his best cynical stare.

"In other news this morning . . ."

Conrad Walters' confidential informant was taking a sick day off from school. That was part of the deal.

Karl Walther, one of Fred's two friends, had gone straight to his father after being interviewed by Malloy. The guy had tried to swear Karl to secrecy about Fred's being missing. Karl had replied that he couldn't keep a secret like that from his parents. After all, he and Fred were classmates and their fathers were alumni of Lakeside, too.

The Superintendent didn't argue the point, but he'd said to tell no one else. Karl had said okay.

Maybe Malloy didn't know that Karl and his father had different last names. Conrad had changed his for professional reasons. Karl, in a fit of teenage rebellion, had reverted to the original spelling. It was a great move. Every time the old man thought about it, he got guilty for being so ambitious.

Karl could understand the Superintendent not knowing about his family's infighting, but if he bought the line about not keeping secrets from mommy and daddy, the guy was just plain dumb.

The only reason Karl had thrown his father this bone was because the old man had found out that Karl had hired two hookers so he could see what a threesome was like.

The boy thought it was scary that someone so gullible was running the whole police department.

He hoped Fred wasn't depending on that guy to get him back.

Glenna Handee saw Conrad Walters' report, because she had quit her job. After a sleepless night, she'd come to the decision that she would now spend all her time looking for her son. She would find him, or die trying.

After calling her boss to let him know of her decision, she went over to Ray's to inform Michael. He was sitting at his usual table, and Harriet was with him. Glenna could see that some of the others present were surprised to see them together. Glenna was, too, but just for a moment. The way she'd been raised, it was natural that people gathered together in times of trouble.

Doc stood up and pulled a chair out for her.

"Thank you, Michael."

Harry squeezed Glenna's hand. "Doc told me about Jerry. I'm very sorry he's missing."

Glenna nodded her head. Doc offered silent thanks that Harry hadn't promised he'd get the boy back.

"I've quit my job, Michael. I'm goin' to spend

all my time huntin' Jerry. If you'll be talkin' to people, I'll keep lookin' outdoors."

Doc had no choice but to say okay.

Then Conrad Walters appeared on Ray's TV and they all watched right to the end.

". . . political favoritism is alive and well in Chicago."

For the first time, Glenna let her rage out.

"What about Jerry?" she yelled. "What about my boy!"

"I can use this, big," Rudd Wetherby said. "Hold on a minute. I got another call."

Doc held for his lawyer to come back on the line. He looked out of the phone booth and saw Harry trying to reassure Glenna. Harry glanced his way and noticed him watching. She saw he was trying to read her, divine her sincerity. She turned her back on him.

"I'm back," the lawyer said.

Doc's voice was hard. "Good. Don't go away again until we're done."

"Sorry," Wetherby said.

His apology was heartfelt, the kind a client who represented a potential multimillion dollar settlement had the right to expect.

"I think we should play this for all it's worth," the lawyer continued. "This shows Malloy for the shit he is. We play that against what a great cop you were. The odds for settling your claim big-time go right through the roof."

"You're missing the point, Rudd. The idea here is to get the department off its ass and looking for Jerry Handee. There's to be no mention that they're goldbricking to get back at me."

There was a moment of silence before Wetherby said, "Doc, listen to me. Their goldbricking is our golden opportunity. Fifteen million in gold. I think we can get the whole magilla."

It was Doc's turn to pause. When he spoke, he spoke softly.

"What I just told you was so we could help Jerry. Got that? Jerry Handee. I'm not some ghoul trying to suck money out of a friend's heartache. You play this any other way than as an anonymous tip to Conrad Walters, telling him about Glenna's problem without mentioning me at all, and I'll withdraw my claim on Armando's money."

There was the longest lull yet. Doc could imagine the lawyer suddenly feeling lightheaded, seeing however many millions his one-third cut represented flying right out the window.

He wondered if Wetherby was buying the threat or not. Doc wasn't going to withdraw his claim. He would take it to another lawyer, though, and then Rudd might sue him. He thought he'd better give the guy something to salvage his pride.

"Rudd, don't take it so hard. Even without linking me to this, the Superintendent will still look bad."

He could almost feel the lawyer perk up.

"Yeah. You're right."

Doc questioned whether he should give him the other thing on his mind. Then he thought, *what the hell*?

"Here's something else you can feed Walters. More than a few cops in this town have noticed that a number of adolescent males have disappeared in the past several months. Officially, they're not connected. Guys talking off-duty aren't so sure."

"Malloy's sitting on a serial killer?" Wetherby sounded as if he could not believe his luck.

"Don't say that, because we don't know that. Just tell Walters to see how many others besides Jerry and Frederick Welles have been reported missing in the last year or so."

"I understand. Even if Malloy's only fucking up, for our purposes negligence is just as good as malice."

"Always a pleasure talking to you, Rudd."

"Likewise. I'll call Walters—anonymously—this afternoon."

"Good." Doc wanted to hang up.

"What'll you be doing?"

"Grilling my neighbors."

Doc hung up.

25

Andy Slick showed up at the morgue looking for cops, but didn't find any. Not that they were after him. He'd been wondering nervously if this was a trap, but he walked through the doors of the Fishbein Institute, Cook County's new morgue, and no one paid any attention to him.

He asked a woman for directions and followed them to a small room where a black attendant sat at a desk studying a correspondence school textbook on his future in real estate.

Andy said, "Hey."

The attendant closed his book around an index finger to save the page and looked up at him.

"Hey?"

"I was told you have my mother." Andy gave the attendant her name. "I want to make sure."

"Make sure, huh? Most folks take our word for it."

"I'm not most folks," Andy said.

"So you want a look?"

"I want to see if you have my mother. Maybe you can help me, if you actually *work* around here."

Black people really scared Andy, so he thought it best to act tough with them. Show them he could deal with them.

The attendant stood up. He had six inches and sixty pounds on Andy.

"Yeah, I *work* around here. I can take you in and show you, too. But you look at someone here, you ain't watchin' TV. You understand what I'm sayin'?"

"I can handle it."

"You better. I took a real dislike to the last guy who puked on my clean floor."

The attendant emphasized his point with a hard stare. Andy wished he could get him in his taxi. But no way he was going to take this gorilla on bare-handed in a public place. He just nodded. The attendant nodded back, put his book down, and led him into a refrigerated room.

Andy looked at the rows of stainless-steel compartments and admired their craftsmanship. They made him think about the possibility of putting bodies in walls.

The attendant stopped and opened a compartment. He rolled out a body.

"That's Mama, all right," Andy said.

He wondered how he could have walked right by and not noticed she was gone. They had been having an argument and weren't talking to one another. That had to be part of it. But still . . .

He wondered if Mama was mad about being dead.

Somebody would have to pay for this, and he knew who.

"That's her," he repeated.

"Yeah. We don't make many mistakes."

"How did she die?"

"Heart failure."

God*damn*!

Andy wanted to scream, but all he said was, "Can I take her?"

The attendant stared at Andy like he was crazy. It wasn't a look he appreciated.

"What do you mean, 'take her'?"

This time Andy felt a surge of genuine anger. He didn't have to put on a tough-guy act.

"You hard of hearing? Can I take my mother?"

The attendant shook his head, incredulous.

"You gonna tote her away? You bring a shoppin' cart, or is she goin' over your shoulder?"

Big or not, Andy was thinking about jumping on the sonofabitch when the guy's point finally reached him. Most people didn't handle dead bodies. Not themselves. Not even when it was their mother.

He watched the attendant close Mama's compartment, and let the guy take his elbow and guide him out of the room.

"Look, you got two choices. You got the bread, you go to a licensed funeral home, sign an order-for-release form, and they come get your mama. You ain't got the bread, tell me now and the county takes care of it."

As they stepped into the anteroom, Andy pulled his arm free.

"I've got money."

"Good," the attendant said. "Cause ain't nobody walkin' out with his mama while *I'm* still here."

26

Sergeant Frank Pankraz had never been in the office of the Superintendent of Police. He was nervous, and when he saw the look Malloy gave him he wished he was anywhere else.

He saluted and introduced himself, "Sergeant Frank Pankraz, sir."

A voice came from behind him.

"Superintendent. Sorry to interrupt. May I see you a minute, please?"

Pankraz looked over his shoulder. He saw a civilian, a black civilian. It took him a second, but he placed the face. The guy's name was Prentice Lee. He worked for the mayor.

"Take a seat, Sergeant," Malloy said on his way out of the office. "I'll be right back."

"Yes, sir."

Frank sat down in front of the big desk, not really sure how he'd let Dumb Dolph talk him into this shit.

The Superintendent was gone long enough for Frank to think maybe he should sneak out. He was debating the issue when the door behind him closed loudly enough to make him jump.

Malloy strode back behind his desk but he remained standing for a moment, establishing an edge over his subordinate.

"You work at the gym, Sergeant?"

"Yes, sir."

"And you have some information for me?"

"Yes, sir."

Malloy was distrustful. He knew about DiGiuseppe's reputed spy network and his friendship with Kildare, and this sergeant in front of him worked downstairs from the Narcotics Unit. It was possible he was part of some trick that dago was pulling.

Malloy sat down.

"You said the information was about Kildare. Tell me."

"Yes, sir. I happened to be upstairs distributing a survey on what kind of a fitness program people might like to see. I was passing by Lieutenant DiGiuseppe's office when I dropped my stack of papers. While I was picking up my stuff, I happened to hear Detectives Petrovsky and Little talking to the Lieutenant."

Frank paused for a minute. He couldn't figure out why he was getting the ball-bearing stare.

"This conversation you heard, it was so remarkable you had to tell me about it. Is that it, Sergeant?"

"Well, sir, the detectives told the Lieutenant that they spotted Hector Guzman going into Mr. Teach's. That's a notorious—"

"I know what it is, Sergeant."

"Yes, sir. The detectives said they thought maybe Hector Guzman was trying to set up a hit on the Sergeant."

Malloy had a hard time keeping a smile off his face when he heard that.

"Kildare is no longer a member of this department. He has no rank whatsoever."

Frank nodded. He decided then and there he'd

never rat on another person in his life. He felt like a turd no self-respecting fly would land on.

"That's all I heard, sir."

Malloy stared at the man. He didn't see how this could be a ploy by DiGiuseppe.

"Sergeant, what did you hope to get out of this for yourself? Coming here and telling me this."

"Nothing, sir."

"Nothing? Not a goddamn thing?"

Frank squirmed in his seat. He wanted to kill that idiot cousin of his.

"I just thought you'd want to know. The word's been passed around about you . . . not wanting personnel taking time from their regular duties."

Malloy smiled acidly.

"Nicely put, Sergeant. Well, I think I understand what brought you here today. I'll have to remember your name."

Frank's gut churned at the thought.

"That'll be all, Sergeant Pankraz."

Frank stood up, saluted, and left. He closed the door behind him.

Malloy determined that the man who'd just left his office was either a brilliant actor putting on a performance whose purpose he couldn't guess, or a lousy snitch looking to suck up to his boss.

He had no trouble deciding which.

Something told him that the goddamn greaser drug dealers were going to solve his Kildare problem for him.

He laughed out loud.

27

Harry had left for work and Doc couldn't put it off any longer. He had to begin his concrete inquisition: pound the pavement, knock on doors, question his neighbors.

He stood on the street corner in front of Ray's and took out the creased delivery map from Szell's Drugstore. One square mile, more or less. *How many people?* he wondered.

He mentally divided the area into a grid. There was no way he knew everyone in The Wedge, but he thought he knew at least one person on every block. In a lot of cases he knew more than one. He'd pump them for information about their neighbors before he called on people he didn't know.

He decided to start out in the same direction he'd taken when he'd followed Jerry's delivery route.

Before he took his first step, it started to rain.

Pat Priest had become a middle-aged woman who'd married and changed her name to Flannery. She still lived in the same house where she grew up, but now she was the mother of three boys. Her parents had passed away. Doc had recognized her the moment she opened the door.

She was the first person that morning to invite him inside. She poured coffee for him in her kitchen.

"How long has it been, Michael? Twenty years?"

"Longer. Since eighth grade at St. Mary's. I can't believe you didn't move away. How come I never see you?"

Pat sat down and stirred three teaspoons of sugar into her coffee.

"Well, do you go to church anymore?"

"No."

"I didn't for a long time, either. But when the kids got old enough to go to school, I started back."

"There should be other places besides church."

"You buy your groceries at Dominic's?"

"No, the Jewel."

"I don't suppose you go to many Cub Scout meetings."

"No."

"Pediatricians' offices?"

"No."

"Disney movies?"

"Only the ones with Bette Midler."

Pat shrugged, and Doc found the gesture hugely discouraging. If he could lose track of a schoolmate he'd known since childhood, someone who'd never moved so much as next door, he had a bigger job to do than he'd ever imagined.

"Don't you ever go to Ray's when you just need something fast, or your kids want a burger?" Doc asked.

"Ray charges more than the supermarket, and he isn't on TV like McDonald's."

Pat reached out and touched his hand.

"But I saw those pictures of you on TV, the ones your lawyer was showing. I think you deserve that money you want."

"Thanks, Pat."

Doc had made a point of missing the press conference. He became aware of the marble for the first time since Harry had put his mind at ease about it.

"Why do they call you Doc these days?"

"Just a joke. Started when I was a cop."

"Was it, like, 'Doc Kildare,' cause you've always been so nice-looking?"

He saw a gleam in her eye and suddenly recalled the Valentines she used to give him at school a lifetime ago. The ticking of a clock made him aware of the quietness of the house, the absence of the machinist husband she'd mentioned and their three children.

He changed the subject. He took out Jerry's picture for her to see.

"Pat, I'm looking for this boy. Do you know him?"

She shook her head. "No. Did he do something?"

"He's missing. His name is Jerry Handee. He's retarded."

"Oh, the poor boy. Did he walk away from a mental hospital or something?"

"No, he lives at home with his mother."

"She must be frantic. I'd be." Pat refilled his cup. "Would you like a cinnamon roll with your coffee?"

Doc shook his head.

"Jerry has a job delivering orders for Szell's Drugstore. Hasn't he ever brought you anything?"

"No. We go to the Soop-Rx. It's cheaper, and

with Bob getting *no* raises for *two* years, I have to save every penny."

"So you've never seen Jerry."

"I'm sorry, Michael. Or should I call you Doc?" she asked coyly.

The marble pulsed in his head. He didn't understand how plastic could throb.

"Just one more question, Pat." He took out his notebook and pen.

"Are you going to write all this down?"

Suddenly she was very uneasy, as if her husband were going to come in and catch them on the kitchen table.

"Just so I know who I talked to."

"Oh. Because I really don't know that boy."

"I believe you, Pat. The only other thing I wanted to ask was if you'd seen anybody strange around your block. Someone you think maybe I should talk to about this."

Time for coffee and flirting was over. Pat looked at him like he was someone who'd crawled in through a window she forgot to lock.

"Is there something I should be worried about? Are my kids in danger?"

Her eyes bounced back and forth between Doc's face and his notebook.

Doc said, "All I can tell you is, this city isn't the same place where we grew up."

He was back on the sidewalk, heading for the next house, glad that the rain had stopped. Excluding him, Pat hadn't seen anyone strange, but he'd bet the Flannery boys would do all their playing indoors for a while.

He still didn't understand why she'd gotten so upset about his notebook. The only possible answer that came to mind was that old Catholic guilt trip about things going on "Your Permanent Record."

Which was ridiculous, since his records weren't permanent. Hell, they weren't even official anymore.

28

Hector Guzman woke up late in the suite at the Drake Hotel that he'd called home since coming to Chicago. Melissa lay sleeping next to him. He blew a soft column of breath against her gently upturned nose. Her eyelids fluttered as she looked at him through a dream.

"I just wanted to see your eyes. Go back to sleep."

She smiled at him, closed her emerald-green eyes, and gently cupped his crotch in her hand.

He remembered the first time he'd taken her to bed. With those vivid eyes, the pale skin and jet-black hair, she'd excited him as though he were a teenager. But the things she'd done to him had gone well beyond any adolescent fantasy.

When he'd woken the next morning there'd been a heart-shaped piece of candy wrapped in gold foil paper on the pillow next to him. The candy was chocolate, with cherry cream filling. Under it was a note. The note was written on scented paper in pink ink.

It said: *Darling, don't say you've never met a hooker with a heart of gold.*

That had been when Hector had decided he was going to make Melissa a movie star, and that she was someone with whom he could share a confidence.

Now, he felt himself engorge under the delicate caress of her polished fingernails. When her hand was filled she pulled him none-too-gently on top of her.

"Your cousin really ate someone's heart?"

They sat dressed in terry-cloth robes, the remains of breakfast in front of them. Hector nodded.

"The thief he killed, the one who murdered my father."

"Okay, I can understand that, the killing part, but why'd he eat the guy's heart?"

"His employer was watching. This was the killing Armando had to perform to prove himself. He ate the heart to show he was capable of more than simple vengeance."

"Even so, eating someone's heart! Yuk!" She pushed away the last of her fruit salad.

"He's mad."

Hector had long ago become inured, at least in the abstract, to his cousin's atrocities. He finished his omelet.

"And you're going to help him get out?"

"He has a billion dollars that I want. For that kind of money, I'll take my chances. Wouldn't you?"

Melissa shook her head.

"You know how much I like you, but if you get this guy out . . ."

"I will. I've hired the men I need to do the job."

"Well, then the only way I'd feel safe was if he was dead. Otherwise, I think we have to stop seeing each other. I mean, I don't mind kinky, but cannibalism gives me the creeps."

Despite his legal training, Hector couldn't find a way to argue that point. So he agreed with it.

"What I want is your company, and his money."

Melissa smiled. "Well, sure, that'd be great."

Hector was loosening the belt to his robe when he heard the knock at the door. Someone was ignoring the standing do-not-disturb order for any time he was in his suite. He pulled the robe tight as Melissa discreetly stepped into the bedroom.

"Yes?" Hector called out.

"It's the manager, Mr. Guzman," a voice answered.

Hector opened the door. He saw that the man facing him was pale, and he'd brought the assistant manager along with him for support.

"Is something wrong?" Hector asked.

"I'm terribly sorry to disturb you, but I'm afraid we have some very unfortunate news. There was an international phone call for you not long ago, but Mr. Congers here was unable to reach you on your room extension."

Hector had ignored the ringing phone when he and Melissa had been in the bath.

The manager said, "We were asked to convey this message: 'Your uncle regrets to inform you that your brother, Fidel, has been killed.' "

Hector was stunned.

Not about Fidelito. He hadn't seen his brother in years, and never really liked him anyway. But now Armando would be deprived of the joy of planning the death of "the traitor." The news would enrage him, and make him much harder for Hector to handle.

The only solution he could see was to suggest that Armando vent *all* his fury on Kildare.

"I'm very sorry, Mr. Guzman," the manager said.

"I am too," Hector replied.

29

"I'm off to lunch, Artie," Tony Szell said with a smile.

Arturo Fuentes looked at his watch. Twelve noon on the dot. He knew Tony would be back at one-thirty sharp. He had ninety minutes to wait until he could take lunch—not a minute more, not a minute less.

"Have a good one, Tony. I'll hold down the fort."

Tony gave a final wave and stepped out of his drugstore at a jaunty pace.

The pharmacist smiled to himself as he thought of Artie's parting words. *Have a good one?* Tony Szell intended to have a great one. Just like every week.

There were times when he wished he could tell Artie about Kandi Gilliam. Then he reminded himself that he was a respected professional and merchant. He had an image in the community to uphold.

Kandi had to be his little secret. He knew it wouldn't look good if people found out he was visiting a young woman each week. It *really* wouldn't look good if they knew he was paying for his visits.

The danger made it all the more delicious. Tony

felt such delight about his rendezvous that he began to whistle.

He thought about Kandi and wondered where she'd come from, and how she got a name like Kandi. He couldn't remember girls having names like that when he was young. He knew that girls back then didn't do the things Kandi did to him. Gerta never had, anyway.

Tony was really dying to tell someone.

There were two more reasons he didn't, and they could both be found in his kitchen at home. They were Gerta and her razor-sharp knife. He'd watched that knife flash like lightning in his wife's strong hand when she butchered the meat for all those wonderful meals she cooked.

He thought of that and resolved that Kandi would be a secret he'd carry to his grave. That was why whenever he visited Kandi he always brought some little item from the store for her. Should anyone ever ask, he was making a delivery.

Even so, he looked up and down the street before entering the brick two-flat where Kandi lived.

And completely missed Doc Kildare, watching him from the living room window of the house across the street.

"The boys next door, they're firebugs. Write that down."

Althea Burns, unlike every other person he'd talked to that morning, had been glad to see Doc's notebook. She was younger than Doc, but already an old-bag-in-training.

"Mrs. Burns, I'm looking for a missing boy."

Althea got indignant. "Well, you never know what those roughnecks could get up to!"

For a moment there she had him thinking. He'd assumed that whoever had Jerry—and someone had to have him—was an adult. But what about kids? Teenagers. They were smart enough, and certainly cruel enough, to torment Jerry.

The notion fell apart when he gave it a little more thought. Kids might be able to decoy Jerry into a bad spot, but it would take the Bears' front four to keep him there if he got scared and wanted to leave. Unless they'd killed him.

He kept thinking of that more and more often.

Kids could have killed him, but kids didn't kill as much as people who were twenty or older. It was when you got to those years that your crazies usually began killing, too. That thought had also been cropping up with increasing frequency.

It fit so frighteningly well with the story Mularkey and Williams had told him about young males disappearing—and with the Welles kid vanishing. Doc hated coincidences as much as any other cop in the world.

"They drink, too," Althea said.

"Pardon?"

"They drink beer when they aren't lighting fires."

As Althea ran down a list of grievances about the desperadoes next door, Doc reviewed his morning.

He'd covered both sides of four blocks. He'd found people home in a third of the places he'd visited. No one had seen Jerry, but many said they knew the boy. Others admitted to having noticed him around, but not recently.

While Doc hadn't been given the names of any neighbors, or told of any strangers, who might be kidnappers, he'd had to listen to all sorts of tales.

There were card games where more than nickels and dimes changed hands. There was a man who dressed in his wife's spare nurse uniforms while she was at work. (He'd made a note to visit that guy later.) There was a couple who gave real good deals on the TVs and microwave ovens they sold from their back porch. There was a woman who ran an unlicensed day-care center in her house. (He'd checked that right away; it may have been unlicensed but it was clean and warm, and the woman who ran it invited him to call any of the kids' parents he wanted. He stopped after the first three told him to mind his own business.) There was a guy who was stealing the premium channels from the cable TV company. (Doc thought he should get together with the people selling the hot televisions.) There was the guy who was screwing *two* of his neighbors' wives.

Everything he'd heard was about the other guy. The man or woman pointing the finger had a letter of reference from Mother Teresa. But that didn't keep them from trying to peek at his notes and see what the neighbors had blabbed about them.

The only reason Doc had put up with all their shit was that he wanted these people to call him from now on if they saw something that involved Jerry. So he kept on listening. There was this . . . there was that . . .

Doc looked out the window, and there was Tony Szell.

Going into a building where a neighbor said there was a hooker.

30

Doc stepped off the curb, intending to see if roly-poly, apple-cheeked Tony was enjoying a nooner, when a car screeched to a stop six inches away from his knee. He was about to call the driver an asshole, but he saw it was Vince and he'd just take it as a hello.

Vince opened his passenger-side door.

"Get in, willya? I'm on city time here."

"I'm sure the taxpayers appreciate your diligence."

"Wise-ass mick."

"Dumb-ass guinea."

Doc got in and Vince hit the gas, leaving rubber from the city's tires on the asphalt of the city's street.

Doc asked, "Where're we going?"

"We're just driving, seeing the sights."

"I've seen these sights all my life."

Vince pulled up to a red light and paid close attention to the backside of a young mother leading her toddler across the intersection.

"Check out the sight in the glove compartment."

Doc knew that Vince wasn't looking at the woman's ass as much as he was looking the other way. He was playing a game. Doc played along.

He opened the glove box and saw a Beretta inside. Nine-millimeter, 15 + 1 magazine. Vince was giving him a gift. An unofficial gift. That meant the weapon was colder than a loan shark's heart. Doc took the gun, stuck it inside his jacket, and slammed the glove box to give Vince his cue.

The traffic signal turned green and Vince took off.

"Junior got word from a snitch about Cousin Hector's doings at Mr. Teach's." Vince turned to glance at Doc. "He's hired a couple shooters."

"Anybody good?"

"We don't have names yet, but you don't have to be Annie Oakley if you got an Uzi."

Doc shook his head.

"I don't understand it. Why is Guzman so pissed off at me? It's not like he's going to see his money or the light of day again."

"It gets worse."

"What does?"

"Your old snitch, Bobby Ro."

"Yeah?"

"He got popped last night."

"Motherfucker!"

"Somebody had a real hard-on about it, too. Burned down his new house in the 'burbs. The firefighters found Bobby tied to a chair inside. Some comedian had stuffed an apple in his mouth."

"What the hell is going on?" Doc demanded.

"I don't know. What I do know is you don't have a badge anymore, and if you get caught carrying a concealed weapon, no matter who's after you, *you're* the one in deep shit. Now if, by some lucky stroke, you found a weapon you could use and throw down and no one could trace to you, well . . ."

Vince shrugged.

Since you didn't thank people for unofficial gifts, Doc changed the subject.

"Harry came back last night."

"No shit. She heard about the money, huh?"

"That's the first thing I thought, too."

"So do you care, or are you happy anyway?"

"I don't know. I'm suspicious, but I'm damn near hopeless when it comes to Harry."

"Every man's got a weakness. For a mick, it's surprising you're not a drunk."

"For a guinea, it's surprising you're not on the pad."

Both of them laughed.

Doc said, "If Harry's going to be around, with all this shit going on, I don't want her hurt."

"Tell her to stay away a few more days. We'll find the cruds Cousin Hector hired and put the clamps on them. In the meantime, you watch your own ass."

Vince pulled into a parking space in front of Nat's Tap.

"Hey, were you able to find out if there are any registered sex creeps living around here?"

Vince said, "Yeah, I found out, and no there aren't. They all must live in better neighborhoods."

"Shit."

"Still no sign of the kid?"

"No. It burns my ass, too. I've lived in The Wedge all my life. His mother says he's here, *I* think he's here, but I can't find him."

Vince rubbed a hand across his face.

"Maybe you aren't gonna."

All Doc could do was nod.

31

Four more hours of listening to people rat on each other had left Doc ready to gag. He hated the fact that he was the one knocking on doors and sowing suspicion. He was making people mistrustful of their neighbors in general and of him in particular.

He was learning more about his tribe than he'd ever wanted to know, and the tribe resented him for it.

On top of it all, he hadn't learned squat about Jerry Handee. The only good thing he could say about the entire experience was that he seemed to be getting in better physical shape from all the walking.

At five o'clock, Doc knocked off for the day. He'd had enough frustration and urban melodrama. He hurried to Ray's so he could call Harry before she left the travel agency.

The tables at Ray's were all taken but there was a spot at the counter available, and the phone booth was empty. Doc reserved his space as he went to the phone by pointing his finger at the open stool and asking Ray for a ham steak, grilled tomato, and fries.

Harry answered the phone on the first ring.

"Spur of the Moment Travel."

"Hi," Doc said.

"Hi."

He could hear the uncertainty in her voice. She didn't know where things stood. It made them even, since he didn't either.

"Any luck finding Jerry?"

"No!" He said it with too much steam. "Sorry. It's been a tough day."

"I understand. I'm worried for Glenna, and frightened for Jerry, too."

"Thanks for not taking it the wrong way."

There was a pause. Harry filled it.

"Doc, about last night . . ."

"Yeah?"

"Once we got undressed . . ."

"Yeah?"

"I didn't think about money the whole time."

He laughed.

"How long did it take you to think that one up?"

"It came to me at lunch. I was asking myself, if I hadn't been shown that story about you, what else might have got me to come see you?"

"You come up with anything?"

"I started thinking about last night."

"So if you *aren't* filled with greed, you *are* consumed by lust. Is that it?"

"I didn't notice you complaining."

The lull this time was more comfortable. Until Doc brought up a new subject.

"I don't think it would be a good idea to see you again for a while."

Harry's voice became cool and defensive. "We didn't promise each other anything."

"It's not you. You know the guy whose money I put the claim on?"

"Not personally, no."

He ignored the sarcasm.

"Vince told me today that a snitch of mine was murdered . . . and that Armando Guzman has arranged for a couple of shooters to come looking for me."

Harry was outraged. "No, goddammit! You're not even a cop anymore!"

"Vince is going to take care of it. The guys from my old team are going to find these guys. But I don't think it would be a hot idea for you to come around for a while."

The silence stretched out long enough for him to wonder if she was still on the line.

"Maybe I'll come and to hell with the danger. Would a gold-digging bimbo do that?"

The question made Doc think. He came up with two answers. The first was no. The second was, if the bimbo was smart she might at least make the offer.

He responded to the first one.

"I can't let you do it, Harry."

"Why the hell not?"

"Even if I hated you, which I don't . . ."

"Gee, thanks."

"I don't want to see you killed."

"Goddammit, I—" Her voice suddenly changed. "We could meet somewhere else."

"Where?"

"A hotel. Someplace fancy. I've got freebies all over town."

He tried to find something wrong with the idea, but couldn't. Especially when he thought of what Harry might wear for him in the bedroom of a luxury hotel.

"Can you book the room under another name?"

"Yes. Where would you like to go?"

"You're the travel agent."

"Okay," she said. He heard her punching

something into her computer, and a minute or two later she was back on the line. "We're confirmed at the Royale under my mother's maiden name, Kersey. See you there at eight."

"Wait. Which Royale? The one downtown?"

"No, the one at O'Hare. In case we need to make a quick getaway."

Glenna Handee was on Ray's TV when Doc sat down to eat.

". . . and when you reported your son missing, Mrs. Handee," Conrad Walters asked, "what did the police do?"

Glenna's hair was pulled back, and she wore a new dress. Someone at the television station had applied makeup for the cameras. The result was amazing. She looked ten years younger.

But despite the cosmetic differences, it was obvious that a white-hot fire burned in Glenna.

"The policeman told me he could call the hospitals and the morgue."

"He didn't offer you any other assistance?"

"No, sir." The words were hard and clipped.

"He didn't suggest you call the Superintendent?"

"No, sir."

"And the reason you called me, Mrs. Handee?"

"I saw your story on the TV. I feel sorry for that Mrs. Welles, but I want folks to know that my boy is missing, too. I was hopin' you could show his picture on TV like you did for that Welles boy."

The shot of Glenna and Conrad Walters dissolved to a photo of Jerry Handee with his name superimposed on it.

Walters spoke in voice-over as it filled the screen.

"This is Jerry Handee. He's seventeen years old, and is learning disabled."

The camera came back to a one-shot of the newsman.

"If you see Jerry, please call the police. Maybe they'll find some time to help."

32

Conrad Walters was pushing this "missing kids" crap so hard because Walter Welles had once rubbed the reporter's face in a jockstrap back in high school. That's what the banker had told Malloy. He'd also told the Superintendent not to worry, the bank's public relations people would handle things. Malloy clicked off the television in his den and looked at his visitor.

An unhappy Warner Carswell looked back.

"Washington wants this whole mess settled quickly and quietly."

"How'd you do in gym class?" Malloy asked.

"I beg your pardon?"

"At school, when you had gym, did you get pushed around?"

"I was captain of the lacrosse team."

"I thought La Crosse was a town in Wisconsin."

The DEA boss had reached the limits of his patience.

"I agreed to meet you at your home only to expedite this matter."

"Yeah, well, the only reason I invited you to my home is because my office is being swept for bugs."

Carswell's face turned to stone. "Your office is bugged?"

Malloy had asked himself that question repeatedly after a very scary thought occurred to him: What if Sergeant Pankraz *was* an incredible actor and *not* a snitch? Maybe DiGiuseppe had sent him to plant a bug. Pankraz had been given all the time he'd ever need when Malloy had stepped out of the office.

Malloy had checked out the story about Guzman hiring two hitmen through another source, and it was real. But what if the whole point of the sergeant's visit had been to get proof of how the Superintendent of Police reacted to the situation?

"I don't know," Malloy said. "I thought we should meet here just in case."

Carswell looked at this over-promoted flatfoot as if he were an idiot.

"If someone bugged your office, why wouldn't they bug your home, too?"

Malloy's face went slack, but only for a moment.

"Nah, the old lady never lets anyone in."

Carswell turned his head toward the window. There could be a laser focused on it right now reading the vibrations of every word they spoke.

Malloy went on, oblivious to developments in technology and everything else.

"You can tell your precious Washington that our problem with Kildare will soon be over, and it won't cost anyone a cent."

"What do you mean?"

"Hector Guzman hired two button men to take out Kildare. That means his cousin Armando wants him dead. When he dies his claim dies with him."

Carswell considered warning Kildare. The question was essentially political. If it were revealed that he was privy to such information and did nothing about it, he'd be finished. If no one were to find out, he'd be better off not getting involved.

Malloy wore a shit-eating grin. "Well, what do you think of that?"

"You're willing to sacrifice one of your men?"

"He's *not* one of my men!" Malloy roared. "And he never was. He was always a goddamn maverick who thought he knew better than everyone else. If he'd played along with me I'd be taking care of him now, and this fucking claim of his would never even have crossed his mind.

The Superintendent was almost hyperventilating, but as his breathing settled down a crafty smile formed on his face.

"The beauty of all this is that there's this wop narc, DiGiuseppe, who thinks he can protect Kildare. Even after I passed the word about not helping the bastard. Now DiGiuseppe is a bastard himself, and there are stories about these files of his. So I can't land on him with both feet."

Malloy's smile turned into a chuckle.

"But nothing says I can't send him on vacation. Which I just did. His replacement is gonna have better things to do than worry about babysitting some one-eyed has-been. Which should take care of our problem real soon now."

Carswell made *two* political decisions at that moment.

One, he'd write a memo to Washington detailing everything he'd just heard, and let them decide whether to save Kildare.

Two, he'd resign his job and go into the private

practice of law, possibly specializing in drug defendants.

The pay was far better, and the class of people you met couldn't possibly be any sleazier.

33

Doc didn't want Harry to watch him clean the marble, but she wouldn't leave. She sat on the edge of the tub in the hotel bathroom and refused to move. That left him no choice. He could feel mucus building up in the socket, and it was driving him crazy.

Harry said, "I saw all those awful pictures on TV." She didn't tell him she'd thrown up. "How much worse could this be?"

Doc took the marble out.

Harry swayed, and he thought for a moment she would fall back into the tub in a dead faint. He wasn't even looking directly at her. She just caught his reflection in the mirror, the same way he saw her.

Then she tensed, starting from her stomach, which he could see clearly through her negligee. He thought she was going to lose her breakfast, but she didn't. She straightened her back, squared her shoulders, and held her head up.

Harry was forcing herself to be strong.

She said, "When you're done with that let's take a shower together. We haven't done that in years."

"How about a bath instead? That tub's big enough; I think it even has a whirlpool thing. We've never done that."

Harry agreed and started the water running. "Nice and hot," she said. She was still watching him clean the hole in his head.

"A normal eye has a drainage system," Doc said. "Tears wash away the crud from your body, or the air, that gets on the eye. That's why the worst you normally have are those little grainy things that stick to your eyelashes. I don't have normal drainage on the left side anymore."

He used an antiseptic solution that Gunther had given him to dab away the mucoid crust that had formed at the periphery of the socket.

Harry had achieved some detachment by now.

"The marble has to be highly polished, because if it gets pitted the irritation can be a lot worse. So it's a good idea not to handle it more than you have to, because that can scratch it."

He was paraphrasing one of Gunther's lectures. It helped him take his mind off the fact that he still thought the socket was ugly as sin.

Harry was actually looking interested.

"Eventually, I'll need a new marble."

"Maybe they'll come up with one someday that can see."

Doc stopped his maintenance routine for a moment.

"Somebody did that, they'd deserve a halo. Anyway, this one'll last two to ten years. Then I need another. Disposable eyes."

He put the prosthesis back in place and blinked. It felt much better now, and it tracked perfectly. Gunther was right; this *was* the one.

"How come it *doesn't* fall out?"

"The eyelids hold it in place." He looked at the tub. "I think that's full up."

Harry turned off the water and Doc, who'd

been naked all along, eased himself gingerly into the water.

"Coming?" he said.

Harry dropped her negligee.

"I certainly hope so."

After they'd made love, they sat on opposite sides of the tub playing footsie under the water.

"Doc?"

"What?"

"How do you feel about . . ."

"You?"

"No. About Glenna."

The question took him completely by surprise. When Harry drew her foot back, though, he knew she was serious.

"She's my friend. Has been for years."

"You've known her longer than you've known me."

"Not in quite the same way."

Harry looked him in the eye.

"I've wondered about that at times, if you—"

"No. The answer is no."

"Still, she has to mean a lot to you. I can see what looking for Jerry is costing you. I just wondered who else you might do this kind of favor for."

Doc scooped up a handful of water and rubbed it over his face. He attempted to speak, but it took him a couple of tries to find a way to start.

"I've told you the story about when Jerry was born."

Harry nodded.

"Being there that day with her, seeing her on the floor ready to give birth . . . finding out later what happened to her husband, I always felt . . . a kind of responsibility to her. To both of them."

"You think Jerry's dead, don't you?"

"Yeah."

"It's not your fault, Doc."

He ignored her absolution.

"I've always admired Glenna for the way she's survived. Especially after what happened to my family." He stopped to absorb the pain of his memories. "She took care of her son, made a home for him, gave him love, made him feel special."

"Did you ever think of Jerry as your son?"

Doc saw that Harry's eyes had tears in them.

"We never really talked about why we didn't have kids, you and I."

"No."

"Never found out who had the problem, or if anything could've been done about it."

"No."

"By the time the idea of kids occurred to me, we had enough problems that I was glad there weren't any around."

The tears rolled down Harry's cheeks.

"Maybe I did think of Jerry as mine."

He moved over to Harry and put his arm around her.

"But I never admitted it before. Even to myself."

34

Hector Guzman flicked clean the restaurant seat with his handkerchief before sitting down.

A pancake house had not been his idea of the perfect breakfast spot. But the cop he'd paid to supply the computer printout of Kildare's personnel record had refused to meet him anywhere else than "this little place I know."

Hector declined to order any food, and let the coffee in front of him cool untouched as he glanced through the file he'd been given.

"That's all there is?" he asked, finishing his reading.

Across the chipped formica table, his dining companion said "Yes" around a mouthful of greasy brown mush. Hector also saw syrup, blueberries, and unmelted butter being churned between uneven teeth.

"You're sure there's nothing more?"

"Yeah."

Pig, Hector thought.

He had spent a very nervous day trying to think of a way to tell Armando about that *estúpido* Fidelito getting killed. He had tried, but failed. Nothing was going to pacify Armando. Not about losing the chance to inflict vengeance with his own hands.

Even Don Ernesto, Armando's father, had been

unable to offer any suggestions. Now what Hector had just read about Kildare made him more apprehensive, and he was scheduled to meet with Armando that afternoon.

The only thing to do was to emphasize what was going right. He would tell Armando the details of the escape plan he was putting into effect. Tell him he would soon be free. He thought Armando would have to be satisfied with that.

Actually, Hector was quite proud of what he'd accomplished. His plan was beautiful. It would likely work, had cost relatively little money, and allowed him to pocket the lion's share of the escape budget.

Best of all, it required Armando to fire Hector as his lawyer.

35

Rudd Wetherby had invited the press to his office this time. He felt that varying the scenery would keep everybody more interested, and sitting behind his own massive desk gave the attorney a feeling of power.

He watched the electronic media set up their equipment. He could afford to be relaxed, because Doc Kildare had believed him when he said *he* hadn't sent Glenna Handee to be interviewed by Conrad Walters. The whole thing had been *her* idea.

Besides, Doc's name hadn't been mentioned once, but he had been right about the Superintendent looking bad. Now that dummy Malloy was trying to let Walter Welles' flacks fix his problems.

Rudd got this cue that the media were ready to go. He could hardly wait to see how Malloy handled this one.

"I've asked you ladies and gentlemen here today because I've become aware of an organized effort to malign the character of my client, Michael Kildare. This effort is being undertaken by a public relations firm in the employ of Mr. Walter Welles, chairman of First Citywide Bank."

The attorney could see the reporters begin to salivate. The ex-cop and the missing rich kid; two juicy stories were about to be tied together for them.

"Now unfortunately Mr. Welles' son is missing, and I'm sure we all wish him a speedy and safe return to his family. Nevertheless a friend of mine in the media, who, of course, must remain nameless . . ."

He had to reassure the press on that score.

"This friend read to me this morning a press release that has been circulated. The gist of it is that Mr. Welles in endeavoring to find his son turned, quite naturally, to a friend. It was only to be expected that a man of his eminence has friends as powerful as the Superintendent of Police. Well, never let it be said that *I* question the value of friendship."

Rudd had them smirking with that one.

"However, the press release implied that the authorities would be better equipped to deal with unfortunate circumstances like the disappearance of Frederick Welles and the equally unfortunate case of Jerry Handee, which you heard about from Conrad Walters last night, if they didn't have to contend in court for monies that were rightfully theirs."

The attorney put on his gravest face.

"Ladies and gentlemen, the money forfeited by convicted drug dealer Armando Guzman, the man arrested by officers under the command of my client, belongs to the United States Government. It does *not* belong to the Police Department unless and until the Attorney General allocates it to that body. As of now, it is up to the District Court to decide how that money will be distributed. Superintendent Malloy and public relations specialists for wealthy bankers have no say in the matter."

A reporter jumped in.

"Those are the legal niceties, but what about the point that the money would be better off in the police budget than in your client's pocket?"

Wetherby smiled, wondering how many in his audience remembered that he'd just said he had a reporter friend.

"A very good question. If you'll allow me to refer to my notes, I'll see if I can give you some very good answers."

The lawyer read from a legal pad.

"The two agencies involved in the raid in question were the police department and the DEA. Under other circumstances, they would be the ones to divide Armando Guzman's ill-gotten gains.

"Let's consider the DEA first. In 1988, this agency spent two million dollars to rent offices in the Washington, D.C., area for its bureaucrats. There was one little hitch. Even though the money was committed, they found themselves unable to move into the offices. Two million dollars for the war on drugs? Poof! Gone like that."

Wetherby snapped his fingers.

Another reporter asked a question.

"We know how Washington screws up, but why should the local cops suffer?"

"They're suffering already, and not by my client's action. The police department in this fair city makes its officers buy their own weapons. To defend yourself as a Chicago cop you have to put out your own money. When the Superintendent was recently petitioned to use confiscated monies to buy every officer a sixteen-shot semiautomatic weapon, to make the balance of firepower a little more equitable, he turned his brave men and women down.

"Seizing money from criminals to fight crime

certainly seems like a good idea, but I'd like some-one to show me where this program has caused crime to go down. I'd also like to see where the money that wasn't spent arming our police offi-cers has gone."

Wetherby paused to take a drink of water. The TV lights were making him hot.

"I'll raise only one more point on this matter, but it's an extremely urgent one. This press re-lease tied Doc Kildare's claim to the matter of two missing boys. As a father myself, this was of great concern to me. Would I be partially responsible for diverting funds which might otherwise be used to help find these children?"

Zinger time.

"Well, again, I can't reveal my source, but it has been brought to my attention that Frederick Welles and Jerry Handee aren't the only two boys to disappear mysteriously from the streets of this city in recent months. In fact, the question of whether we face something altogether horrible here has been the subject of speculation among our *working* police officers for some time now."

The frenzy began. This was a bigger story than any of the reporters had ever expected. This was the stuff of front-page headlines and top-of-the-hour stories. A female voice cut through the uproar.

"Are you saying there's a serial killer out there?"

Wetherby replied, "I'm saying that boys have been disappearing for a long time before my client filed his claim, and the man most responsible for this city's public safety hasn't done enough about it, no matter how much money he's been given."

36

Doc looked at the names above the doorbells and saw his choices were VIJAY PATEL and KANDI GILLIAM. He pressed Kandi's bell. And pressed it again. And twice more.

"All right, for Christ's sake. I'm coming."

The shout came from behind a wooden door at the first-floor landing. Doc stood outside a glass door in the outer hallway. After unbolting several locks, the inner door swung open and a bleary-eyed young woman looked out at him. She had fairly nice breasts, and didn't seem to mind that they all but hung out of her robe.

"Cop," she said.

She was the first, the very first, person who'd ever made Doc that way. But she was wrong.

"Ex-cop," he said.

"Yeah, I saw you on the news."

He felt better that she hadn't made him after all.

"What do you want?"

"I'd like to talk with you."

"Are you the one I heard is going around asking questions all over the place?"

"That's me."

She went inside and closed the door on him. He leaned on her bell until she shouted again.

"Go away or—"

"You'll call the cops? Go ahead."

"Shit."

She opened the door and stepped back out. This time she covered her assets. No more peep show.

She said, "I don't know anything about anybody. Go ask somebody else your questions."

That's when it hit him. Not to ask somebody else questions, but to ask questions about somebody else. Somebody other than Jerry Handee.

Still, he had one thing he wanted to pin down with her.

"How long has Tony Szell been coming to see you?"

"Who?"

Doc smiled. She knew who, all right.

"I could always send his wife over. Big, strong German woman. Got arms like a pipe-fitter, and has these old-fashioned notions about the sanctity of marriage."

Kandi sighed.

"Look, I know *all* about his wife. I know about *everybody's* wife. That's why I ain't one myself. And I don't need to see Tony's."

"How long has he been seeing you?"

"A year, I think. Since I first moved to this wonderful neighborhood. I met him in his store. I had a 'scrip for tetracycline and he thought it was cute giving it to me for free. He said if I ever needed anything else he'd be happy to bring it over."

"Romantic."

"Look, he ain't a bad guy. He's the only one I let come here, but it's strictly business between us. He brings me knickknacks from the store and I give him a little better time for a little less money than the other johns."

"What kind of knickknacks?" Doc asked.

She knew what he meant. And she didn't like it.

"Hey, I ain't no fucking junkie! You put your money down, you can come in and take a look anywhere you want. Around me or my apartment."

"Tony must love you for your sparkling conversation."

She slammed the door on him again and he stepped outside.

He wasn't sure why he'd come to see Kandi today, other than because she was a loose end. Maybe it was because if Tony could have a secret about a hooker, he could have secrets about other things. If he did, seeing as he was Jerry's employer, Doc wanted to know them.

He'd get around to Tony, but first he wanted to follow up on his new idea. Since he was getting nowhere finding Jerry, why not ask how Frederick Welles had come to be among the missing?

Because he'd bet every last cent of his claim and his pension that the same person—*killer*, he admitted—was responsible for both of them.

He stopped at the first phone he could find and called Vince.

37

Andy Slick had arranged for *two* funeral homes to go pick up Mama. He'd made sure the second one got to the morgue a half hour after the first had already taken her away. He knew he got the timing right, because he sat parked across the street from the morgue and watched.

The first guy had loaded Mama into an unmarked van and driven away. Funeral homes didn't pick up bodies with hearses; they used first-call cars, either station wagons with blacked-out windows or unmarked vans.

Andy had made a point of learning how bodies were transported when he'd realized one night that eventually Mama's basement was going to run out of room. The driver from the second funeral home had come out of the morgue swearing, the way anyone would who'd been jerked around.

The second driver was ready to pull out when Andy jogged up to the van. He had a small, sharp nail sticking out of the toe of his boot and he pushed it into the sidewall of the left front tire. He was taking no chances that the guy would drive away on him.

"Scuse me," Andy said as politely as he knew how. "You from Cuddy's Funeral Home?"

The driver stared at him.

"Yeah, how'd you know?"

This driver's van was unmarked, too.

Andy ignored the question. "I think I caused you a problem. I asked you to pick up my mother."

The driver looked relieved that he'd have someone to bitch at. He picked up a clipboard with his order-for-release form attached to it. He read a name off the form, mispronouncing both halves of it.

"Is that you?" he asked.

"Yeah," Andy said.

"Well, your mother's gone. Donatello Brothers already took her."

"Goddamn. My fucking uncle can't even let me bury my mother the way I want."

"What?"

"I called you guys to do the funeral. But my mother's buttinski brother called Donatello. I didn't know a thing about it until he called me half an hour ago. I race right over here and you say she's gone. Pisses me off."

The driver nodded his head in sympathy.

"Hey, this ain't right. You're her son. You want, we'll go over to Donatello right now and get her."

"Yeah, that's just what I'd like to do, but you know what a pain in the ass relatives are."

"Tell me about it."

"Listen, I'm gonna straighten this mess out with my dumb uncle, then I'll call you guys to come get her. Sorry about the hassle."

The driver looked skeptical.

"Besides," Andy said, "I think you got a flat tire here."

"What?"

The driver shoved his door open and dropped the

clipboard on the seat. He stooped to look at the tire. The tiny puncture was imperceptible, but the tire was flattening visibly. The driver cursed as he searched for the source of the trouble.

As he did, Andy snatched a copy of the order-for-release form from the clipboard. Besides bearing Mama's name, it was inscribed with the signature of Francis Cuddy and bore the license number of Cuddy's Funeral Home. Andy slipped it inside his jacket.

"I have to take off," he said. "I'll tell Donatello I want you guys to handle my mother."

"Yeah, sure."

The driver just wanted to get his tire changed and go back to work.

Andy walked out of the morgue's lot thinking everything had gone perfectly. Now he'd go to Donatello with the release form and say he was there to take the body to Cuddy's. Then he'd take Mama and call Cuddy's and say, no, Donatello was going to handle things after all.

Since he'd let both places keep their deposits, he didn't expect trouble from either of them. This way he'd have Mama and no one would know it.

Because Mama was going to be buried only one place and by only one person.

Andy got into his unmarked van and went to pick up his mother.

38

"Dead?"

Armando Guzman was stunned when Hector gave him the news.

"The traitor is dead?"

Hector nodded. He was pleased Armando hadn't exploded immediately. Pleased, but puzzled.

"Don Ernesto told me that he tried to take over your operations but the bosses wanted no more Guzmans in business. They killed him."

"How?"

"A bomb."

"In his car?"

"Yes."

"How do you feel, Hector? He was your brother."

Hector shrugged. "We weren't close."

"So, I hated him more than you loved him?"

"Yes."

"Tell me, cousin, what *do* you love?"

"My life."

Hector felt the weight of Armando's stare.

"You mean the money, the houses, the women, everything that makes you like the smile you see in your mirror."

"*Sí.*"

"How much of that would you have without me?"

Hector didn't reply; they both knew the answer. Fear wasn't the only reason Hector hated his cousin.

"I was going to kill Fidelito, but I respected him. He saw an opportunity to seize my power and he could not help but take it. In his place, I would have done no less. Unlike you, cousin, your brother was a man."

Hector swallowed his pride. He knew his moment would come, and then he would see how macho Armando was.

"I am tired of this *Yanqui* jail," Armando said. "When do I get out?"

"Soon."

Hector described his plan and Armando accepted it all. He voiced no objection to hiring a new lawyer. He made only one change. His equanimity made Hector uneasy.

"What about our greedy cop?" Armando asked.

"That news is not so good. You can kill him, but it will have to be hit-and-run."

"Why?"

"He has no one he loves. No one to hold hostage, no one to bring him to you."

"No family?"

"His family is dead. Four deaths, one quickly after another in a span of two years."

Armando nodded with new understanding.

"I see now. Life has stolen from him, so he steals from me. Has he no woman?"

"An ex-wife."

Armando shook his head immediately.

"No. We could take her and he could laugh at us. We could say come, and he could disappear."

Hector agreed.

"You will go look at this cop, Hector."

"What?"

"Look at his face. See what I have made of him.

See where he is weak. See what will bring him to me."

"But . . ."

Armando's voice dropped to a whisper.

"Do it, cousin. Do it if you value your precious life."

39

Doc stepped into the gym before going upstairs to the Narcotics Unit. He looked around and felt uneasy, as if he'd entered the enemy camp. He wondered if this was how bad guys felt every time they got busted.

When Marv Gold, one of the department's PE instructors, saw him, his jaw dropped. Then he smiled. He quickly wiped the expression from his face when he remembered his politics. Next, he looked around and decided it was safe to give Doc a wink.

"You working up an act, Marv?"

"Something I can do for you, sir?"

"Yeah, my car's outside," Doc joked. Actually, he'd given in and taken the CTA. "Have the Superintendent wash it and fill the trunk with cash."

Marv fought it but he laughed out loud. He was smart enough to turn the laughter into a coughing fit. His face still ended up bright red.

"I'm here to see Vince," Doc said.

"I believe you know the way."

"I believe I do."

Doc went upstairs. Vince's office was in the far corner of the floor, and Doc had to walk past every cop in the place. No one said a word to him, but their expressions and gestures spoke volumes.

The ones on his side gave him discreet smiles, winks, and thumbs-up. Detective Terri Quinn even copped a quick feel as he passed her. The others got squinty and tight-mouthed. He could practically hear them wondering how they could rat on someone who didn't have a badge anymore.

Doc knocked on Vince's scarred wooden door.

"Whoever you are, you're interrupting police work here."

Doc went inside. Detective Frank Wallis had his feet up on Vince's desk and was leafing through a porno mag.

"Imagine that," Doc said. "He can do police work with his zipper up."

"Doc! How the hell are you?"

"Not bad. You get loaned out to Vice?"

"Nah, the dicks over there just wanted an outside opinion on whether this stuff is obscene. I volunteered."

"Big of you."

Doc glanced at the magazine.

"Can't be obscene. Doesn't involve any endangered species."

Frank laughed. Vince entered the office with a file under his arm.

"Wallis, if you can get up without embarrassing yourself, get that shit outta here."

The detective stood up and looked at his crotch.

"No embarrassment, no obscenity."

He went out and closed the door behind him. Vince locked the door.

"That the file on the Welles kid?" Doc asked.

"Yeah. A friend faxed it to me. We're getting high-tech as hell around here lately."

"What's it say?"

Vince tossed it to him and told him to read. Doc skimmed through the pages. From the number of detectives working on the case, it was obvious it paid to go straight to the top—if you could.

Frederick Welles had definitely been home between leaving school on Wednesday afternoon and being reported absent on Thursday morning. He'd come home after the housekeeper had done her work for the day and left his own distinctive mess for her to find in the kitchen the next morning.

The building's daytime doorman, Ezra Fobb, saw Frederick arrive home from school Wednesday in a Red Ball Taxi. He didn't get the number of the cab, but he knew he had the company right. He knew because he remembered that the cabbie seemed to be in a hurry when he approached, as if he didn't want the doorman to see him.

Other than that, the team of detectives hadn't done any better finding the kid than Doc had finding Jerry Handee. If everything was in the file.

"Lots of manpower here."

Vince smiled.

"Malloy tried to run it himself at first, and that's how Conrad Walters got ahold of the story."

"I didn't see any follow-up on this taxi angle."

"I noticed that too, so I asked."

"And?"

"What, you want me to let you in on the department's big secret?"

Doc didn't bother to respond.

"Red Ball can't find any record of a cab making a trip to that building within an hour of the time the doorman says the kid was let off. At first they said sometimes their drivers leave the meter off, charge a flat fare, and pocket the cash."

"Don't their drivers lease?"

"No. They're one of the few outfits left that split the meter with the driver. Anyway, they said maybe someone was dippin' in the till. But we had them check out the taxis they had out on the street at that time. Every driver could account for his whereabouts. All of their logs have entries for the time in question. All of their receipts balance to the penny. Now the passengers are being tracked down, to corroborate the drivers."

"The doorman's sure he saw a Red Ball?"

"Positive."

"How're his eyes?"

"He got his driver's license renewed last month without needin' glasses."

"Does he drink?"

Vince shook his head.

"He's a part-time Baptist preacher."

"So someone's got his own private taxi."

Vince nodded.

"And maybe specializes in giving last rides."

Vince took the file from Doc and unlocked the door.

"Come on, I want to show you some more high-tech."

Doc got up and followed Vince. For a moment he thought they were going to the Captain's office, but they stopped just outside the Captain's door, at the desk of the administrative officer. Neither the Captain nor his clerk was at his post.

Vince dropped his copy of the Welles file into what looked like a fancy wastebasket. The thing whirred, and in seconds the file was so much confetti.

"Paper shredder. Wasn't it your lawyer who asked how the department spends its money?"

"Yeah."

"No money to stop manpower cutbacks. No money to buy the troops automatics. But we've got all the gizmos you could ever ask for."

Vince shook his head.

"Let's get outta here. I'll drive you home and tell you all about my vacation."

40

When Doc got out of Vince's car he saw Glenna waiting for him on his front porch. He noticed the difference in her immediately. Any sense of apprehension she'd felt was gone. Left in its place was a vengefulness that filled her eyes with a cold harsh light.

She carried a big tattered purse over her shoulder.

"Glenna," Doc greeted her.

She got up off the glider.

"Conrad Walters come by to see me. Some crazy bastard's killed Jerry, ain't he?"

Doc knew there was no way he could lie or even evade.

"I think so."

"I'm gonna find him, Michael."

"Glenna, the department has a lead. They haven't told anyone yet, but they have a lot of people out looking."

"They're lookin' because of that Welles boy, ain't they?"

"Yes."

"Well, I'll be lookin' because of my boy."

She started to leave, but Doc caught her arm.

"Wait a minute. Jerry and the Welles kid aren't the only ones missing, and they aren't the only ones who *might* have been killed. If there is a guy out there doing all this, he's crazy as a shithouse rat and just as dangerous."

Glenna stepped back from him. She opened her ragged purse and took out an old Smith & Wesson .44 Special, with a barrel long enough to make Clint Eastwood envious.

"If he's a rat, he'll die like one."

Doc knew that she had no more right to carry her .44 than he did the Beretta that was under his jacket. He also knew Glenna was no more likely to give up her weapon than he was his.

"Do you know how to use that monster?"

She nodded grimly.

"Everybody from my part of West Virginia can shoot. This was my daddy's gun. He promised it to the child of his that was the best shot. I had five brothers."

Doc thought about what Vince had told him on the ride home, about him being sent on vacation and the guys being kept busy. Vince planned to stay plugged into the doings of Cousin Hector and his hit men. The whole team would come down with the blue flu if they were needed. But all things considered, maybe he should take a vacation of his own.

The problem was, he didn't feel like going away.

"Are you any good at teaching?" Doc asked.

"Shootin'?"

"Yes."

"Why?"

Doc showed her the Beretta.

"I might need to kill a few bastards myself."

They rode the bus out to the forest preserve, looking like all the other passengers who couldn't afford their own cars. Doc speculated on whether they were the most heavily armed people on the bus.

He'd told Glenna who was after him, and why he'd need to sharpen his shooting skills. She'd shaken her head and asked how the world had become such an evil place. He'd had no answer for her.

She told him if she took care of her business quick enough, she'd be happy to help him with his. Doc thanked her but said he'd be happy if she could just help him improve his aim. Glenna replied that she wasn't the marksman her daddy was, but . . . but she'd even been able to teach Jerry to shoot. She reckoned she could help him.

He wasn't so sure. Jerry, whatever his other limitations, had possessed two eyes; with only one eye Doc didn't have stereoscopic vision, and he couldn't judge distances worth a damn.

Gunther had explained things to him. When you had two eyes and you looked at something, the image registered on a focal point of each eye. The brain then determined the angle of convergence for the line of sight from each eye to the object. It was the degree of the angle that told the brain how near or far the object was: depth perception.

It was easy to understand, Gunther had told him, if you held a pencil right in front of your nose. The pencil was so close you almost had to cross your eyes to see it. The angle of convergence was acute. On the other hand if you stared at a point on the horizon, your eyes barely converged at all.

When you had one eye, it had nothing to converge with; this made judging the distances of traffic and targets a very tricky business.

Doc just hoped Glenna could show him something that would give him a better chance of hitting the bad guys than shooting his dick off.

"I don't understand all this depth perceptin' talk. Let me try this."

Glenna covered her left eye with her left hand. The huge revolver looked far too heavy for her to hold at the end of her extended right arm, but it was rock-steady.

She blew a beer can fifty feety away into shrapnel.

They'd walked half a mile into the woods, collecting cans and bottles as they went. Their arms were full by the time they stopped at a hillock in a clearing. Doc lined up rows of targets so the slugs would be stopped by the rise behind them.

He didn't think he could miss the whole damn hill. He was also fairly sure that on a chilly, overcast day, a month before picnic season had any chance of beginning, their fire wouldn't attract any attention.

So far, he'd been right on both counts. He hadn't missed the hill entirely, and no one had complained.

But while Glenna picked off her targets routinely, Doc missed far more often than not. He'd shot short; he'd shot long. Occasionally, he'd nicked a target. From distances of twenty to fifty feet, though, he hadn't hit one squarely, in half an hour of trying.

"Let me try the other way," Glenna said.

She covered her right eye with her right hand and shot with her *left* hand. She turned a bottle into powdered glass.

"How the hell do you do that?"

Glenna frowned while trying to think of the answer.

"I . . . I just *feel* where I should be shootin'. I expect my hand knows as much about where to shoot as my eyes."

"You don't have to think about it?"

"I never *think* about it. All your mind has to do is keep your eyes open and your hand steady. Maybe not even that much."

West Virginia Zen, Doc thought.

"I don't mean to be insultin', Michael, but could you shoot much before you got hurt?"

"Yeah. I was pretty good."

"Well then, you should *know* how to shoot somethin' fifty feet away without thinkin' about it."

She was right. He should know. With all the hours he'd put in at the practice range, it should be in muscle memory or something.

He turned from Glenna, and in one motion raised and fired his weapon.

He blasted a bottle to bits.

The one in front of the beer can he'd been aiming at.

"See," Glenna said, "nothin' to it."

"Yeah."

Maybe he'd better go on vacation, Doc thought. Or ask Vince for an Uzi.

41

There was a jar filled with change, dollar bills, and an occasional five spot on the back bar at Nat's Tap. A hand-printed label read HELP US FIND JERRY. Above the jar, between the cash register and a bottle of Old Granddad, was a copy of the boy's picture that Doc had distributed.

Doc had a question for Nat when the bar owner brought him a beer.

"Who gets the money?"

"What?"

"Who gets the money in the 'Find Jerry' jar?"

"Well, he does, of course."

"How can you give it to him when he's missing?"

The look on Nat's face showed that while his heart might have been in the right place, the United Way didn't have to worry about his gaining on them.

Doc said, "Why don't you give it to Glenna? Help her make next month's rent."

"Well, that's certainly a worthy cause."

Nat was Glenna's landlord.

"But wouldn't that make the sign kinda deceivin'?"

"Glenna's looking for Jerry harder than anyone. She's out looking right now. Keeping a roof over her head would make things a lot easier."

Nat nodded. He'd bought the idea.

"I don't see how anyone could argue with that."

"Me neither."

Nat left to wait on another customer.

The place was fairly full, but Doc had the far end of the bar to himself. In the fifteen minutes he'd been there he'd overheard several conversations, all on the same subject: Had Jerry Handee been killed by some maniac?

There was a Doppler effect to these dialogues. They'd start in quiet, distant tones, appropriate to the grimness of the subject. Then they'd roar up fast and loud in the heat of emotion. Finally they'd fade away to silence, as heads turned to look at Doc.

Everyone knew he'd been asking questions, and everyone wondered if he could possibly suspect one of *them*.

It was a reasonable suspicion. He *was* watching them and wondering who, if any, among them had the skill to mock up a taxi, and the mad brutality to commit a string of murders. The bonds between Doc and his neighbors, some of life-long duration, seemed to be dissolving with each round of drinks.

The strain everyone felt spurred new and larger donations to the cash jar. Now even a few tens and a twenty were being deposited.

The dynamics of the room changed the moment Hector Guzman walked through the door. Everyone looked at him. He pushed his Bogart hat back on his head and returned their looks. He noticed Doc at the far end of the bar and grinned.

Hector had decided two things before he set out to obey his cousin's order. First, he had to put on the boldest front possible. Second, he would run without shame if necessary.

He gave Doc what he hoped was sufficient attention and made his way to the bar. He noticed the picture of the boy and the appeal for money. Hector immediately started to feel better. He knew that people who eased their guilt with money were not to be feared.

They were to be manipulated.

When Nat came over to ask his pleasure, Hector said, "This poor child is missing?"

Doc watched Hector, more than a little surprised by his presence. He saw Nat nod in response to the question.

Doc would never have guessed Hector had the nerve to confront anyone outside a courtroom. But here he was, and Doc knew it was some kind of challenge.

A disturbing thought made him quickly check the windows: What if the hit men Hector had hired were about to come busting in and hose down the whole place?

He relaxed when he saw no bogeymen outside. He should have realized that a daily-manicure guy like Hector would be miles away before any shooting started.

"What happened to this young man?" Hector asked Nat.

"He's a retarded kid, name of Jerry Handee, and he never came home from work a few days back. Everybody's real worried, and that fella"—Nat nodded at Doc—"he's been lookin' for him ever since."

Doc sat bolt upright. He didn't know why, but he didn't like Hector hearing all this.

"What do you want, Cousin Hector?" Doc asked.

Cousin Hector? the lawyer asked himself. The cop's casual familiarity turned his bowels to ice.

He considered running, but was afraid any motion would cause him to soil his pants. If he had to stand still, he would try manipulation.

"Why, I want to make a donation."

Hector produced his wallet and counted out ten one-hundred-dollar bills, laying the money on the bar.

"Would a thousand dollars help?"

Everyone in the place looked at the cash. Nat picked it up, but turned to Doc before he put it in the jar.

"This on the up and up, Doc?"

Doc never had a chance to answer, because Ray burst through the door, red-faced and bug-eyed and straining for breath.

"I saw him!" he gasped. "I just saw Jerry Handee!"

42

Doc dragged a wheezing Ray into the night-time alley behind his corner store. All the others followed on the run.

"He's not here anymore, I told you."

Ray bent over and labored to get enough oxygen into his sixty-seven-year-old lungs.

"Which way did he go?" Doc asked.

Ray pointed down the alley, and Doc followed the gesture with his eye. The alley ran the length of the standard one-eighth-mile city block. The distance was illuminated by four streetlights. The only sign of life Doc saw was a cat looking back at him from atop a garbage can.

Doc said, "Okay, Ray. Take your time and catch your breath. When you're ready, tell me the whole thing from the beginning."

Ray took Doc at his word. He waited for his heart to return to its normal, sedate rhythm. People got impatient with his recovery rate. They fidgeted and gave him restive looks.

"Jesus Christ, Ray. Don't take all night here," Red Penwell bawled.

"Shut up!" Doc told him.

"Hey, who do you—"

"Shut the fuck up, Red."

Red looked at Doc and, even knowing the guy

had only one eye, he didn't like his chances. He kept quiet.

Doc was sure that Red and everyone else felt a terrible pressure to do something fast. Everyone felt it except him.

He knew the important thing was that Jerry was still alive. Ray had been sure it was him. Given that, and the fact that he hadn't left the neighborhood, getting all the facts straight would be more helpful than running around helter-skelter.

"I was working late," Ray finally began, "putting all the stuff together for my accountant to file my tax return. Otherwise, I'd have gone home at my regular time."

"Yeah," Doc said.

"So when I got through with all that, I still had my regular cleanup work to do."

Nat said, "Come on, Ray. Get to the point."

"Let him tell it his own way!" Doc said harshly.

Nat looked insulted, and moved closer to Red Penwell.

Ray continued, "Well, the last thing I did was put out the trash. That's when I saw him. I pushed open the back door and there he was. Jerry. He was eating out of my garbage cans. He had a mouthful of something I'd rather not think about."

"Did he say anything?" Doc asked.

"No. I didn't know which of us was more surprised. We both must've looked like we'd seen ghosts. Then I said, 'Jerry, come inside and let me fix you something nice.' That's when he ran away."

"And you didn't go after him?" Red asked.

Ray's face flushed with anger.

"Yeah, I went after him. I went ten feet by the

time he went fifty. I couldn't have caught him if I was half my age. And nobody with a gut like yours could, either."

Doc didn't need any arguments.

"Look, everybody, Ray's going to tell his story, and *I'm* the only one who's going to ask questions. If that doesn't suit any of you, you can get the hell out of here."

Everyone except Ray gave Doc openly belligerent looks, but no one spoke out. No one left, either.

"Ray, did Jerry look like he was hurt? Did he have any cuts, or were there signs of a gunshot wound?"

"No, nothing like that. He smelled to high hell, though, and was covered just about head to toe with grease."

"Did he look like he might have been sick or disoriented?"

"No. The *only* thing I could see wrong was he looked so scared you'd think the devil was after him."

"Excuse me," Nat said sarcastically, "but something would have had to scare him bad if he was practically right across the street from his own home and he ran away. Maybe we should find him before he disappears again."

"You're right," Doc said.

"Well, thank *you*."

Doc waited to see if any of them made the connection. Jerry was alive and scared out of his meager wits; there were reports out that some loony was running around grabbing people. That suggested a very nasty conclusion, but none of them picked up on it.

They were all too pissed off at him. In the hope that he could keep them distracted, Doc apologized.

"I'm sorry, everyone. I got carried away. Maybe you should go looking for Jerry, but if you do, don't *anyone* go alone."

"Why not?" Red asked with a sneer.

Doc looked at him closely for a moment, then shrugged.

"He's too fast. You'd never catch him."

They agreed that they would look in two groups, eight in one, seven in the other.

Doc knew that they'd never find the boy. Jerry would be back in his filthy hidey-hole by now, the one Doc hadn't been able to find. It was a thought that comforted him.

Nat said to the others, "Hey, wait for me. I gotta go lock up." His face dropped as he remembered something. "Hell, I left that dude all alone in my bar!"

Doc looked around and saw that Nat was right. Cousin Hector hadn't come with them. But he'd seen all the commotion.

Then Doc noticed the Mercedes sitting opposite the mouth of the alley. The window was down, and Cousin Hector was smiling at him.

Hector had picked up the thousand dollars Nat had left on the bar when he and all the others had run out. He went behind the bar and put the money in the jar. They wouldn't be able to call him an Indian-giver, he thought.

Then he took the picture of the boy and left.

Now, sitting in his car, he watched them bicker. It was obvious they didn't have the boy. Hector took the picture out of his coat pocket and looked at it. He remembered that the bartender had said the boy's name was Jerry Handee. He took a pen from the glove compartment and wrote the name on the back of the photo.

It struck him as curious that so many people would care so much about an *imbecil*. They collected money for him; they chased after him; they quarreled over him. Still, Hector was not one to argue with luck.

Everyone else was looking for the boy, so he would, too. If he got the *pobrecito* first, he would have his hostage.

Hector noticed that the cop was looking at him. He smiled and let the Mercedes ease off down the street. He thought that this night's work deserved its proper reward. He picked up his car phone.

He would see if Melissa was free. Well, *available*, anyway.

43

Doc's phone rang the minute he sat down on his front porch. He knew who it was immediately, and cursed himself for forgetting. He got the door unlocked and picked up the phone as it rang a third time.

"I'm sorry," he said.

"You don't have to be, if there's a good reason."

He'd forgotten all about Harry's suggestion that they have dinner at some little out-of-the-way restaurant.

Doc took a breath and told her why he'd forgotten.

"Jerry Handee is alive."

Harry's voice was joyful. "He's home? That's wonderful."

"I didn't say—"

Looking through his living room window, Doc saw a Red Ball Taxi pass by.

"Hold on a second, Harry."

He laid the phone down and ran out on the porch. The cab slowed for the intersection, turned the corner past Nat's Tap, and was gone. Doc went back inside.

"I'm back."

"What was that all about?"

"I thought I saw something. Maybe I did, I'm not sure."

"Why do you sound so worried if Jerry's home?" Alarm entered Harry's voice. "It wasn't those creeps looking for you, was it?"

Doc answered her first question.

"Harry, I said he was alive. I didn't say he was home."

"I don't understand."

He told her about Ray spotting Jerry, and the boy running away.

"Why would he do that?"

Doc had an answer. It was speculative, but every bit of experience he had told him he was on the money. He had it right.

"Because there's a monster out there killing people, and Jerry knows who it is."

"Oh my God, that poor boy." Then Harry asked the obvious question. "But why wouldn't he go home to Glenna?"

"Think about it a second, Harry."

A second was all she needed.

"Because the monster is someone who knows Jerry, too. Someone who knows where he lives." Harry sounded stricken.

Doc added a further consideration. "Maybe even someone who threatened to come get Jerry *and* his mama if he goes home."

Someone who might cruise by in a Red Ball Taxi every so often to keep an eye on things.

"Oh, Doc, I can't imagine anything more horrible than this."

Until tonight, neither could he.

"It gets worse. Hector Guzman, Armando's cousin and lawyer, dropped by Nat's tonight, and was on hand when Ray ran in and dropped his bomb. Just before that Cousin Hector had been taking a keen interest in Jerry's trouble, because Nat had this damn donation jar up collecting money for the kid. Hector even laid out a thousand bucks to help the recovery effort. Now I think he's going to look for Jerry for a whole different reason."

"What reason?" Harry asked hesitantly.

"If he can find Jerry, he has a hostage to get to me."

"Doc, you can't let him do that! You can't!"

There was real fear in Harry's voice.

"If he gets Jerry, how can I do anything else?"

The phone rang again before he could step back outside. This time Vince was calling *after* Harry.

"Got some news."

"What?"

"Just heard from a friend at DEA that Armando's cousin Fidelito, down in Columbia, got hit."

"How come?"

"My friend says he was trying to pick up the pieces of Armando's organization. The guess is he wanted it for himself. Apparently the big boys down there wanted it for *them*selves."

Doc thought about it a minute.

"Could be another reason."

"What?"

"Bobby Ro gave me the tip that Armando was coming to town, remember?"

"Yeah."

"Bobby had to get the information from somewhere. Why not from Fidelito? Who'd be in a better spot to know?"

"You think Armando's cousin sold him out?"

"If he intended to take over, sure."

"Makes sense," Vince said. "Not that he'd ever

tell us, but Armando has to know who ratted on him."

"So he arranges for Bobby and Fidelito to get it."

"You're on the list, too."

"I haven't forgotten," Doc said.

"Yeah, you might have figured it out. Or maybe there's just some pharaoh's curse on this money. You watch yourself."

"I will."

Doc hung up, and it struck him how serious their conversation had been. Neither he nor Vince had sworn once.

44

"I never get tired of looking at you," Hector said.

"You will. The first time you see a wrinkle."

"No, you'll never get old."

"Everything gets old. Even sex."

"Bite your tongue."

Melissa looked down at Hector as she straddled him. He was still inside her, but softening.

"I'd rather bite something else."

"See, you still like it."

"I'm not old yet. Neither are you."

"I won't get old. And if I do, that's why we have plastic surgeons and Swiss clinics."

"Be sure to send me a postcard."

"You'll be with me. I'll have them make you almost as beautiful as me."

She patted his chest affectionately and started to climb off, but Hector put his hands on her hips and held her in place. "What's wrong?" he asked.

"You know."

"No, what?"

"We talked about it last time."

"Armando?"

She nodded.

"He scares you that much?"

"I never met a cannibal who didn't. I never met a cannibal at all, and I don't intend to start."

Hector still hadn't found a way to argue the point.

"I think he scares you too," she said.

"He does."

Melissa leaned over and kissed him lightly.

"Not many guys would admit that. You're special."

"But you're still going to stop seeing me."

Melissa drew a fingernail down his chest, from the hollow of his throat to his belly button.

"Can you keep a secret?" she asked.

"I'm a lawyer. We're like priests, professional secret-keepers."

"Priests don't charge."

"Okay, pay me just one dollar. You'll have attorney-client privilege."

"Tell you what. We'll barter. You keep my secret, and tonight's on me."

Hector smiled. "Tell me."

"I killed a guy once."

He felt himself shrivel, until she reassured him.

"Not a client. A guy who tried to take me over. A pimp."

"How did you do it?"

"I shot him."

Melissa started to rock her hips as she remembered, and despite himself Hector felt a stirring in his loins.

"I went to meet a client at his hotel, but when I got there I found this guy instead of the client. Big guy with an ear-to-ear grin. Said he'd put my client in another room and told him to spend the night reflecting on his evil ways. When I asked who the hell he thought he was, he told me I was looking at my new owner.

"I didn't argue. I told him okay. I said there

was no need to hurt me. He said fine and dandy, but he liked to break in his new girls personally."

Melissa rocked harder atop Hector.

"He wasn't very imaginative, just rough. He didn't want anything special until the end. He said it was important that his girls knew how to kiss ass. So, right at the end, he flopped over on his stomach and pulled his cheeks apart."

Melissa's heat was bringing Hector erect.

"He thought he had me so scared I'd do it. He still had his ass in both hands when I reached into my purse, got my little gun, and blew his brains all over the pillows. Must've been a sight for the cops who found him."

She looked down at Hector. He was hard inside her.

"That's what you have to do, honey. Pretend to kiss a little ass, then kill the bastard that wants to own you."

He reached up and pulled her to him.

She whispered in his ear.

"Really. Do it. You'll respect yourself more. And so will I."

45

Doc was back on his front porch by the time Nat had locked up. The others had grown tired of waiting for him and had gone off on their own. Nat was still pissed at Doc, but he came over to ask which way his search party had gone.

Doc nodded his head. "They went thataway."

"What the hell is with you?" Nat asked.

"What?"

"The way you're acting. Everyone has to tiptoe around you like *we're* the pervert you're after. Then we're just pissants getting in your way. Now the whole thing's some kind of joke to you. Did that gunshot wound do you some brain damage?"

The question was meant as an insult rather than an inquiry, but Doc answered it regardless.

"It may have."

"You just going to sit around?"

"Yeah."

"You *are* crazy."

"Maybe."

"Sonofabitch," Nat muttered.

He started off, but before he could get two feet Doc spoke up.

"Nat?"

"What?" he asked angrily.

"Did Cousin Hector leave the money?"

"Yeah, he did. Put it in the jar himself. Surprised the hell outta me."

"Was there anything missing?"

Nat shook his head. "Every cent was in the register."

"How about the picture of Jerry?"

Nat thought a moment.

"Damn, you're right. That was gone. But for a thousand bucks, he's entitled. Look, you sit on your ass if you want, but I'm going."

Nat left, giving Doc one last look of disapproval. Doc stayed where he was through the night, holding the Beretta under his crossed arms. He heard the voices of his neighbors calling Jerry's name, but there were no cries of discovery or pleas for help. He saw no more Red Ball Taxis or signs of hit men.

At dawn, he saw Glenna Handee drag her indomitable spirit home. One look and he could tell that she'd somehow failed to bump into any of the others, and hadn't heard the news. Doc crossed the street to tell her that her son was still alive.

And still in grave danger.

46

The train pounded around the curve in the "L" tracks at dawn, and Jerry Handee felt both scared and safe. He huddled in a tool crib that extended from the tracks between the Kelvin Avenue and Perry Street stations like a misplaced outhouse.

He was shivering, filthy, and sick to his stomach from the garbage he'd been eating. Every time a train went by it made the crib vibrate so hard Jerry was afraid it would fall to the alley twenty-five feet below. At the same time he felt relieved that Andy hadn't found out where he was, that he hadn't been sneaking up on him. He couldn't have been, or the train would have run him over.

Jerry kept hoping for a train to run Andy over. *Something* like that, anyway. It had to happen, or Jerry would never get home.

For a minute last night, when he saw Ray, he thought he should let Ray make him some food. But he knew that Ray would call Mama and she'd take him home, and Andy would get both of them.

He knew that Mama had Granddaddy's gun, but he feared that Andy would sneak up on them after they were both sleeping and the gun wouldn't do any good. They'd wind up like that boy he saw Andy taking down to the basement.

Jerry did not want to wind up in that basement.

So he stayed up all night and peeked out of the crib's windows. He wasn't going to let Andy sneak up on him. Through all the hours of darkness he watched, fully expecting Andy to climb up onto the tracks and come straight for him. He knew he couldn't count on a train hitting Andy, either, so he held on to the heavy wrench he'd found in the crib.

He was just lucky he'd heard some of the neighborhood kids talking about this being a great place to hide. If he didn't have the crib, he knew Andy would have got him by now for sure.

For a little while, Jerry'd thought he maybe could go to Doc. Doc was a policeman, and he could put Andy in jail. But then he remembered what Mama had told him. Doc lost his eye and all, and he wasn't a policeman no more. He wasn't very nice lately, either. He'd say hello if you said it to him first, but sometimes he'd pretend not to see you and walk right by.

Jerry peeked out one of his little windows. There were no trains coming. He couldn't see anybody on the street that crossed under the tracks up ahead, and he couldn't hear anybody in the alley below. Andy wasn't sneaking up on him.

He opened the door of the crib and peed between the ties. Then he went back inside and prayed for Mama.

He prayed, too, that somebody or something would kill Andy. Real quick.

Then he went to sleep for the day.

47

Andy Slick had buried twenty-three bodies, but none of them neater than Mama's. He'd given her a special place, too. It was right in the middle of the second room, in a plot big enough for four normal burials. That was only right, because Mama had started the whole thing, had shown him the way.

She'd killed his father.

Henri Lisse had been a monster. Not that he'd looked it. At a glance, he seemed to be an ordinary guy. Well, he *was* a little standoffish—and he *did* mutter to himself under his breath. Still, he functioned. He had a wife and a kid. Held down a steady job as a plumber, and brought home better money than most men. He owned his home free and clear.

It was inside that home, with the wife and son as prisoners, that the monster surfaced and ruled. Henri demanded blind obedience, and both his captives would gladly have given it except he kept changing the rules on them. Day to day. Sometimes one minute to the next.

His wife had to have his dinner ready the moment he came home from work. Except when he didn't feel like eating right away. In either case, the food had to be hot. But not overcooked. His son didn't dare neglect his studies for television. Except when Papa didn't want to watch TV alone.

Andy had to be quiet in the house. Even if it meant leaving his shoes off when the floors were freezing cold. But heaven help him if Henri thought he was sneaking around. Mama had to keep the house spotlessly clean. But not pick up after one of the messes Henri made before he was through making it. Which might be a matter of minutes, or days.

The monster had rules for every facet of human behavior—and contradicted every rule he made, and then reversed the contradictions, but not necessarily to his original position. There was really no way mother or son could know how to please Henri. Making the simplest decision was an occasion for fear.

Because they knew only too well what happened whenever the monster was displeased.

First he would rant at them, bunching his fists and shouting at the top of his voice. His face would turn red, his eyes would bulge, and spittle that they didn't dare wipe away would fly from his mouth onto their faces. Whatever the offense, the monster's accusation was always the same: Mama and Andy didn't respect him. He slaved at his job every day to give them everything they should have, and they thought they could treat him like a piece of *merde*. Well, he'd show them they couldn't.

Then the beatings would begin.

The monster had beaten his wife from the beginning of their marriage, and his son from the beginning of the boy's life. Andy had never known a time when he wasn't afraid of his father. Mama would comfort him after each attack, and usually take comfort, too, because she *always* tried to defend her son. Even though she knew it meant absorbing more punishment for herself.

As he grew older, Mama's courage made Andy feel guilty. Not because he didn't need her protection and solace. He would have died without them. But because he knew he wasn't as brave as his mother. Most of the time Andy would rush to his mother's defense as quickly as she came to his. He'd try to divert the monster's pummeling fists. He'd let himself be hurled aside and rush back to help.

Most times he'd do that. But not always. Some nights his pain and fear were just too great. He'd hear the monster scream at Mama. The sharp, terrifying crack of the first blow would follow, and Andy would hide and pray that he'd be spared.

He seldom was—more than once he'd been awakened from a sound sleep to find the monster beating him—and then the guilt and pain were all-consuming.

The night that changed everything came when he was eight years old. He was in bed when the monster started yelling. His father called Mama such bad names that the blood roared in Andy's ears. The boy was torn between wanting to help Mama and thinking desperately of a new place to hide.

Then something happened he'd never heard before. Mama screamed.

Before she was hit.

And it wasn't a cry of pain. It was a . . . a . . . shout . . . a shout of *rage*! As bloodthirsty a roar as any the monster had ever produced.

For a moment there was silence, followed by the most terrifying scream Andy'd ever heard. He couldn't tell who it had come from, and he had to see if something had happened to Mama. He raced to his parents' bedroom. When he skidded through the doorway he was frozen stiff by what he saw.

The monster was standing in the middle of the room, with Mama's knitting needle sticking clean through his neck.

His father saw Andy, gobbled something at him, and fell to his knees. The monster yanked the bloody needle free, but he wasn't able to breathe. He flopped around for a minute, rolled over, and died.

Andy stared at the body, waiting, wanting to be sure. When he was, he cheered. And laughed. And clapped his hands. He crossed the room and kicked the monster in the head.

"How's it feel? How do you like it?" he asked. Then he added gleefully, "Don't you know you're supposed to keep your room neat?" And he gave the corpse another kick.

He kept kicking and laughing until he was breathing hard. Until Mama put her arms around him and eased him away. Andy turned and embraced his mother.

What Mama had done was a revelation to him. For a long, long time he'd wanted to kill his father, but he'd never dreamed you could actually *do* it. Mama had finally had enough. She'd killed their captor. She'd taught the monster a lesson.

She'd taught Andy, too.

If people deserved it, you could kill them.

The thing was, Mama didn't understand what a good thing she'd done. She was scared. She gently held Andy's face, with the monster's blood still on her hands, and made him promise never, *never* to tell anyone what had happened to his father. If he did the police would take Mama away, and Andy would be all alone.

Suddenly the boy's elation was tempered with fear, and he promised never to say a word. Not one.

Mama rolled the body up in a sheet and had Andy help her drag it down into a corner of the basement. They buried it in the dirt floor. His mother asked God to forgive them. She told the Lord that they'd just buried a *bad* man. Andy nodded and thought, *Forgive us, but not him.*

He'd had to rebury his father twice more. The first grave was too shallow, and a sickening stench filled the house. He dug the next grave deeper, and years later, when he was in high school, he put the skeletal remains in a cube of cement. He didn't mark the burial spot, but he drew a floor plan of the room and indicated his father's place on it by printing BAD DADDY.

No one was ever going to find the body, but Mama continued to be terrified that they'd be caught. She told the few people who asked that her husband had run off with another woman. Then she sat in the front window waiting to see if anyone might come looking for him. Or her. She had bars put on the windows and dead bolts on the doors. She changed the name on the doorbell to her maiden name, so people would forget the monster faster.

Andy wanted to change his name, too, but Mama said that he'd been in school too long under his father's name. If he switched now it might look suspicious.

After the killing, Mama wouldn't leave the house. She sold the old man's car and their summer cottage over the phone. They lived on the money they got from the sales, along with accumulated bank accounts and savings bonds. Andy started working part-time when he was ten. Things were tight, but they pulled through.

Andy ran all of Mama's errands for her. When he went out he heard people saying that he was the boy with the crazy mother. He thought they'd better be careful. Just get the wrong person mad at you, and see what'd happen.

The only time Mama ever left home again was one day when Andy was a teenager. He came home from school and found Mama slumped in her chair, clutching her chest. Andy called a cab and took her to the doctor. The physician wanted to send her to the hospital but Mama refused. He started to argue, but he stopped when he saw the look on Andy's face.

They went home with a prescription for medicine that the doctor told Andy to be sure Mama took daily.

Because he had a secret to keep, Andy withdrew into a shell of silence at school. At first his friends asked what was wrong. He not only wouldn't tell them, he thought it best not to talk to them at all. That way he wouldn't let something slip by mistake. After a while his friends didn't care what was wrong with him—they weren't his friends anymore. All the kids decided he'd just "gone weird." His teachers didn't notice anything unusual because his grades remained high, and he'd always been a fairly quiet boy.

When the time came to go to high school, Andy's academic record would have qualified him for any college prep school in town, but he chose a technical school instead. He wanted to get a decent-paying job as fast as he could. He and Mama had scrimped long enough already.

He studied auto mechanics and body work. He was good at both, but he liked body work better.

It made him happy to take cars that were all broken and bent and pound them back into shape, make them smooth and shiny again.

Just as before, Andy kept strictly to himself and worked diligently. For three years, his classmates were content to ignore him. They were more interested in talking about girls and sneaking cigarettes into school. The work they did on their cars wasn't nearly as good as Andy's, but excellence was no big deal to them; good-enough-to-get-a-job was their goal.

Things changed when Tommy Fain arrived. He transferred in for senior year. He arrived with a customized '55 Chevy, the only girlfriend around who admitted going all the way, and the claim that he knew more about cars than anyone else in the class. He was immediately the coolest kid in school. "Untouchable Tommy," they called him.

Only two things bothered Tommy, and he kept them to himself. The first was that Andy didn't become one of his acolytes like all the other guys. The other was that the say-nothing doofus did better body work than him.

Andy's body work wasn't fancy like Tommy's. It had no pizzazz, no moxie. But, man, was it clean. It was like Andy had a better idea of what a car should look like than the guys who'd designed and built it.

As a technical school, the institution demanded no final exam for graduating seniors, but a "final project" instead. Each student had to take a car that had been all but totaled and, on a fixed budget, improve it as much as possible in one month's time.

The finished cars, along with their "before" photos, would be shown to a panel of judges from body shops and used-car dealerships. The student whose car got the highest rating from the body men and the highest price from the dealers was the winner. And would have all the job offers he could handle.

For most guys in the class, it was a foregone conclusion who the winner would be. But Tommy Fain didn't kid himself, he knew he would be in for a real fight. That's why he didn't mind cheating. He added to his budget by demanding ten bucks from each of his twenty guys, and they were happy to give it. They couldn't wait to see how cool Tommy could make his car with an extra two hundred dollars.

Tommy started with a miserable piece of shit and was soon turning it into a real rod. When he was finished with it the thing would go like hell and be just as hot to look at. Still, he couldn't help feeling nervous. He kept eyeballing Andy's car. Couldn't help himself. It was like the damn thing wouldn't let him be.

Mr. Mute was doing his usual boring number. But he was doing his usual job on it, too. He was taking something that nobody'd look at twice and making it into something you'd never get tired of looking at. It wasn't flashy like Tommy's; it was more of an old man's car. Okay, a real *nice* old man's car.

Then a horrible thought struck Tommy: Old men were going to be the judges of this contest. Guys over thirty or even forty, halfway ready to croak. They'd be the guys deciding the winner. The ones who handed out the jobs.

It was too late for Tommy to try to do something like Andy had done. He couldn't do that stuff, anyway. His strength was knocking your eyes out, not getting all the tiny, fussy details right.

Tommy knew Andy was going to beat him.

So he had to destroy Andy's car.

Andy never said a word to Tommy, but he watched him. He saw the way Tommy looked at his car. He could tell how worried he had Tommy. And he enjoyed it. Andy knew he could never take Tommy's place with the other guys—he didn't want to—but he thought it would be fun to knock Mr. Bigshot off his perch.

Then Andy saw the change in Tommy's eyes. The worry was gone. Something hard and cold and mean had replaced it. The new look scared Andy—for the first time since that long-ago night, someone reminded him of the monster.

Andy knew then that if Tommy couldn't *find* anything wrong with Andy's car, he'd *make* something wrong.

Tommy was going to wreck his car.

So he took it home and put it in the same garage where his father used to park his car. He wasn't supposed to do this. One of the project rules was that everybody had to leave his car at school. That way no one could cheat by having somebody else do his work. But the teacher knew the kind of work Andy did, knew that he'd never let anyone else touch his car, and when Andy told him he wanted to put extra hours into his car the teacher made an exception.

Andy started sleeping in his car with a lug wrench on his lap. He figured Tommy and his friends would find out where the car was and come to pulverize it one night. He didn't know if he could fight them all off, but he was going to try.

But he was wrong. When Tommy came, he

came alone. No friends. Then Andy figured it out. Tommy didn't want anyone to know that even with an extra two hundred bucks he couldn't win. Andy knew about how Tommy was cheating, but, staying right in character, he hadn't said a word.

Andy had been half-asleep when he'd heard the side door to his garage rattle. He'd quickly slipped out of his car; earlier he'd removed the dome light so there would be nothing to give him away. He peeked out the window. There was Tommy with a crowbar, prying the padlock off the door.

Tommy's crowbar against Andy's lug wrench. Pretty even. But Tommy didn't know Andy was waiting for him in the dark. And Andy knew right where Tommy would enter.

The moment before Tommy came in, Andy heard the voice in his head for the first time.

It was Mama.

She said, *Kill Tommy.*

Andy knew for certain that Mama wasn't in the garage with him. She was in bed. Mama didn't even go out to dump the garbage anymore. But he heard her voice clearly. She said Tommy was bad, just like Daddy had been. Hadn't Tommy scared Andy? Wasn't he going to destroy Andy's car? Did Andy think Tommy would let him stick around to tell everyone what Tommy had done?

The door to the garage opened, and Andy's wrench cracked Untouchable Tommy Fain's skull with an audible ring. The blows that followed got progressively quieter; it got to be like beating a mushy watermelon. Andy finally stopped when he noticed he was splattering blood on his car.

There was only one thing to do with Tommy. Andy took him to the basement.

No one ever found out what happened. Tommy

hadn't told anybody of his plan to wreck Andy's car. Of course his parents called the police the second day he was missing, but all the cops could do was ask Tommy's friends if they knew anything, and they didn't. When they asked Andy if he knew anything, he said no. He said he'd had nothing to do with Tommy—and no one could contradict him.

Andy's car won the project. He had his choice of job offers.

It was several years later that he hit upon the idea of having his own cab. Andy still took care of all of Mama's needs, but now he lived in his own place. He still buried his bodies at Mama's, but that was only right. She was the one who told him who to kill.

Andy was looking for some extra income when a taxi was brought into the shop in need of a new front end. After working on it, Andy and the driver got to talking. The driver told him that taxi money would be okay if he got to keep the whole meter instead of splitting it with the company.

So Andy bought a wrecked cab that the company thought wasn't worth fixing and restored it at home. He told the company that the meter was also a total write-off, but he fixed that, too. Then he went down to Police Headquarters at 11th and State, took the city geography test, got fingerprinted and photographed, and walked out with a chauffeur's license.

The license was in his father's family name, but Andy had used his mother's surname ever since leaving school. The way he looked at it, when he drove his secret cab he had a secret identity.

The money he made was even better than he'd expected. But then he put in more hours on the street than he'd planned, too. About the only drawback was that driving a cab meant dealing with a lot of passengers who scared the hell out of him. Same as any driver.

After Mama started telling him which passengers he could kill, however, that wasn't a problem anymore. All he had to do was set up his taxi to make sure he had the edge. Once he'd done that, he even got a little charge when he went cruising.

Working two jobs made it harder for Andy to run Mama's errands for her. So when Szell's Drugstore hired a delivery boy, Andy let him bring Mama's prescription. He didn't worry about it. He'd seen this Jerry kid around, talked to him the first time he made a delivery. Generally checked him out. Andy knew that the boy was both polite and a retard. Having Jerry save him some time would be no problem.

Or so he had thought.

One night, after his terrible fight with Mama—he still couldn't figure out why she'd insulted him—he was bringing a body to Mama's house to put in the basement. Some shabby asshole who'd tried to panhandle him by putting his hand in his pocket and telling Andy he'd *better* have a few dollars to spare. What Andy'd had in *his* pocket had settled the whole thing right away.

Between being angry with Mama and pissed about the grimy thief who'd been stinking up the trunk of his cab, he hadn't even waited until it was completely dark to bring the body inside. He'd just carried it rolled up in a tarp, from the garage out back into the house.

But he'd been careless and left the back door open. Jerry must have shown up right after that and, seeing the door open, stepped right in. All Andy knew for sure was he'd reached the bottom of the basement stairs when a shadow fell over him. He looked up and saw Jerry staring at him.

He wondered what the boy was doing there. He didn't think it was time for Mama's medicine again already. Then Andy recognized the look of horror on Jerry's face, and he glanced down. The head of the asshole he'd just taken care of was hanging out of the tarp.

Jerry screamed and ran.

Which was just what Andy wanted to do. Because seeing the boy there, and knowing his secret had been discovered, scared him worse than anything in his life.

He wanted to run away and hide, but he dropped the body and ran right after Jerry. He couldn't let his secret come out now, not after being so smart all these years. He couldn't let a retard ruin him.

By the time Andy got to the kitchen, Jerry was already out the back door and through the yard.

Andy yelled, "I know you! I know where you live!"

He slammed the back door behind him, making sure it locked. He ran to the garage and started his taxi. Cursing his luck, he drove as fast as he could without getting a ticket and parked in an alley a half-block from Nat's Tap. He had been waiting in a doorway only a few minutes when he saw Jerry running home.

His mistake had been showing himself too soon. He'd thought he was fast enough to catch the boy. But Jerry was considerably younger, and rightfully feared for his life. When he saw Andy appear between him and his house, he cut into the alley behind Ray's and disappeared.

Andy followed, knowing Jerry was hiding somewhere nearby, but he couldn't find him. He looked for half an hour. As he poked and peered he kept whispering the same message.

"I'll get you. If you go home, I'll get you. You go home and I'll get your Mama, too."

Now, Andy stared at the spot on the basement floor where he'd buried *his* Mama. She'd died because Jerry had run off with her medicine.

He'd get Jerry for that. *Soon*.

48

Superintendent Malloy was getting sick and tired of hearing bad news every time he turned on the TV. It was a goddamn Sunday morning, and he *still* had to look at that tweedy DEA shit Carswell talking to Conrad Walters about his resignation.

He listened to the weasel say that he'd dedicated all the time he could to government service. His kids were approaching college age and he had to think of his own retirement. So he felt compelled to enter the private practice of law, where he could earn a more substantial income.

Walters asked the bastard if his practice would include defending the same kinds of people he'd been trying to arrest. Carswell responded with a straight face that everyone was entitled to the ablest defense he could afford.

"Goddamn hypocrite!" Malloy yelled at his television. "You're leaving me holding the bag!"

Carswell's move had left Malloy in a lonely spot. He was now the only miserly bureaucrat standing between that valiant martyr Doc Kildare and his claim on the drug money.

The Superintendent wanted to puke.

Kildare wasn't his only problem. The Sunday *Trib* said, in effect, that he was playing favorites for bigwigs when their kids disappeared and didn't give a damn when some dipshit moron turned up missing. The *Sun-Times* wanted to know why the department was keeping the public in the dark about a serial killer who was running amok.

It made Malloy furious that he couldn't even help himself out by revealing that they had a pretty good lead in finding out what had happened to the Welles kid. Doing that would warn off the creep who'd grabbed him.

Then the thought hit him.

He couldn't reveal the lead about the phony Red Ball Taxi. That would be professional suicide. But he could announce that there *was* a lead, a promising but unspecified lead. And if some overzealous news shithead, Conrad Walters, say, found out, through someone's carelessness, what the lead was and went public with it, it wouldn't be his fault.

What it would be was a way to get him off the hook by hammering the irresponsible media over the head.

They were to blame. *They* were irresponsible. *They* distorted things like his relationship with Walter Welles. *They* offered misplaced support for Kildare.

The way Malloy saw it, he had nothing to lose. Those missing kids had to be dead by now, anyway. There was no harm there. He might even scare the killer out of town by letting him know they were closing in on him.

And by the time the uproar died down, maybe those goddamn beaner hit men would finally have popped Kildare.

He called the captain who handled his PR and told him to arrange a press briefing for tomorrow.

49

"He doesn't deserve this, not my poor boy!"

Doc had just finished explaining to Glenna about Jerry's being alive, and how he had not just one monster after him now but two. He'd given her the whole story about Ray seeing Jerry; about the Welles boy and the phantom taxi; about Cousin Hector taking Jerry's picture from Nat's Tap.

Glenna got up from her lumpy sofa, where they'd both been sitting, and reached for her ragged handbag with the cannon inside it.

"You won't find him," Doc said wearily.

She started for the door. "I aim to try."

"We *don't* want to find him today. We want him to stay put."

Glenna stopped with her hand on the doorknob. She looked at him in dismay.

"How can you talk like that?"

"Think about it. Just for a minute before you go out again, *think* about it. I've lived in this neighborhood all my life. You've lived here the better part of twenty years. We still can't find him. How the hell else will anybody else find him?"

Glenna was physically exhausted, but not yet emotionally drained. Her anger sustained her.

"What if they do?"

"They won't," Doc said. "Jerry is safer hiding right now than he would be with you. Some very bad people want him. Your trusty six-shooter might not be enough to hold off a homicidal maniac and a bunch of Colombians."

"I won't just sit here doin' nothin'."

"I don't want you to. We have to get more help from the people around here."

"How can anyone help more than they have?"

"They have to help us nail the creeps who're after him. They have to get more personally involved. When it was just your kid in danger, they'd help only to the extent that being neighborly didn't inconvenience them."

Glenna shook her head.

"You're wrong. Everyone's been real concerned."

"Yeah. They all said how awful it is. They all fed me some dirt about the people next door. They even pretended to be a posse riding to the rescue when they got a chance. But they've all got their own lives, and only so much time for anyone else."

"People have to work, to mind their children and tend their homes. What else can they do?"

"They can drop everything and help us, goddammit!"

Doc's emotions were raw. Along with a fatigue that was grinding his bones to dust, he felt an aching need to strike out at *someone*.

He said, "They *will* help us, too. Because we're going to give them monsters on the loose. The killer crazy meets the Colombian drug fiends. Coming to a street corner near you. We're going to tell them that one of them *is* a homicidal maniac, and that a plague of South American killers has invaded. We're going to spread the word until their neighborhood is ready to devour any outsider who comes in or any insider who speaks above a whisper."

"That's what you want me to do?"

"Yes. People will listen to you. I wouldn't win any popularity contests these days. You have to spread the word and scare the hell out of them."

Glenna gave him a long, hard stare.

"Tomorrow."

"What?"

"If I can't find Jerry today, I'll do it tomorrow."

Then she went out and left him standing there.

50

The moment she stepped onto the street, Glenna stuck her hand in her purse and wrapped it around the .44. She knew it would take all the concentration she could muster to find Jerry, but she was ready to drop and now her thoughts were awhirl.

She wondered if she could frighten her neighbors the way Michael had said. They were good people, and they'd saved her skin enough times that even thinking about it was painful.

Glenna remembered how Nat had let her go six months without paying rent when she'd first brought Jerry home, let her live free until she found a job. Ray's wife, Dottie, had brought free meals to her, and Mrs. Turello babysat Jerry for years like she was his own granny. Those two kind ladies had gone to their reward, but Ray and Nat were alive. So were many others who had been good to her.

But she couldn't deny that Michael had always been a true friend, too. He'd always given her any help he could.

Glenna had never told him, but there was a time before he met Harriet when she'd hoped he would marry her and be Jerry's new daddy. Even after he got married, Glenna was pleased that she could feel a special bond between them, and between Michael and her son.

She understood that what he wanted her to do had to be even more painful for him. After all, this place was his home. He had to feel he was betraying kin. Still, it didn't seem to matter to him.

Glenna stepped into an alley and looked around. "Jerry? Baby, can you hear me?"

There was no answer, no one in sight.

Without the company of a friendly face, the city suddenly seemed cold and randomly cruel. Glenna hadn't gone back to West Virginia when Jerry was born, because she knew there would be only welfare checks for her and ridicule for her son. She'd thought it would be better here.

Now, standing alone with a gun in her hand, she had to reconsider. Because if she didn't find Jerry today, she couldn't see any other choice than taking Michael's advice. As painful as it would be, she *would* scare everyone as much as she could. Then she'd have to leave.

Her shame would never let her stay.

51

"What are you thinking, Doc?"

He and Harry sat in the kitchen, having cups of cocoa. The Beretta was on the table in front of him.

"Nothing."

Harry gave his hand a gentle squeeze.

"You don't have to tell me, but I can feel it. It's not Jerry, and it's not that drug bastard. It's something else. I only want to know if it's me."

He looked at her. Her hair was brushed straight down after spending the day in bed with him. She held her cup in front of her mouth with both hands. He could see what she'd looked like as a little girl.

Harry had come over with plans to go to a resort hotel an hour outside of town. She'd reserved a secluded bungalow with a fireplace and view of Lake Michigan. She'd said it would be wonderful.

Doc wanted to stay home. She asked what had happened to the danger, and whether she should leave. He told her to stay, and if anyone tried to break in on them he felt like shooting someone, anyway.

Harry looked at him for a moment and said if that was the case she'd feel better where she could hide under the covers. They'd spent the day in bed making love and napping. Only hunger had made them get up, and then they hadn't wanted more than cocoa.

"It's not you, it's us."

"What about us?"

"That's the question I've been asking."

"Oh."

She sipped her cocoa.

"I love you, Harry. . . ."

"I love you, too."

"But I'm not sure I'm good for you."

"Fuck you, I'll decide that."

He smiled.

"You're starting to sound like Vince."

"Goody gumdrops."

"Maybe not."

"Come on, Doc. Tell me what you're thinking."

"I think the shit's about to fly."

She sat and waited, knowing there was more to come.

"You said that my job was the problem, but I'm not a cop anymore and I still seem to attract plenty of trouble. I'm not sure how I feel about that, but I know the odds are it doesn't make you happy."

Harry went to the stove, picked up the kettle, and refilled their cups.

"It doesn't," she said, sitting back down.

"I don't want to get back together just to break up again."

"Neither do I."

"I'm thinking about making some changes."

"Like what?"

"Like selling the house."

Harry almost dropped her cup. She slopped cocoa onto the table.

"Yeah," Doc said, "how about that?"

"Where would you go?"

"I don't know yet. What I do know is we're both going to have to learn from our mistakes if we want to take a second shot at it."

Harry nodded.

"What's my part of this bargain?"

"You don't leave."

"Is that all?"

"If I get shot again, you visit me in the hospital."

52

Armando Guzman killed Attorney Jeffrey Weinblatt with a two-handed karate chop just as soon as they were alone in the conference room at the Federal Courthouse. A British mercenary had taught him the technique, but it was the unfortunate attorney who had insisted, per his instructions, that his client be allowed the dignity of being handcuffed in the front.

The man died with only the smallest of grunts, and Armando caught him by his collar before he could fall to the floor and make any noise. The guards outside didn't hear a thing.

Hiring Weinblatt had been an essential feature of Hector's plan. Just as it had been conceived, Armando's new lawyer had brought him into court this Monday morning for his previously scheduled appeal hearing. Weinblatt argued that Mr. Guzman's former counsel, Hector, had to be incompetent to allow Mr. Guzman to be so obviously railroaded at his first trial. This meant that the accused had not received an adequate defense and, therefore, hadn't had a fair trial.

While the hearing was in progress, Armando whispered to his new lawyer. He said they needed to talk. Maybe, Armando suggested, there were a few things he could tell the feds that would allow them to give him *some* consideration.

Weinblatt approached the bench and asked for time to have a brief conference with his client. He hinted that Armando might have something to trade. The prosecution said no deals were going to be made. Weinblatt offered that there were always bigger fish to catch than Mr. Guzman.

Everyone knew by now that Armando was a token offering. The prosecution thought of the potential for greater glory, and a conference was allowed.

All of it went the way Hector had predicted. It almost worried Armando that his cousin was so smart.

Now Jeffrey Weinblatt lay dead on the conference room floor, his quarter-million-dollar fee doing him no good at all, and Armando was crawling through a vent in the ceiling.

The vent was supposed to be sealed, but its screen swung down easily on oiled hinges. Only a small magnet had held it in place. The same preparations had been made in each of the four conference rooms to which Armando might have been taken.

This was Hector's doing, too. He hadn't even needed to bribe anyone in authority. He'd simply paid off a worker whose company maintained the heating and air-conditioning in the building. The man had been paid a handsome sum to do the work and killed as soon as it was completed.

Armando found a penlight and a diagram inside the vent. He pulled the screen up after him. The space was small and oppressive, and the directions indicated a long trip. With the light clenched between his teeth he crawled off as fast as he could, grateful that he'd never allowed himself to become a *puerco* like so many of his colleagues.

Hector had told Armando that his diminished value as a prisoner would work in his favor. The guards would be less attentive, and more patient before opening the conference room door. Still, they wouldn't wait forever. By the time Armando pushed open another hinged screen and lowered himself into an empty utility room, he was nervous and sweating.

He saw the workman's coverall that was noted in his escape instructions. He reached into a pocket and found the key to open the handcuffs. Once his hands were free, he put the coverall on over the suit he'd worn to court. He pulled on the Cubs baseball cap that had been left for him.

Also in a pocket of the coverall he found a photo ID badge with a phony name, and a picture that looked vaguely like him. He clipped it on.

Forcing himself to relax, Armando stepped out into the corridor. There were people walking by, including cops, but nobody gave him a second glance. His instructions led him to a rear service entrance that was supposed to be lightly guarded.

Actually, the guard sitting at the desk between Armando and freedom was mountainously fat. But he was busy reading his newspaper. Armando felt greatly reassured. There was no way the guard would be so relaxed if the dead lawyer had been found and the alarm had sounded.

El Gordo looked up at Armando and squinted at his ID.

"Checking out early, Diego?"

Armando smiled under the lowered bill of his cap and shrugged with his palms out. His whole posture said, *If I didn't get to it today, man, it'll be there mañana.* He sauntered past.

The guard chuckled and went back to his paper.

Armando was out the door, breathing free and forcing himself to maintain a casual pace. He saw the car waiting for him at the end of the alley.

Hearing the guard say the phony name on the ID badge stirred a memory in Armando's head. A moment later it clicked into place. He knew the name Hector had chosen for him. It came from an old *Yanqui* TV show.

Diego DeLaVega. *Don* Diego DeLaVega.

Zorro.

Armando thought sometimes that fucking Hector got too cute.

53

Glenna Handee walked into Ray's while the breakfast crowd was still there. She hadn't found Jerry yesterday, having given up only when she couldn't go another step. That meant that this morning, Ray's was the place to start.

Spread the word, Michael had said. Scare the hell out of them. She hated to do it, and wouldn't blame anyone if they hated her for it. But she had no choice. She was determined to get her boy back.

Ray saw her first when she stepped inside.

"Glenna, where have you been? I tried to find you all day yesterday. I saw Jerry!"

Then everyone crowded around Glenna. They all repeated the news, sharing what were meant to be glad tidings. She let them talk themselves out.

"I thank you for all you've done, but Michael already told me."

She saw the joy go right out of them.

"Yeah, well, he was the only one who didn't bother to help," Red Penwell said.

"Sat on his ass," Nat added.

"Please don't be mad at Michael. He's done all he could, and he has terrible troubles of his own."

Red wouldn't be appeased.

"Nobody leads the life of Riley around here."

"I know, I know," Glenna said. "But Michael's found out a few things he thought everybody should hear by way of warnin', and he's asked me to tell you."

"What kind of 'warning'?" Ray asked.

Glenna remembered her instructions: Scare the hell out of them. She also decided to watch closely and see if anyone took it a little too personally when she said there was a killer among them.

"Well," she began, "it's real bad news. . . ."

54

The *caleta* was a huge, empty, L-shaped tenement building that ran the length of a short dead-end block. The stem of the building abutted the elevated structure of the Kennedy Expressway, and the ascender ran parallel to it. Nobody had any business coming onto the block unless it was to visit the building.

Since the stash house was now Armando Guzman's hideout, nobody had any business visiting the building if they wanted to stay alive.

From a top-floor window Armando watched the endless stream of *Yanquis* roaring past on the highway. *So many of them,* he thought. With a smile he amended himself: *So many of them my customers.*

Armando turned when he heard the door behind him open.

"*Hola,* cousin. All is well?"

He nodded to Hector.

"I killed the lawyer. I felt safer that way."

Hector shrugged. He didn't care. His name hadn't been used as the referral.

"I saw your two guards below. They are satisfactory?"

"Yes."

Armando sensed an unusual bravado in his cousin. It made him suspicious.

"What about the cop?"

"What's that you say, 'Thank you for freeing me from captivity'? Why, think nothing of it, cousin."

"What about the cop?" Armando repeated, his tone hardening.

Hector shook his head, as if to despair of ever teaching Armando any manners. Then he shrugged and smiled.

"Good news there, too. Our hostage-to-be."

He handed Armando the photo of Jerry Handee.

"This is his son? I thought you said he had no family."

"He doesn't. But he cares about this boy *like* a son."

"How do you know?"

Hector explained what he'd discovered, making himself sound dashing in his encounter with Kildare. Armando didn't believe a word of his cousin's boasting. How could anyone who wore such a ridiculous coat and hat expect to be taken seriously? But the picture of the boy, and the story that went with it, seemed real.

"If this simpleton is missing, how do we find him?"

Hector shrugged.

"How hard can it be? As you say, he's simple. Let me have one of your men and we will find him."

Then Hector added with great mocking concern, "If you'll feel safe with only one guard."

Armando's face turned to stone.

"Take them both. They gave me my own weapon."

He picked up an Ingraham machine pistol that lay on a table in the corner.

"Me, too," Hector said.

He opened his coat with one hand. The other hand extended through a vent in the lining and held an identical weapon. It was almost but not quite pointing at Armando.

Hector had decided to take Melissa's advice about killing Armando, and he was already in love with the way it made him feel.

What he'd completely forgotten was the part about kissing ass first.

55

The video cameras began to roll, and the Superintendent started to talk.

"I've asked you here to speak with you briefly about a matter of public concern."

Malloy's speech was duplicated word-for-word in a press handout that had been distributed to the assembled media. Each of them was identical except for the one that went to Conrad Walters, and since each one had the reporter's name on it, there was no worry about Walters getting the wrong handout.

His had a note about a certain taxicab that an anonymous and untraceable leaker had provided. Malloy's money was on Walters breaking the story as soon as possible.

"Firstly, I want to say that I wasn't very happy when a certain attorney revealed that we have a situation with young men and boys disappearing in this city. This was an attempt to smear the department and gain sympathy for another matter that I won't go into now."

"Smart," a voice in the back said.

The Superintendent ignored the wise-ass. He knew who'd have the last laugh.

"I wasn't happy, because this department has an ongoing investigation into this matter."

He'd defy them to prove it hadn't.

"Bringing the subject under public scrutiny only makes our job that much harder. Secondly, I'd like to say that this department serves and protects every citizen of this city equally. The rich and powerful are afforded no special treatment. As long as I'm responsible around here, that's the way it'll stay."

He took a sip of water. He knew the news assholes didn't buy that one, but he was pretty sure the public would.

"Lastly, since the matter of our investigation into the disappearance of Frederick Welles has become a matter of public knowledge, I feel it's important that the people of Chicago know we have a significant lead in the case."

He had been going to tell them that he couldn't reveal the nature of the lead without jeopardizing the investigation. He never got the chance.

Some sonofabitch ran into the room right in the middle of his press conference and shouted . . .

"Armando Guzman's just killed his lawyer and escaped from the Federal Court Building!"

56

Doc spotted the car with the people living in it as he walked past the alley that ran alongside the "L" tracks. He knew that they were living in the twenty-year-old station wagon, because he saw their sleeping bags spread out in back and they were cooking with an electric skillet that someone had gimmicked to plug into the cigarette lighter.

A regular Reagan-era RV.

The city's homeless numbered in the thousands, but these were the first Doc had ever seen in The Wedge. He wondered if this was how Glenna and Jerry would wind up. That would be rich. Finally find the kid and return him to his jobless mother, and have them both end up on the street.

Doc went over to the car and knocked on the driver's window. The man behind the wheel didn't look too happy to see him. He rolled the window down only a crack.

Doc said, "Hi, I was wondering if you could help me."

The man shook his head vigorously.

"We ain't got any money, and my wife and me ain't eating so the kids can."

Doc looked at the woman. She was making grilled cheese sandwiches. He could see a loaf of white bread between her feet and a package of

American cheese on her lap. Two pre-school faces peered at the food from the backseat, ignoring Doc completely.

"I'm not looking for food or money."

"Then you're two jumps ahead of us, mister."

Doc pulled a twenty-dollar bill from his wallet and slipped it through the crack.

"What's this for?"

"Your next meal."

The man tucked the money into his shirt pocket.

"Thank you, sir," his wife said.

"I'm looking for a boy. He's seventeen years old. Dark hair, dark eyes. About five-eight, one seventy-five. His clothes are probably covered with grease. Have you seen anyone like that?"

The man had enough pride left to want to work for the money he'd received. He gave the question an honest effort, but after a minute's thought shook his head.

"We've seen lots of boys, and a lot of them ain't been bathin' regular. But I don't think we seen anyone who fits your description."

He checked the accuracy of his recollection with his wife. She shook her head, too.

"I'm sorry, sir."

The man said, "Listen, if we spot him, where can we find you? I like to pay my debts."

"How about if I stop back here tonight?" Doc asked.

The man laughed bitterly.

"We won't be here. See that crew working on the tracks, outta that truck up the alley? They told us we were on city property here, and if we weren't gone in an hour they'd call the cops."

Doc handed the man another twenty and told

him how to get to Ray's if he saw anybody match-
ing Jerry's description.

The track maintenance crew was a bunch of
wise guys.

"Young boy, huh? Hey, if you're lookin' for a
date, Mort here has a cousin you might like to
meet."

"Yeah, he wears sunglasses almost as nice as
yours."

"Hey, maybe this guy's not a fag. Maybe he's
like a Fearless Fosdick private eye."

The only guy who didn't rag Doc was an older
black man up in a cherry-picker, doing something
with a big wrench to the underside of the tracks.
He was the only one doing any work. He was the
only one who didn't have to zip his lip when Doc
pushed back his jacket to reveal the Beretta.

"There's a badge that goes with this," Doc lied
convincingly, "and if I don't get some cooperation
from you assholes, I'm going to arrest you for
loitering and impersonating city employees."

The older man turned from his work and re-
garded the scene below.

One of The Three Stooges piped up. "Hey,
man, we didn't know you was a cop."

"Yeah, don't get bent outta shape," said another.

"Shut the fuck up until I talk to you," Doc said.
"You can't *imagine* what happens when I get bent
out of shape."

The older man called down to Doc.

"Pardon me, officer. You have to understand
about those three, they wasn't raised right."

The wise guys didn't say anything, but they
gave their coworker dirty looks. He didn't seem
to mind. The huge wrench rested easily in his big
hands.

"Have you seen the boy I described?" Doc called up to him.

"No, sir, I haven't."

"How far has your work taken you today?"

"We started just south of Kelvin Avenue. We're supposed to go to Perry Street." The man looked down at the others and shook his head. "It won't surprise me if we don't get the whole stretch done on time."

"You'll be working this line again tomorrow?"

"Tomorrow and for some time to come. Gotta make sure these old tracks don't come down like the Walls of Jericho."

"Thanks for your time. I might be back."

"Always happy to help a fellow city *worker*."

The man gave him a big smile and Doc left with the impression that he'd made his day.

57

Andy set out to hunt Jerry in his van. He thought about taking the taxi, but decided it wouldn't look right to have a cab idling through alleys. Besides that, he'd have to drive slowly down a lot of side streets and he didn't want the hassle of being hailed for a ride. So, even though he felt more powerful in his taxi, he took the van out of Mama's garage and left the taxi locked inside.

He'd stayed at Mama's since he buried her. He'd felt the need to be close. Now he drove the van out of the alley behind the garage and turned onto the street.

Andy looked around and asked himself where, oh where had that little bastard Jerry gone? He hadn't been able to find him in a week of trying. It made him think that maybe the kid just played at being retarded. The whole thing could be a joke. His way of laughing at people. If that was the case, Andy would really teach him a lesson.

He was sure, though, that Jerry hadn't gone home yet, or to the cops. Andy knew that if the boy had been either place the cops would have set a trap for him at Mama's, and they hadn't.

Still, there was no getting around the fact that the longer he let Jerry live, the bigger the chance he was taking. He had to get him soon. Today, if he could.

Andy stopped for a red light. There were no cars behind him, no oncoming traffic. No pedestrians crossing the street. No one to see him.

So he whispered aloud, "Mama?"

He waited for an answer and, receiving none, tried again louder. "Mama."

Nothing. Getting agitated, he yelled, "Mama!"

Volume didn't help, and now he was sitting at a green light. He stepped on the gas and the light turned yellow. It was red before he'd cleared the intersection. For a second he thought he'd better floor it. The last thing he needed was a cop giving him a ticket. But when he checked his mirrors he saw no one behind him. He calmed down and kept his speed legal.

Uncaring now of who might see him, he said, "Mama, please talk to me."

But she didn't. And she hadn't since he'd buried her. Andy had never thought that death could separate them. He wanted to tell her he was sorry for getting mad at her, for not making sure she got her medicine. But he wanted *her* to apologize, too. She'd insulted *him*. She'd said he was starting to look like his father.

Suddenly a new thought occurred to him, and it was horrifying: If Mama had stopped talking to him in his head—did that mean the monster was going to start?

"This is all your stupid fault, Jerry!" Andy yelled. He struck his fists against his head in frustration.

This time someone was looking at him. A guy in a pickup truck. Sitting next to him at another red light. Andy didn't remember seeing the light, much less stopping for it. He screamed at the guy in the truck, "What the hell you looking at?"

Nothing, that's what. The guy made an abrupt

turn and got the hell out of there. "Ha-ha, look at that chickenshit go. I bet he—"

Andy stopped short. He realized he was muttering to himself under his breath. Just like the monster used to do. And Mama'd said that now he *looked* like the monster, too. And Mama wouldn't talk to him anymore. How would he know who to kill if Mama didn't tell him?

Well, one thing was for sure.

He *was* going to kill that little retard Jerry.

58

Tony Szell smiled at Doc as he walked into the drugstore.

"Good morning, Doc."

Doc didn't smile back. He looked more grim than usual, Tony thought. Then he remembered that Jerry was still missing.

"Any news of Jerry yet?" Tony asked soberly.

Doc said, "I'm glad you asked. Let's go back to your office and talk."

A sudden chill raced down Tony's spine, and Doc saw it.

Artie Fuentes looked over from behind the glass partition where he was filling a prescription.

"Hey, Doc," he called, "anything happenin' with Jerry?"

"Tony and I are just going to talk about him. Why don't you keep an eye on the store a few minutes?"

As Doc put his arm around Tony and led him back to his office, he seemed to shrink inside his white smock.

"Have a seat," Doc said, closing the door behind them.

Tony started to sit in a visitor's chair.

"Take your own seat, Tony."

He bobbed his head in apology and went

around his desk to sit in his chair. Doc took a seat across from him.

He'd come here because he'd never gotten around to talking with the pharmacist about his little liaisons with Kandi Gilliam, and to see if Tony might be hiding something else. Just looking at the man, Doc knew he had a big secret. He could have seen that with *two* marbles in his head.

Funny, that was the first time he'd thought about the damn thing in quite a while.

"Something I can do for you, Doc?" Tony asked meekly.

It was obvious Tony was trying to decide how to play things. Doc didn't want him playing at all. He wanted him broken down and talking right away.

"I know about Kandi Gilliam. I saw you go into her apartment, and she told me about your weekly visits."

Tony turned so white, held so still, that Doc thought he was having some kind of seizure.

The pharmacist choked out a single word. "Gerta?"

"No, she doesn't know."

"Please, Doc. Please don't . . ."

"I don't want to, Tony." He paused. "I won't have to, if you remember something maybe you forgot to tell me last time."

"I . . . I could get in trouble if I tell."

Tony's voice sounded the way it must have sixty years ago. He was a child unsure of owning up to the mess he'd made.

"You're in trouble now, Tony. It's just a question of how much. And what we can keep quiet and what we can't."

Hope grew in the frightened eyes. "Could we keep it quiet?"

"Start talking."

"You want to know about Jerry, of course."

For one dizzying moment, Doc thought Tony was going to confess to being the killer.

"I should never have given him that prescription to deliver."

Doc said, "Uh-huh."

"I mean, I knew she had to have it. It was heart medicine, for God's sake. The prescription got called in every month like clockwork."

"Yeah?"

"The problem was, the prescription had expired. The doctor was supposed to renew it every six months. But for an old customer with a chronic heart condition, you ask yourself where's the harm."

Tony shook his head. He was dismayed at how a simple act of generosity had turned on him.

"The prescription hasn't been renewed for four years, but I had it ready every month when I got the call, anyway."

That's when Doc remembered. *Heart medicine.* He and Mularkey and Williams had looked all over Otille Coultier's house for heart medicine.

"This month I didn't get the call. I waited one day, then two and three. I got worried. You don't skip nitroglycerin and not suffer for it. I wondered if she'd had the prescription renewed and started using one of those damn discount chains."

Doc asked to be sure. "Otille Coultier?"

Tony bobbed his head affirmatively. Then he got angry.

"When people do that, take their business elsewhere after I treat them so well for so many years, the least I expect is they should tell me! How else can I keep my records neat?"

"That's only fair," Doc sympathized.

"Doc, I wasn't supposed to send that prescription out. Legally, I was safer to mind my own business and let a customer die. As it turned out, I heard she died anyway. And who knows what happened to Jerry?"

Doc realized that Tony hadn't heard the news.

"He was still alive as of Saturday night. Ray saw him behind his place."

"That's wonderful!"

Doc explained why it wasn't so wonderful and, as he'd instructed Glenna to do, scared the hell out of Tony.

"My god, my god! How could such things happen around here? I think it's time I sold out to Artie."

Tony realized how that sounded.

"A younger man, a stronger man could cope better."

Doc gave him a moment's silence, but Tony seemed to have unburdened his soul. The pressure to confess was gone, the need to plead remained.

"Doc, I hope and pray Jerry comes home safely . . . and I beg you not to tell anyone what I've done."

He knew Tony meant on both counts.

"It wouldn't serve any purpose. Can I use your phone?"

Tony jumped out of his chair.

"Please. Sit here." He was only too happy to help. "I'll leave you alone. You can have your privacy."

"Thanks, Tony."

Doc took the pharmacist's chair. He watched

the old man practically bow his way out of his own office. *Wonderful world, when you had to terrorize your neighbors to get what you wanted.*

Tony had just closed the door behind him when he realized he'd forgotten to mention that Otille Coultier's son was the one who'd always called in the prescription for his mother.

He put his hand on the doorknob to go back in. Then he stopped. It had been awful for him in there, but apparently Doc was willing to keep his mouth shut. He couldn't see any reason to risk that by mentioning an insignificant detail.

Tony took his hand off the doorknob and tried to control his shaking as he went back to work.

Hearing that Otille Coultier hadn't called for the medicine she needed to stay alive, Doc decided to find out if there was anything else he should know about her death.

He called the science library at Northwestern University. The reference librarian listened to his questions, put him on hold, and came back to say she'd found someone in the stacks who might be of help to him. She put a man on the phone. He said he was a botanist, but bugs were his avocation.

He told Doc that the length of time it took fly eggs to mature into larvae, or maggots, varied according to the air temperature. Doc said, if he remembered correctly, the weather for the period in question ranged from the mid-fifties to the low sixties. Then under those conditions, the man told him, he was looking at three to four days for maggots to develop.

Doc asked if there was any way it was possible for them to develop in eighteen hours. The man said that even in really hot weather it took closer to twenty-four. Doc thanked him for his trouble.

The information told Doc that the old woman with the maggots in her mouth had been dead by the time Jerry arrived with the prescription that Tony shouldn't have sent. Where the hell that left him, he didn't know.

Jerry could have seen the dead body in the window, but that certainly hadn't been what scared him so badly. Had it? Jesus, he thought, maybe for someone with an eight-year-old's mind, it had. Which would mean all of his other assumptions were wrong.

Then he remembered Frederick Welles. *He* hadn't run away from a dead old lady. That kid had been involved with the bogus taxi. And what could a taxi have to do with Otille Coultier's death?

Doc thought it might be helpful to get a look at the biddy's post mortem results. He knew that as a civilian, and one on the Superintendent's shit list, he wasn't likely to get any cooperation from a pathologist on the Coroner's staff. But there might be one thing he could try. He called the morgue.

The voice that answered his call said, "I can't talk now. I got to go to the bathroom."

"What?"

"Listen, man. I had some bad gumbo last night and it wants out. Like *now.* Gimme your number quick and I'll call you back."

Doc was going to Ray's next. He gave the man that number.

Then he made two more calls. The first was to the locksmith who'd opened Otille Coultier's house last week. The second was to Harry at work.

"Spur of the Moment Travel," a voice trilled.

Had to be the infamous Shirley, Doc thought.

"Harry Wilkerson, please."

"I'm sorry, she's away fr—" There was a pause. "Hey, is this . . . I mean, may I ask who's calling?"

"No."

"You're him, her ex, aren't you? I saw your picture in the paper the other day. Has *Harriet* ever described me to you?"

In great and scathing detail.

"I'm a younger woman, you know. Hey!"

Harry was apparently no longer away, because Doc heard her hiss a string of threats at Shirley. Then she said hello.

"I think you could get arrested for doing all that. Or any of it."

"Doc?"

"Yeah. Harry, I need to ask you something."

"What?"

"Do you believe in curses?"

She snorted, and Doc tried again.

"Not that kind. The kind that kills people."

She snorted louder.

"The kind that got my snitch Bobby Ro set on fire with an apple in his mouth."

"Jesus, Doc!"

"I'm sorry, but it was a serious question. It's one of the things I've been thinking about."

He listened to the line hum for a minute.

"I . . . I almost believe what happened to your family . . ."

She didn't have to finish, and he didn't respond.

"Otherwise, I'd believe in a curse only if there was money behind it."

"There could be tons of money."

"Doc, quit scaring me and tell me what's going on."

He told her that besides having guys looking for him and Bobby Ro getting popped, Fidelito Guzman had also bought the farm. He couldn't be sure how he and the other two were connected, except that they were all tied, in one way or another, to Armando Guzman's money. If Doc wound up getting some of that money, he was considering the merits of a long vacation.

He asked, "Could you fix it so we could go far away without anybody knowing where we went?"

"We?"

"As long as you keep your end of the bargain."

She'd told him the other night she'd have to give it some thought.

"Would the curse affect me, too?"

"Might affect everyone in the car, plane, or room, depending on where I am."

"Doc, how bad do these people want to kill you?"

"I don't know. That's why I'm thinking of traveling."

Harry's tone became businesslike.

"Are you thinking domestic or international?"

"International. Far, far away."

"Is your passport still valid?"

It took a moment to remember. "Yes, it is."

"I can do it. Where'd you have in mind?"

"Someplace warm where they speak English. Don't mention any names if your bosom buddy is still around."

"She isn't. I'll work out the possibilities for you."

"For me?"

There was only the slightest hesitation.

"For us. I accept my part of the bargain. And

I'll fix it so the richest goddamn curse in the world won't find us."

Before leaving the drugstore, Doc made one more call. He talked to Ray, and asked him to round up the oldest of The Wedge's old-timers and have them get their ancient backsides over there as fast as they could.

59

"Is it true some bug's goin' around puttin' the snatch on youngsters these days?" Ben Haskins asked Doc.

Ben was eighty-two. His back was bent but he could still see without glasses, and he'd raise his fist to anyone foolish enough to try to help him across the street.

He was also the youngest of the four people sitting at Ray's back table. Monie Watkins was eighty-three. Ella Tolbert was eighty-five. Sy Wasserman still got around at ninety.

"And what about these gangsters we hear are after you?" Sy asked.

Doc looked at these four wonderful survivors, and for a moment his heart ached to see his mother and father.

He said, "Yes, somebody is grabbing boys and young men, and the only reason that makes sense for Jerry Handee to be hiding out is he knows who's doing it."

"You didn't answer Sy's question, dear," Ella said.

"You know about my claim?"

They did.

"Well, apparently Armando Guzman has decided he doesn't want me to have any of his money, even if he's going to be in prison for the rest of his life."

Suddenly, Ray and the four old people looked disturbed. Doc couldn't understand why.

"Haven't you heard?" Ray asked.

"What?"

"Armando Guzman's escaped. They've been having bulletins on the radio and TV all morning. He killed his lawyer and got away from the courthouse."

Doc was stunned. "He got away?"

"Sure did, the little greaser bastard," Ben answered.

"And he killed his cousin Hector?"

Sy shook his head. "No, his lawyer was a boy named Weinblatt. I think I knew his grandfather."

As ye sow . . . Doc thought. He'd advocated scaring people, and now he was unable to deny the flash of apprehension he felt. If Armando was out, it would make sense for him to run. But he knew he couldn't count on that. He decided that if he saw *anybody* whose looks he didn't like, he was going to empty the Beretta and face the consequences later.

Monie brought him back to the moment with her delicate voice.

"What did you want to talk with us about, dear?"

Doc looked at her. "I wanted to ask if you know of any cab drivers who live in the neighborhood."

It had occurred to Doc that maybe it wasn't a phony cab that was involved with the Welles boy but a real one. A driver could falsify his trip log; he could contrive passengers no one would ever be able to contact; he could pay the meter out of his own pocket. So, if there was anyone in The Wedge who drove a cab, he might just be worth a visit. And who would know better who lived in the neighborhood, than people who'd spent the better part of the century in it?

"Specifically, do you know anyone who drives a Red Ball Taxi?"

"I don't think I ever knew a taxi driver," Ella said.

Sy said, "I knew plenty. I even knew some taxi *dancers*. But all of 'em are dead now."

Monie's social circle didn't include cab drivers.

Ben Haskins, though, was rubbing his chin.

"Ben?"

"I don't know any drivers, but it's funny you should mention that particular company."

"Why?"

"Well, last week, I think it musta been the same night the Handee boy disappeared, I had to get up and pee. I have to go so often these days I think my bladder musta shrunk up smaller than a thimble."

Sy nodded knowingly.

"Anyway, I like fresh air at night. So, I had the top half of my bathroom window down a ways, and I'm looking outside while I take care of business. I see this Red Ball Taxi pull into a garage across the alley. Drove right in like it belonged there."

"Whose garage was it?"

"Otille Coultier's. Which is pretty funny, since that dame hadn't been outta her house in ages."

Doc got excited; he felt very close to something. He paid no attention when the phone rang and Ray went to answer it.

"Who was driving the cab?"

"My eyes are good," Ben said, "but they can't see in the dark, and that yard over there is always dark. The only one I could guess is Otille's son.

His name's André Lisse, but he calls himself Andy."

"I didn't know she had a son." Doc had always thought the old woman had lived alone.

"How old are you?" Ben asked.

Doc told him.

"He must be ten to fifteen years older than you. Moved out quite a while back. Likely you never met him, but maybe he's your cab driver."

Ray poked his head out of the phone booth. "Excuse me, Doc. I think I got a call for you here. From the morgue."

None of the oldsters liked the sound of that.

Tony Szell was just about to go to lunch—no Kandi today, thank God—and his nerves were finally getting settled, when Artie told him he had a phone call. He started shaking all over again. It got worse when he heard Doc's voice on the line.

Doc asked, "Who called in Otille Coultier's prescription, her or her son?"

Tony almost fainted. Why hadn't he told Doc?

"H-he d-did," Tony stammered.

"Every time?"

"Y-yes."

"Thanks," Doc said.

Doc wondered if he should tell Tony to relax. He decided not yet.

60

Hector Guzman drove through The Wedge in his Mercedes, looking around and asking himself where he would hide if he were an imbecile. The thought struck him as ridiculous, so he framed it another way.

Where would he hide if he were *Armando*?

Still ridiculous. In the block ahead he saw Fausto, one of the two killer-bodyguards he'd hired, plodding along the sidewalk. He had dropped Fausto and Eraldo off an hour earlier to conduct the search on foot. Hector was about to speed up and ask him if he'd seen anything, when he noticed something very strange.

There was a skinny woman, a scarecrow to his connoisseur's eye, following Fausto.

She didn't just happen to be behind him going the same way. She was following him with a purpose. Hector had seen such things in too many movies to be deceived. Fausto apparently had no idea of her presence. Undoubtedly, Hector thought, he would be amazed that anyone would follow a killer who handed out machine pistols like they were lollipops.

Nevertheless, that was what she was doing. No. It was even more incredible than that. She was *stalking* him.

Hector pulled the Mercedes over to the curb

and got out behind the woman. The opportunity was too good for him to pass up. He intended to capture the bag of bones who hunted the killer. He would tell Armando he'd brought him some female company. Hector tried not to laugh.

He looked around to make sure no one was watching, and saw that the street was empty. Then he realized that he hadn't seen anyone on a sidewalk for the past half-hour. He wondered what was going on in this place. It was strange. Right now, though, he was grateful for the lack of witnesses.

Hector stole up behind the scarecrow as quickly and quietly as he could. Unfortunately, his hunting skills were less developed than his sense of drama. He'd closed to within only ten feet of her when she turned on him. He was chagrined to see Fausto, that oblivious fool, disappearing around the corner ahead.

Hector did what he did best in any awkward situation. He smiled.

The scarecrow didn't smile back. In fact, the merciless look in her eyes made Hector regret having left the safety of his Mercedes.

Glenna stared at the man in front of her. He was practically close enough to reach out and touch. She was sure this had to be one of Michael's Colombians. Nobody around The Wedge dressed in a coat and hat like that.

All morning she'd been going around telling stories about the bad men coming into the neighborhood. She'd been scaring people, and the more she scared them the more she scared herself. Now one of the bastards had turned the corner, and this one was right in front of her.

Well, Glenna decided, this fancy one would

never get a crack at her boy. She reached into her tattered purse.

Hector froze when he saw the monstrous gun the scarecrow was pulling out of her handbag. He forgot the machine pistol under his coat. He forgot how to run. He forgot how to yell for help. This skinny woman was going to kill him, and he could do nothing about it.

It was absurd!

He refused to believe he could die like this. The best years of his life were ahead of him. He was going to get into the movie business. He had beautiful women to love.

That was it, he thought. God liked his little jokes. All the beautiful women he'd had, and one who looked like this would kill him.

Then the scarecrow's giant *pistola* snagged on some loose threads hanging from the inside of her shabby purse. The thrall was broken and Hector could move again. He couldn't run, though, because she might free the gun and shoot him in the back. He took the only action he could.

He leaped forward and struck the woman on her face as hard as he could.

Hector almost wept with relief when she fell to the ground unconscious. He didn't even care how much his hand hurt. He stared at her a moment to make sure she wasn't trying to fool him. When he felt secure, he picked up her handbag and eased the gun out. He was awed by its size, and shuddered when he thought what it would have been like to be shot by such a brute.

He saw that the woman carried identification papers in the bag, too. When he read her name Hector laughed out loud. This had to be the *devil's* sense of humor.

The scarecrow was the imbecile's mother!

She even carried pictures of the boy. Here was the perfect hostage. He didn't need to waste his time looking for the imbecile now.

He picked the woman up—she was light as a bundle of sticks—and put her in the trunk of the Mercedes. He would collect Fausto and Eraldo and take his prize back to show his cousin.

Armando would not be impressed by the capture of a skinny woman. Until Hector showed him the gun he had taken from her, and explained who she was. Maybe he'd wave the gun, ever so casually, under Armando's nose.

61

Ben Haskins had driven Doc to the Fishbein Institute, but said he was too busy to wait around a morgue for him. Doc had found Marcus Worth, the would-be real-estate mogul, recovered from his gumbo poisoning and back on duty.

He said, "Yeah, we have to be talkin' about the same guy. He wanted to leave with his mama, like he could take her home in a grocery cart or somethin'."

"But he didn't, did he?"

Marcus got indignant.

"Do I look like a fool to you?"

"No."

"I got a family to support with this job until I get my real-estate license."

"Sorry."

Marcus accepted the apology with a nod.

"That's okay. Cause the funny thing was, once I got this fool straight that only a licensed funeral home or the county was gonna take a body off my hands, he got *two* funeral homes to come by for her. The second guy was some kinda pissed, too, when he didn't find a body to pick up."

Doc rolled that around in his head.

"You remember the names of the funeral homes?"

"Yeah. Cuddy and Donatello."

"You mind if I use your phone?" he asked.

*   *   *

Getting to the locksmith's shop took two buses and fifty-five minutes. The man was inclined to listen to Doc, because he labored under the misapprehension that Doc was a cop. What else would he be? The last time he'd seen him Doc had been standing with two uniforms waiting to go look at a stiff. Doc did nothing to disabuse him of the notion.

"So what was it you left behind?" the locksmith asked.

"My notebook. I had it out to write some things down and I must've left it there. I looked to hell and gone for it before I realized where it had to be."

Doc shrugged, as if to say, *Who doesn't screw up occasionally?*

"This notebook of yours is important?"

"It has all my case notes in it."

"I mean, it can't wait 'til I'm done eating?"

The man's sandwich, one bite gone, lay on a sheet of waxed paper on his work table.

"Listen," Doc said, "you don't have to come out at all. Just give me the keys you used and I'll bring them back when I'm done."

"You want me to give you my masters?"

"I'll bring them back."

"I don't know." The locksmith shook his head.

Doc looked around as if he were about to confide a secret.

"It's kind of embarrassing for me, you know, to forget my notebook like this. It's like not tucking back in after you take a leak; you're not supposed to forget these things. I could get a lot of grief from the guys if this gets out. So, really, it's better if I go alone, anyway."

The locksmith's expression was softening.

"You do this favor for me, maybe I can do something for you sometime."

A gleam entered the locksmith's eye.

"Can you fix a speeding ticket?"

Doc winked. "Who knows?"

The man handed him the keys he needed and told him which locks they fit.

"Hey," he said, "I just realized. I don't even know your name."

Doc looked at him and smiled.

"Vince DiGiuseppe." Doc gave him Vince's number. "Call me right before your court date comes up."

62

Jerry's delivery bike was still locked up to the light pole in front of Otille Coultier's house. Doc cursed Malloy's name. Screwing him was bad enough; not helping Jerry was unforgivable. Only six days had passed since he'd first seen the bike there, but it seemed a lot longer than that. He wondered how long the time had seemed to Jerry.

Doc reviewed all the things he'd learned in the last week.

Teenage boys and young men had been disappearing off the city's streets. Frederick Welles' disappearance had brought things to a boil, because his parents were wealthy and had clout. Somebody with a Red Ball Taxi had been the last person seen with the Welles kid. Ben Haskins had seen a Red Ball Taxi pull into Otille Coultier's garage.

Otille Coultier had been dead before Jerry disappeared. She had a son named Andy who always called in the prescription to Szell's Drugstore for her heart medicine. Except the last time he hadn't.

After Otille bit the dust, sonny boy went to fetch her from the morgue. Since Doc's calls to Cuddy and Donatello revealed that neither had buried her, Handy Andy had presumably frustrated the best intentions of Marcus Worth.

If someone was crazy enough to steal his mother's body, and presumably had access to the garage where a Red Ball Taxi had been seen being parked, and might have been visiting Mama when Jerry Handee came by, did that make him a killer?

As a jury of one, Doc voted guilty.

But with Armando Guzman running around loose, this guy Andy wasn't the only problem Doc had at the moment. Of course if Doc caught or, more realistically, popped Armando, he'd probably not only get the money he wanted but a medal and a parade, too.

On the other hand, breaking and entering a dead woman's house wasn't likely to win much public sympathy. And no judge in the country was going to fork over government millions to a guy doing time as a common burglar. Despite the conflict of interests, Doc couldn't help thinking there might be something in Otille's house that would land old André in deep shit and put a serious crazy away.

It was a lot to think about.

Doc walked briskly up the sidewalk that ran alongside Otille Coultier's house and pushed through a gate into the yard behind it. He crossed to the garage and looked through a window.

Sonofabitch. A Red Ball Taxi.

Doc looked at the house. He checked to see if anyone was peeking out a window at him. Was the crazy bastard at home? Doc didn't see anyone, but who knew?

There was nothing for him to do now but make it look like he had every right in the world to be there. He returned to the front of the house and opened the dead-bolt locks, one-two-three. He stepped inside, closed the door behind him, and pulled his gun.

Doc swung his head back and forth, the gun following his gaze. He didn't want any maniac with a meat cleaver coming out of his blind side.

He didn't see anyone, and the house was quiet. Not even a goddamn clock ticking or a fridge buzzing. All Doc could hear was his heart banging against his ribs. He was scared, and he was pissed off that he couldn't call for backup.

He pushed off from the safety of the door and started searching the house. He not only swung his head back and forth, he listened as hard as he could for anyone sneaking up from behind. When that wasn't enough to calm his fear, he did half-turns and pirouettes.

The first floor was as innocuous and fustily feminine as when he'd seen it before. He still checked every room and closet. He checked the pantry, the fridge, and the stove. He looked behind and under any piece of furniture big enough to conceal a man. Before going upstairs he jammed chairs under the knobs of the front, back, and basement doors.

A goddamn squeaking step on the stairway almost caused him to squeeze off half a clip. He stopped to listen. All he heard was two birds bickering as they flew past outside.

He made it to the second floor without his heart failing. There was nobody home up there, either. What he did find was a picture of Andy. It had to be thirty years old and the color was hand-tinted—looked like a high school graduation shot. The guy had brown hair, a straight little nose, and a small unsmiling mouth. A very ordinary face.

Except for the pale blue eyes. Even back then,

they looked like they wouldn't flinch at the sight of death.

Doc went back downstairs. There was only one place left to look. The basement.

63

Andy felt uneasy the moment he pushed through the door.

He hadn't been inside Ray's since the late Fifties. He recognized Ray right away, even though his face was heavier and his hair, what was left of it, had gone gray. No one else was in the place.

Ray looked up from the newspaper he'd been reading at the soda fountain with a start. He seemed nervous. It was obvious to Andy that Ray didn't recognize him.

"Can I get you something?" Ray asked.

"Burger and fries. You still carry RC Cola?"

"In the cooler there."

Ray got up and went around to the grill. Andy couldn't figure out why he was so nervous, or how he'd stayed in business so long if the place was always this dead.

"How'd you like your burger?"

"Well done. Real well done."

For a moment, Ray seemed to remember him. Maybe it had been the cooking instructions. Then the recollection escaped him, will-o'-the-wisp.

Ray got to work on the food while Andy grabbed the bottle of pop and took a seat at the counter. He looked around. The place hadn't changed much. Same old fixtures. Candy bars in the same place. Even the grease on the walls and the ceiling seemed to have a familiar texture. Andy found it all very comforting.

He'd been driving around for hours when he saw Ray's sign at the corner. He'd almost decided not to stop and come in, but he hadn't eaten since breakfast and the frustration of his failed hunt— and Mama's refusal to talk to him—had aggravated his hunger.

In the end, he'd decided it was safe to stop into Ray's. It wasn't as if he were wearing a sign. People wouldn't know who he was or what he was doing. They wouldn't know more than they ever did. Jack shit.

Sitting at the soda fountain, he couldn't understand how Jerry had eluded him for so long. Wherever that little bastard was hiding, he was really pissing Andy off. His anger was so intense it made him stop and think. Maybe a worsening temper was yet another sign he was becoming like the monster.

"But I'm really a good boy."

Andy almost repeated himself when he looked up and saw Ray staring at him from the grill where he was cooking Andy's burger.

"You say something?" Ray asked.

Muttering. He'd been muttering again, and Ray had heard him. *Stop it*, he told himself. *Stop it!*

"You okay?" Ray said.

"Yeah." Andy pulled himself together. "I just said I want my fries well done, too."

Ray nodded, turning back to his work. "Whatever you want."

Andy smiled. That's the way people should be, he thought, like Ray. Helpful. Agreeable. If everyone was that way, maybe he wouldn't have to kill any more of them.

He watched the burger sizzling on the grill and

saw the spuds turning to gold in the deep fry. Smelled the meat and potatoes. Delicious. Almost ready. His mouth was watering. He took a deep swig of his RC and savored the cold, sweet taste. He was calming down.

Andy took a deep breath and thought that after he got rid of Jerry, he'd have to come back to Ray's more often.

After all, this was the neighborhood place to eat, and he was a part of the neighborhood like anyone else.

64

Doc found the clipboard when he stuck his hand into the space under the back of the cement pedestal on which the gas furnace stood in the corner of the basement.

The furnace was the only place to look for something. There was no place for anyone to hide down here. Even the washer and dryer were upstairs, just off the kitchen. The basement was just two big empty rooms, covered with an ugly green indoor-outdoor carpet.

The carpet felt like it was laid over differing surfaces. In the first room, the floor was unyielding. In the second there were a few hard spots, but most of the floor flexed slightly under his weight.

Doc brushed off the crud that had fallen on the clipboard and looked at what he'd found. It was some kind of a chart.

Jesus Christ!

BAD DADDY. BAD JACK. Row after row of names, all of them "bad." The only interruption was a space indicating the position of the furnace. The place was a crypt. Doc looked down at the floor under his feet and almost gagged. Suddenly he felt very cold, and he could imagine dozens of ghostly hands reaching up to grab him.

He turned quickly toward the basement stairs and pointed his gun in that direction. This son-ofabitch was *not* going to get him. But he almost wished Andy would come down the stairs right now; he'd feel a lot better, a lot safer, if he could blow him away immediately.

This had to be what had scared Jerry. *Jerry!*

His mind reeled and he quickly scanned the chart. No "Bad Jerry." He noticed a second page and read it, too, sighing with relief when he'd finished. Glenna's boy was still out there some-where, hiding.

There were only two names on the largely empty second page. BAD FRED. That *had* to be Frederick Welles. The other name was written larger and bolder than any of the others: MAMA.

Doc really didn't want to do it, but he knew he had to look under the carpet. He went into the second room. The presence here of only two bodies made it somewhat less mind-rending.

He went to a corner of the room and took hold of the green fiber. The carpet fitted neatly against the walls, but it came up with little resistance. Doc dragged it back to the middle of the room. What he found underneath was a grid frame of two-by-fours into which sheets of ply-wood had been laid. It looked like an acoustical tile ceiling brought to earth.

There were only three exceptions to the pat-tern. Mama's oversize plot was filled to the top of the frame with cement. The standard-sized plot in the corner had also been filled with ce-ment. This was marked on the chart as the last resting place of Bad Fred.

The only other exception was the plot adjacent to Frederick Welles's. Its plywood cover had been removed to reveal a dirt floor.

Apparently, Andy had plans to do more digging.

65

Superintendent Malloy had been called on his private line and told to report to the mayor's office. *Now.* The caller hadn't even identified himself before hanging up. There was just this snotty voice giving him an order like he was a rookie. The problem was, very few people had his private number, and he couldn't afford to ignore any of them.

So, after the mayor's unsmiling secretary told him to go right in, he straightened his uniform and headed for the imposing set of double doors. One thing he knew for sure, they weren't going to stick him with Armando Guzman getting away. That was the goddamn feds' screwup.

Of course, with nobody filling the city's top DEA spot at the moment, the search for scapegoats inevitably led his way. He'd be goddamned, though, if he'd let them get him. He was going to tell the mayor that if they embarrassed him, he could embarrass people, too. He knocked perfunctorily and went in under a full head of steam.

The mayor wasn't there. His hatchet man, Prentice Lee, was. So was Conrad Walters.

Lee said, "Close the door and sit down."

All of Malloy's steam evaporated. He knew something was very wrong here. He shut the door and took a seat. Lee was sitting in the may-

or's chair, behind the mayor's desk. There was a
folder in front of him. He was looking at Malloy
like he was a lump of shit he'd just put his Guccis
into.

*That fucker Walters actually had a goddamn grin on
his face.* Malloy wanted to get out of there fast.

"I'm really very busy, Mr. Lee."

"No you're not. Sit down."

He took the seat across from Lee.

"I thought the mayor wanted me here."

"He does. He just has me put out his trash."

Lee opened the folder and tossed some papers
at Malloy.

"You recognize this?" Lee asked.

It was Conrad Walters' personalized press briefing, complete with the leaked tip on the Red Ball
Taxi. The Superintendent looked at Walters as if
he'd betrayed him. If you couldn't count on blind
ambition, what the hell was left for a man to believe in?

Walters just shook his head. He really couldn't
believe how dumb this guy was. Did he think a
newsman wouldn't know when he was being set
up? All Walters had had to do was ask to see a
few of the other handouts to tell that he was the
only one being fed inside information. And why
should that be? Because somebody on the cops
loved him? *Come on . . .*

So, no matter how nicely this package was gift-
wrapped, Walters had been sure it was ready to
explode. The trick, then, was to let it blow up in
someone else's face. He might have to forego an
exclusive story, but once the word spread that
he was responsible for getting the Superintendent
axed, well, that was the kind of thing that made
a guy a journalistic legend.

"What do you have to say?" Lee asked.

Malloy turned to the hatchet man and bluffed.

"This is confidential police information. I can only thank Mr. Walters for his sense of civic responsibility. I assure you I'll get to the bottom of this."

"You've already *hit* bottom," Lee said. He turned to Walters. "Thank you for your help, Mr. Walters."

The reporter stood up.

"You'll be in touch?"

"Very shortly."

On his way out, Conrad Walters smiled at Malloy and hoped he could read his mind. He was thinking, *one down, one to go.* Someday he was going to get that asshole Walter Welles, too.

As soon as the door had closed, Lee slid a sheet of paper across the desk.

"This is your resignation. Sign it."

Malloy almost blacked out just looking at the paper. Then he got mad.

"No. No goddamn way!"

"If that's the way you feel . . ."

Lee took out another piece of paper and held it against his chest.

"This is an order from the mayor suspending you from duty immediately. You will not be allowed to return to your office; you will not be allowed to enter any police facility; you will not be allowed to communicate with any of your aides. This order empowers *me* to investigate how confidential police information was leaked to Mr. Walters."

The Superintendent wished he still carried a gun. He'd have nailed this sonofabitch right where he sat.

"You think you can get away with canning me

for some chickenshit thing like this? Try it. I'll make you and a lot of other people pay."

Lee smiled like a hungry cat.

"You really are a self-basting turkey."

"And you're an overpriced nigger."

Lee's smile only got wider.

"See? See what I mean? I insulted you, but I didn't get ethnic about it. You're behind the learning curve, man."

"You just tell the mayor that—"

Lee slammed his hand down on the desk so hard everything in the room seemed to jump, including Malloy.

"You don't get it, do you, you dumb fuck? Your days of giving orders are over. You're finished. You sign that resignation now, you get a pension. You don't . . ." Lee's smile returned. "Baby, you don't, you'll be fucked worse than you tried to fuck Kildare."

The Superintendent felt as if he'd been poleaxed.

"That?" he muttered. "That's what this is all about?"

"You could've found a spot for Kildare. That would've been good PR. You could've gone along with Carswell's idea to pay him a million. That would've been acceptable politics. But what do you do? You put your hands together and pray for the guy to be murdered while you tell your men to turn a blind eye. That's too fucking dangerously dumb to tolerate."

Malloy was stunned again. *Carswell* had betrayed him, too. One cop ratting on another. That was worse than what Walters had done.

Lee shook his head. "You see why you gotta go?"

"There's no—"

"We're gonna *have* to settle with Kildare now.

For a lot more than it would have cost a while
ago."

"You wouldn't . . ."

". . . give Walters the story about you hoping
for a hit on one of your former finest?" Lee didn't
answer the question he'd helped Malloy to finish,
he just said, "Sign the resignation."

Malloy signed.

66

Doc recognized Andy the moment he walked into Ray's and saw him sitting at the end of the counter calmly munching on a burger. There was a little gray in his hair now, but the old photograph at Otille's house nailed him perfectly. Doc reached under his jacket for his gun.

He reached for it, but decided he'd better scratch his ribs instead. What the hell was he doing to do, make a citizen's arrest? With an illegal weapon? Relying on information from an unlawful search? He'd end up with a longer sentence than Andy.

He was tempted just to wait until the guy stepped outside, blow his brains out, wipe the gun, and throw it down a sewer. Except he couldn't afford to lose the Beretta with Armando Guzman running around free.

As much as he hated to do it, he had to call the cops.

He strolled past the grocery section of the store to the soda fountain. Then another thought hit him. What if Ray asked how the search for Jerry was going? Damn, Ray was looking at him now, and so was Andy.

"Hi, Doc. Any—"

"Make me a shake, will you, Ray?"

"Sure, but—"

"Talk to you in a minute. Gotta make a call."

He saw Ray give him a funny look, but he stepped into the phone booth before he could say anything more.

Doc closed the door of the booth behind him and turned his back on the killer. He was sure if he even glanced at the bastard he'd be off and running. Doc dropped a quarter into the phone and called Vince's home number.

"Hello?" It was Beverly, Vince's wife.

He kept his voice down, but not so low he'd have to repeat himself.

"Bev, this is Doc Kildare. I need to talk to Vince right away."

"He's not here, Doc. He just got another call and rushed right out not five minutes ago."

"Goddamn," Doc muttered.

"What?"

"Nothing, Bev. Was the call a police matter?"

"That's what I asked. He laughed and said, 'What else?' "

"Thanks, Bev. I'll try him at his office."

"Sure. The way he drove out of here, he'll be there already."

Doc hung up and he couldn't help himself: He peeked over his shoulder.

Andy sat at the counter staring at the phone booth. The guy looked right at him. He tried to be sneaky about it, just a quick glimpse before he made a second call, but he definitely looked at him. Why'd he do that?

Andy tried to remember if he knew the guy in the booth. He was sure he hadn't seen him in his cab. He didn't think he'd seen him anywhere. So why was he also sure the guy knew him when he looked around?

It scared Andy, reminded him of a dream that an Indian doctor had given him. The guy had come into the body shop in his suit and turban, and while he's waiting for his Mercedes he starts talking to Andy about reincarnation. Andy had cut him right off, saying he didn't believe in that stuff. But that night he'd had a nightmare. He'd dreamed that all the guys he'd buried in Mama's basement had been reincarnated and were coming after him. He'd woken up screaming.

Now here was this guy he'd never seen before, but Andy was sure the guy knew his secrets. It made him think he'd been right to be nervous about coming back to Ray's.

Taking great care not to speak aloud, Andy thought, *Mama, what's going on here? Where are you? I need you, Mama. Help me, please!*

It was getting hot in the booth when a voice in Doc's ear said, "Police gym."

"I asked the switchboard for the Narcotics Unit."

"Who do you want? I'll transfer you."

"Vince DiGiuseppe."

Doc could almost feel the frost form on the other end of the line. He could certainly hear it.

"The lieutenant's on vacation."

Doc told himself to be polite.

"Yes, but he may have come in anyway. If he hasn't, he'll probably be walking through the door any minute."

"Who is this?"

Doc covered the phone with his hand while he said, "Shit."

"This is a citizen with information on the Welles boy."

"What's your name?"

"What's yours?"

It was neck-and-neck who was becoming more impatient.

"This is Sergeant Frank Pankraz. Now who the hell are you?"

He had no choice. "This is Doc Kildare. Now, if Vince has come in, will you please connect me to his fucking line?"

For a moment there was no response.

"The lieutenant's on vacation, and this sounds like a fucking crank call to me, anyway."

Pankraz hung up on him. Doc tried to think of someone else he could call.

But when he took one more little peek, he saw that Andy was gone.

67

Armando had not had a woman for far too long, but this thin creature with the black circles under her eyes that Hector had brought back left his loins cold and limp. He couldn't see what her value was.

"Tell me again why this woman is here," he said in Spanish.

"She is the imbecile's mother," Hector explained for the third time. He couldn't comprehend how he and this dense turd could possibly be related.

"Is the cop looking for her?"

"It doesn't matter if he is or not!"

That was the first time Hector had ever raised his voice to Armando, and he was so exasperated he failed to notice the deadly look that came into his cousin's eyes. He carried on, gesticulating as if talking to an idiot.

"She is now our hostage. Because even if Kildare finds the boy, what will he do with him? He needs to give him back to someone. If we have the mother, what will he do with the imbecile? Keep him?"

Armando looked at the woman. Fausto and Eraldo had bound and gagged her before going back to their posts.

"I think," Armando said, "you kidnapped this

woman because you lack the *cojones* to confront a boy who has no more brains than a burro."

The insult was too much for Hector.

"Perhaps you wouldn't think our little scarecrow here so helpless if she pointed this at you!"

He reached for the Smith & Wesson under his coat, but he never got it clear. Armando was on him before he knew it, grabbing the gun and slapping him backhand and forehand. Hector was still dazed when Armando relieved him of his Ingraham machine pistol, too.

Glenna's heart sank when she saw the new bastard grab the fancy bastard's guns away from him. She'd hoped Mr. Fancy would shoot the other one. He was going to be much harder to deal with entirely.

Armando pressed the barrel of Glenna's revolver between Hector's eyes.

"Tell me why I shouldn't kill you, cousin."

Hector was shaking, but he replied immediately.

"Because you need me to get Kildare, and you want to kill him even more."

Armando stared into his eyes for a moment, then let the gun fall to his side and laughed.

"My father was right. You are very, very smart."

Hector had just started to smile when Armando's arm whipped the long barrel of the .44 across his cheek, drawing blood and sending him crashing into the wall behind him. Armando waited until his cousin's senses had jelled before tapping the gun against his chest.

"Just remember, all the brains in the world won't help if I decide to kill you. You better hope your scarecrow brings me someone I *really* want to kill."

68

Jerry Handee didn't know if hunger woke him or the strange noises. Noises had to be new to bother him. He slept through the racket of "L" trains roaring by all day. This was more of a banging sound, irregular but coming from a fixed point.

Jerry heard a man's voice and got really scared. He thought that Andy had found him. He prayed for a train to get him quick. He peeked out a window and saw a black man stick his head up between the ties and look around. He wasn't Andy. Andy was white.

Jerry didn't know what the man was doing, but he worried that he would find him and take him back to Mama. But the man didn't. He ducked his head and Jerry didn't see him anymore, and the banging noise stopped.

All that had been when the sun was going down. Now it was night, and Jerry knew he had to leave the crib. Not only was he hungry and had to pee, he knew that the black man could come back tomorrow. And if he didn't make his banging noise first, he could find Jerry when he was sleeping.

The idea scared him, but Jerry knew he was going to have to find a new hiding place. He looked out a window and saw the light of an approaching train. The light and the *clunkita-clack* noise of the wheels came around the curve in the tracks before the train did, before the engineer could see the tool crib. Jerry scrunched down until the train had passed.

After it had, he got back up and saw it disappearing toward the Kelvin Avenue station. No train was coming from the opposite direction. It was time to go. He opened his door and stepped carefully out onto the tracks.

He knew that he shouldn't touch the raised third rail. Mama had told him that would be just like going to the electric chair. He didn't know what an electric chair was, but he knew he didn't want to go to one.

The ties of the tracks were each six inches wide, but the spaces between them varied almost whimsically. A full moon shone like a spotlight, so Jerry could see where he was going; there was no wind, so he kept his balance without any problem. Still, when you walked the "L" tracks at night, you had to watch your step.

The other thing he had to remember, besides not touching the third rail, was to count just the right number of ties. He had to count exactly nine of them from the one that was even with the crib's door. When he got to nine he'd lower himself, facing back the way he'd come, and slip through the opening between the ninth and tenth ties.

Just below, his feet would find one of the huge X-shaped braces that supported the pillars that held up the tracks. Once he got his feet planted on the brace, he could shinny his way down to the ground.

With laborious concentration Jerry started

walking and counting out the ties. One, two, three . . . When he got to nine it didn't look right. Something about the space looked different. It looked too small and neat or something. He wondered if he should go back and start again.

It wasn't necessary. The moonlight was bright enough to see all the ties from where he was. He'd counted correctly. This was the right space, but it was *different*.

Then Jerry noticed something else that was different. The metal things that held the tie in place weren't old and rusty anymore. They were shiny and new.

He connected the new hardware to the black man. That must have been what he was doing. Jerry was grappling with this new situation when he heard the *clunkita-clack*.

A train was coming!

He couldn't go back to the crib. He'd be running right at the train. He couldn't run ahead to the Kelvin Avenue station. He'd never make it. To get to the other side of the tracks, he'd have to cross *two* third rails, one for each direction. He was too scared to try that.

Jerry quickly tried what had always worked before. He lowered himself between the ninth and tenth ties. His legs went through okay, but the space *was* smaller. He touched his feet onto the brace below, but when he tried to squeeze his chest through he got stuck. The new opening was too small for him.

He could see the train's light but he couldn't hear its noise. It had stopped at the Perry Street station around the curve. Jerry had forgotten that every other train stopped there. He could've gone back to the crib. Now, the train wasn't going to mash Andy, it was going to mash him.

He heard the *buzz-buzz* the conductor made to tell the engineer all the doors were closed and he could start up the train again. A second later came a *clunk, clunkita-clack*. The train had started. As soon as it got around the curve, it would pick up speed.

Jerry squirmed down as hard as he could. His shirt tore, and skin ripped off his chest and back, but he was inching slowly downward. He put his feet on the outsides of the brace and used his legs to pull. He felt like he was crushing his chest.

The train came into view and Jerry screamed, but he couldn't be heard above the noise of the wheels. He got low enough to put his hands under the tie and push. Only his head, shoulders and upper chest were above the tracks now. He shrieked at the train.

The motorman had started to open his throttle when he saw something sticking out of the tracks ahead. He knew work was being done on the line, but couldn't believe some damn fool had left debris on the tracks. He slammed on his brakes but, despite the animal squeal of locked wheels, he knew he was already too late to stop. He only hoped he could slow the train down enough that it wouldn't derail.

When he saw that what he'd thought was debris was a boy's head and shoulders, he screamed.

Jerry screamed, too, as the train bore down on him. He could practically feel the sparks that flashed blue-white from the screeching wheels. He shoved and pulled with all the strength in his body. With a final convulsive effort he popped down through the ties, tearing flesh from his chin, his nose, and his forehead.

The train passed overhead, howling like a banshee.

Jerry clung to the X-shaped brace for dear life, bleeding and terrified and sobbing in the night.

69

Harry was sitting in Doc's living room going over the list of possibilities for their travel plans when the phone rang.

"Hello," she said.

Silence.

"Hello."

A voice with a faint Latin accent came on the line.

"Put the cop on."

She didn't like the sound of that.

"How do you know I'm not a cop?"

More silence.

"You don't sound like a cop."

She followed up on her bluff. "Come over, and I'll show you my gun."

There was a brief argument in the background, and a new voice with a much heavier accent came on.

"Look, *chica*, you want to play guns, you come, too. But you tell that greedy cop, Kildare, we have the inbecile's *madre*. The skinny woman who had her own big gun that we got now. I'm goin' to give you directions. You tell the cop to come or we kill the woman. You come, too, if you look good enough to eat."

"Is this Armando Guzman?"

There was a chuckle.

"Yours truly, *chica*."

Suddenly, Harry wanted Doc to be there very badly. She was in way over her head with a bastard like this. She wrote down the directions.

"You got all that, *chica*? You better."

Guzman hung up. The meeting was in three hours, but Harry's problem was, Doc wasn't home and she didn't know where to find him.

If she did locate him, though, she'd probably be sending him to his death. But if she ignored the message, Glenna would die, and if Doc found out later that she'd held back on him . . .

Her dilemma resolved itself when the ghosts closed in on her. They wouldn't allow Harry to sit by and do nothing. She pleaded with them not to let Doc die. Not now. She remembered Doc saying that his sister Pat was his guardian angel. She begged Pat to protect him tonight.

Then she got her coat and her car keys and went out to look for Doc.

70

The goddamn Red Ball Taxi was gone.

It had been taken from Otille Coultier's garage, and in its place a dark gray van had been left. Doc banged his fist in frustration against the side of the garage. Like a shit-for-brains fool, he hadn't even made a note of the number on the phony cab.

He didn't know what the hell he could do now. How did you find one cab that looked like a thousand others? The answer came to him so fast he left the yard on the run. If you wanted to find a needle in a haystack, you got rid of the fucking haystack.

Doc sprinted down the street looking for a public phone.

The first thing he'd done when he'd seen that Andy had left Ray's had been to dash outside. The killer had been nowhere in sight. The only place Doc had thought to look had been Otille's house. As he'd run over there, he'd decided to kill Andy with the Beretta. If he had to shoot it out later with Armando, he'd use his own automatic and let Rudd defend him for it.

Doc skidded to a stop in front of a laundromat. It was open, empty, and it had a public phone. He went inside, waited until his breathing had returned to normal, and made his call.

"Red Ball Taxi. Where should I send your cab?"

"This is Deputy Superintendent of Police Conklin," Doc told the dispatcher. "Is your fleet manager there?"

"Deputy Superintendent? Right, and I'm the Sugar Plum Fairy."

Doc used his best hard-ass cop voice.

"What's your name, lady?"

"Billie Hundley."

She'd answered before she could catch herself. Doc's voice turned soft, but was filled with implied threat.

"Okay, Billie. I'm calling about a very serious matter here. You can be a big help, or you can be a wise-ass and end up *responsible* for a lot of grief. Am I making myself clear?"

"Yes, sir."

"Is the fleet manager in?"

"No, sir."

"You're a dispatcher?"

"Yes, sir."

"Then you'll have to carry the ball. Have you read the story about kids being grabbed off the street?"

"I seen it on TV."

"So you know how serious it is."

"Yeah, I got a little nephew I been worried about."

"And you know the department's been looking into a connection between the disappearance of Frederick Welles and a Red Ball Taxi driver."

"Hey, we—were told to keep that quiet. Listen, sir, I'm sorry I wised off. We get a lotta jerks callin'. . . ."

"We're past that now," Doc said. "The department has found out that the guy we want *is* using one of your cabs, or a car painted like one."

"Oh, shit."

"We think he's going to hit tonight, and we think we know where."

"Kill the bastard."

Doc smiled.

"I've got some very important suggestions to make to you, so listen closely."

Doc advised her that all Red Ball Taxis should stay out of The Wedge. There were going to be some very nervous cops out there tonight, and he didn't want any innocent cabbie getting shot by mistake. The ban would start immediately and stay in effect until dawn. The dispatcher should notify her drivers in such a way that didn't alert the suspect, since it was thought he might have a scanner capable of monitoring her company's radio frequency.

Could she do all that?

She could and she would. She asked him to remember just one thing.

"Kill the bastard."

Harry spotted Doc coming out of the laundromat and honked her horn. She pulled over to the curb. Doc's hand went to his gun, and he checked the backseat just in case before getting in. The car was okay, but Harry wasn't. She looked desperate.

"What's wrong?"

She told him about Armando Guzman's call.

"Doc, you can't go. You've got to call the police."

He laughed bitterly. He told Harry about Andy and seeing him in Ray's, and what had happened when he'd called the police then.

"The fucker hung up on me. The cops aren't taking my calls anymore."

"Call Vince."

"I tried. He's out running around somewhere. He's probably with the rest of the team looking for Armando."

"But you know where Guzman is, or at least how to get to him."

"Yeah, but I don't know how to find any cops that will help me. The ones I can reach don't give a flying fuck."

"This is crazy!"

"Sure the hell is. What's really crazy is, I have to do this myself anyway."

He told her why. Harry wasn't thrilled, but she couldn't argue with his reasoning.

Doc tapped his hand against the Beretta holstered under his jacket for comfort. He looked at his watch.

"We've got some time until Armando wants to see me. Let's try finding Jerry first."

"Doc, you've been looking for days."

"Yeah, but I have two new advantages."

"What?"

"I've got you to drive me around. And now I know where Jerry goes to eat."

71

Armando brushed off his cousin's coat and settled Hector's hat back onto his head.

"You understand what you are to do?"

Hector nodded, but avoided Armando's eyes.

"Yes."

"You will bring me my cop?"

"Yes."

"You will have Fausto and Eraldo with you, so you will not fail."

"No."

"Good." Armando turned to the contract killers. "Don't let any harm come to my cousin."

They understood their orders perfectly. If things went wrong, Armando wanted Hector for himself. That's why they had weapons and Hector didn't. He'd have no chance to escape. Or kill himself.

"*Vaya con Dios*," Armando said.

The three men walked out of the room, leaving Armando with Glenna. He looked at her again. Try as he might, he could work up no excitement for her.

Maybe this was a strength she had, Armando thought. He could see that she knew she was going to die. Still she showed no fear, only hate. He was proud of her. Feeling that such a spirit should be free to express itself, he removed her gag. One such as this wouldn't scream, she would curse him.

He was surprised, though, when she said nothing. Armando was forced to speak first.

"You are brave. If you were more *guapa*, I would take you to Spain with me."

Glenna looked up at Armando from where she sat bound on the floor. She'd watched him beat Mr. Fancy and strut around afterward. She thought she knew one way she might have a chance.

"You like pushin' people around."

Armando smiled.

"The strong always push the weak."

"That's undeniable. But you *like* it."

"Yes, I do."

"Never met a man you couldn't lick?"

Lick? He didn't understand. For a moment he thought she was calling him a *maricón*. Then he comprehended the *Yanqui* idiom.

"Never."

"You're gonna kill me."

"Of course."

Glenna paused to take a breath. She knew she could be hurrying her own death, but she felt her idea was the only hope she had.

"Well, why don't we make things interestin'? Give me a fightin' chance."

Armando smiled again.

"What do you mean?"

"I mean, untie me, and let's see who leaves this room alive."

Armando laughed. "Such a one! As *flaca* as you are, I'm almost ready to take your skinny body with me to Spain."

He stopped laughing when he looked into Glenna's eyes again. There was nothing funny there. They were eyes such as you might see on a hawk as it swooped for the kill.

Glenna taunted him.

"What's the matter? Scared? Of a poor, tired woman?"

Armando had no reply. He thought of the gun Hector had taken away from her. A woman who could use such a weapon was not to be taken lightly. It disturbed him that he couldn't reconcile his sudden feeling of dread with the fact that Hector had disarmed her.

"Big mouth, little pecker," Glenna said.

Another idiom, Armando thought. This one insulting.

"If you sent that fool and those two others to fetch Michael Kildare, you better pray they don't succeed."

Glenna saw that he wasn't going to untie her. She had nothing to lose by speaking out.

"He'll kill a little varmint like you for sure."

That Armando understood perfectly. He started beating the skinny woman.

72

The mustard on both sides of the corned beef had held the sandwich together. There was hardly a bite taken from it, and it rested on a clean styrofoam plate. Jerry took it from the garbage can in back of Rothman's Deli.

There weren't even any bugs on it, because Aaron Rothman always sealed his perishable garbage in plastic bags.

Jerry had gotten to the food before any of the neighborhood's stray dogs. It was the best find he'd had in days. He wolfed the sandwich in a few quick gulps. The mustard stung when it ran down into a cut on his chin. He had a hard time keeping from crying.

He looked for something else to eat, because he was still hungry. He was still scared, too. He knew Andy was going to get him for sure, now that he couldn't stay in his tool crib anymore. He couldn't think of another good place to hide.

He thought it might be time to go home. He could sneak in when Mama wasn't around, get Granddaddy's gun, and shoot himself. That way Andy couldn't get him because he'd already be dead. Mama could bury him in the cemetery with Daddy and he wouldn't wind up in Andy's basement.

Then Jerry got another idea.

He could go home and tell Mama how he knew Andy was going to sneak in and get them when they were asleep. But if they stayed *up* all night, like he had in the tool crib, then they'd be *awake* when he came.

And they could shoot Andy!

It was a good idea, and Jerry wished he'd thought of it sooner. He could go home, and he didn't have to be scared anymore. He couldn't wait to see Mama.

Before he took a step, a Red Ball Taxi turned into the alley.

Doc decided that Jerry would be too scared to go back and scavenge for his dinner at Ray's again. So he and Harry hit Lujack's Diner, the Gold Cup Coffee Shop, and the day-old bakery store, without luck. The garbage cans he'd checked had all been unmolested.

The only thing in their favor was that they were making great time. There were no cars on the street, no people on the sidewalks. The campaign of terror had The Wedge locked up tight. Doc's neighbors weren't going to devour the monsters that had invaded, but they weren't going to be eaten alive, either.

He'd overrated their courage, but one problem was solved. Anyone he and Harry saw tonight was likely to be either predator or prey. There would be no innocent bystanders.

"Where to next?" Harry asked.

Doc thought about it.

"We're about halfway between Rothman's Deli and the Donut Hole. Let's figure a kid would go for something sweet before something kosher."

Harry made a left turn.

She said, "I just don't understand how anyone

could do something so monstrous to all those people."

Doc had taken Andy's floor plans with him when he'd left the Coultier house. He handed them to Harry.

"Here's how."

73

As he drove into the alley, Andy saw a figure duck behind a garage. He wasn't able to tell if it had been Jerry, or some derelict who thought he'd seen a cop car.

Andy pulled over close to the wall of the building on his right. He'd gone home to get his taxi as soon as he'd run out of Ray's. He'd needed *something* to make him feel that he wasn't falling apart. He made sure he left enough room in the alley for any car that might need to get by. He didn't want some jerk honking for him to get out of the way if he found Jerry.

He got out of the cab and drew his knife from a hip pocket. The five-inch blade jumped open with a soft click. He walked slowly and quietly along the right-hand side of the alley. His heart was in his throat. If it *was* Jerry he'd seen, he couldn't afford to blow it. There was no telling if he'd get another chance like this.

Just past the wall where he'd parked the taxi was a high wooden fence that enclosed the building's backyard. A door stood in the middle of the fence. He tried it with a gentle touch. It was locked from the inside. No room for mistakes now. If Jerry was around, Andy didn't want the boy sneaking out behind him.

Next came a brick garage with three bays. Each

bay had a rollup metal door and was sealed with a padlock. Andy eased past them, taking pains not to make any noise that would give him away. But he was amazed that people for blocks around couldn't hear the beating of his heart. To him it sounded like a great drum, beating fast and furious.

He sensed something in the air. *Fear*. Someone else's fear. Jerry *was* here. Andy's sense of relief was so great his knees almost buckled. Now, all he had to do was flush the boy out and kill him.

The sharp tang of rotting food reached his nose. Of course, he thought, the little bastard had been eating.

Andy took a deep breath and turned the knife in his hand. This was it. He'd kill Jerry, and then Mama would forgive him. She'd talk to him again. She'd never let the monster get inside his head. And she'd say she was sorry for insulting him. Everything would be fine again.

Just as soon as Jerry died.

Andy stepped around the corner of the garage and whispered, "Jerrrr-ry."

He stood facing a ten-foot wide passageway between the garage he'd just passed and the one beyond it. He could see three doors. Ahead, to his left, a door led into an apartment building. He knew that in The Wedge people didn't leave such doors unlocked. Ahead, to his right, was the door to the back of Rothman's Deli. It was protected by a security gate. The last door was set into the side wall of the garage he'd just passed, and it didn't fit right. Andy could see it had been forced open and imperfectly closed again.

A shiver ran through him when he thought how scared Jerry must've been to do that.

Suddenly Andy was afraid again, too. He flashed

on his nightmare about reincarnation. He got the cold, sinking feeling that maybe it wasn't just a dream. Maybe it was a premonition. What if Jerry wasn't alone in there? What if everyone—even the monster—was in there waiting for him?

Could that be possible?

To his great surprise, Andy hoped so. In a lightning-fast shift of emotion, his fear was gone—stomped flat by anger. A rage so intense he felt his skin burn.

The monster had always beaten him when he was a small and helpless boy. Now he'd have to face him as a full-grown man. Andy Slick! Wait 'til the fucker saw what happened to him this time. Him *and* Jerry. Getting the two of them together would be perfect. And he'd do the others all over again just for fun.

Then there'd be no doubt that Mama would come back to him.

Andy closed his knife, put it in his pocket, and took out his gun.

"Jerry, you're making me mad. You don't want to do that. You make me mad, I'm going to hurt you. Come out now and I promise . . . it won't hurt to die."

The brick rocketed down out of the night and crashed into Andy's skull.

Jerry grabbed another from the roof where he stood and threw it down at Andy with all the strength in his body. It was harder to hit him now because he was down on his knees, but the second brick got him on the head, too.

There were three more loose bricks on the garage roof and he threw them all. Andy was flat on the ground now, but Jerry hit him with two more shots to the head and one on the back of the neck.

Jerry stood at the edge of the roof looking down and breathing hard. He'd known when he'd seen the cab turn into the alley it had to be Andy; he'd just felt it. He'd seen the door to the garage was open, but had been afraid to go in because it was dark in there. So he'd climbed the drainpipe up to the roof.

Staying in the tool crib had taught him that high places were good for hiding. He could see down and nobody ever looked up. At first, he was just going to lie flat. But Andy started talking. Telling him it wouldn't hurt to die.

Let Andy die then, if it didn't hurt! And he'd thrown the first brick.

Now, Jerry pulled one more brick from its crumbling mortar and started down the drainpipe. He was going to make sure Andy never scared him again.

74

Detective Junior Little brought the unmarked car around a corner.

"Ain't got a lotta night life around here, do they?"

"I keep expecting to see zombies coming up out of the sewers or something," Detective Frank Wallis said from the backseat.

Detective Steve Petrovsky, as usual, kept quiet.

Lieutenant Vince DiGiuseppe, riding shotgun, scanned the streets of The Wedge and didn't like what he saw, which was nothing. They'd been driving around the area for forty-five minutes and they hadn't seen a single person on the street. That was pretty damned eerie for a mild spring night.

When Vince had gotten the word that Malloy was out, he'd rushed right down to his office. Little and Petrovsky had been there already, and he'd called Wallis to come in. Then the four of them had gone out looking for Armando Guzman and any friends he might have picked up in his travels.

After checking the obvious places, Vince had decided to cruise Doc's neighborhood to see if the Colombian asshole might actually have the nerve to try to hit Doc. They hadn't seen any sign of

Guzman, but then they hadn't seen any sign of *anybody*.

"Signpost up ahead," Wallis said, making Vince jump. "You're entering The Twilight Zone."

Vince gave him a look.

"I don't know what's going on around here, but it stinks. Let's go knock on Doc's door and see what he knows."

Doc and Harry saw the Red Ball Taxi the first thing as they drove into the alley behind Rothman's Deli. Then Doc looked ahead and saw a figure dragging a body out from behind a garage.

Doc yelled, "Stop the car, Harry."

He pulled his gun and jumped out while it was still rolling.

"Stop right there, motherfucker! Put your hands in the air."

The bastard had to be forty feet away. Doc was going to start his aim low, work up, and fire the entire clip. He ought to hit the mark at least a couple of times that way. But the guy put his hands up. And started crying.

When the figure turned, Doc was looking at Jerry Handee.

Doc's hands trembled as he slowly lowered his gun. He tried to see if the figure on the ground was Andy, but the man's head was a bloody pulp. Jerry's hands were covered with blood, too.

"Jerry, it's okay. It's me, Doc."

"D-doc," the boy blubbered, "c-can I g-go home now?"

Doc put his gun away. He looked at Harry. She was still in the car, staring at the battered corpse. Doc caught her eye and motioned for her to accompany him. She got out and together they walked over to Jerry.

Doc put his arms around the boy and Harry stroked his head.

"Was that Andy?" Doc asked.

Jerry glanced at the body and nodded. He laid his face against Doc's chest and asked them not to be mad at him because Andy had been doing real bad things. Jerry told them everything he'd seen and where he'd been.

The boy asked, "Can I see my mama now?"

Doc exchanged a look with Harry. One bogey-man down, one to go.

Doc surveyed the scene. "We have to do a few things first. Will you give me a hand?"

"With what?"

"Well, we can't leave Andy here."

"Am I gonna get in trouble?"

"No. But I don't want you to tell anyone what happened tonight, okay?"

Harry was about to say something, but Doc shook his head emphatically.

"Okay," Jerry said.

Doc took care to avoid streams of blood and what he guessed to be gobs of brain tissue and chunks of skull, and went over to a garbage can and emptied a black plastic bag. He put the bag over Andy's gory head and tied it off around the killer's neck.

"We'll put him in the trunk of Harry's car," Doc said.

Harry was startled but didn't object. Doc and Jerry loaded the body and closed the lid over it. Doc retraced his way back to Rothman's garbage cans. He sifted through them as Harry looked at him, wondering if he'd gone crazy. Doc apparently found what he wanted in two cylindrical containers.

"What the hell are you doing?" Harry asked.

Jerry watched without a word.

"Destroying evidence."

"Why?"

"So no one comes asking Jerry any awkward questions."

"Oh."

From one container Doc shook a pungent yellow gel, taking care to cover all the mortal remains of Andy's head. Over this he poured a thinner liquid from the other container.

"What is that stuff?" Harry asked.

"Kosher napalm. You want to know the ingredients?"

"No thanks."

"You got a light?"

Harry went to her car and pushed in the cigarette lighter. When it popped back out she gave it to Doc. He used it to light a scrap of waste paper.

Doc looked around. He didn't see anyone peeking out a window. The way people in The Wedge were feeling, they weren't likely to eavesdrop on things that went bump in the night. A fire on the other hand . . . Doc hoped he'd gotten his kitchen chemistry right. Just before he burned his fingers, he touched off his concoction.

The flame raced along its oily path and burned brightly. Out of the corner of his eye, Doc saw Jerry smile. Within seconds the fire had consumed its fuel down to the pavement and gone out.

For a moment smoke lingered in the air, carrying a scent Doc prayed he'd soon forget. Then it was carried away by a breeze. Doc looked around. Still no snoops. He examined his handiwork.

The blood and soft tissue were gone. The bits

of bone were charred and unrecognizable. Doc kicked them down the alley, anyway. There were scorch marks on the concrete but that couldn't be helped, and he couldn't imagine what use they'd be to any investigation.

He looked at the taxi and decided to leave it right where it was. None of them had touched it. There was no way to connect them to it. A random alley was a good place to abandon it.

Doc looked around one more time to see if they'd left *any* sign of their presence.

Jerry asked what he was doing, and Doc told him.

"Andy had a gun," the boy said. "It's around the corner there."

"Show me," Doc said.

They went to the side of the garage and Jerry pointed a foot toward a shadow. Doc found the pistol, a Browning automatic. He picked it up, put the safety on, and checked the clip and chamber.

Jerry said, "He was going to shoot me with that." Then he added fiercely, "But I got *him* first!"

Doc looked at the boy and had an ugly thought. The problem was, ugly or not, it was the first idea he'd had that might let them get Glenna back, and let him save his own ass in the bargain.

"Jerry, your mama told me she taught you how to shoot. Is that right?"

"Sure, Doc."

"Are you a good shot?"

"Sure."

He wasn't bragging, just stating a fact.

Doc paused. He asked himself if there was any other way to do this. He was damned if he could think of one, and he put his arm around the boy.

"Jerry, I have to tell you something, and you

have to promise that you'll be strong. As strong as you were with Andy tonight."

Jerry's face clouded. "What?"

"It's about your mama. . . ."

Doc came out of his house with a loaded shopping bag and a huge old leather jacket with slash pockets that had once belonged to Big John. He walked over to where Harry's car was parked out front. He was handing the items to Jerry in the backseat when he heard a horn honk and saw Vince and the guys pull up across the street.

"Nice to see *somebody* alive and kickin' around here," Junior said with a smile.

"Doc, c'mere a minute," Vince said.

Doc closed the passenger side door of Harry's car and crossed over to Vince. He squatted and put a hand on the fender of the unmarked unit.

"You heard about Guzman, right?"

"Yeah."

"You hear about Malloy?"

"What?"

"He's out. The mayor canned him."

"Long overdue. But you didn't round up the Mouseketeers to tell me that."

Wallis laughed. Little and Petrovsky smiled.

"We're out lookin' for your old friend Armando. I just wanted to tell you that I'm back on the job, and you can expect the department to protect you the same as anyone else."

"I'll sleep easy."

Vince snorted. He looked across the street and saw Harry. He waved. He smiled when she waved back. Then Vince noticed the filthy, scraped-up boy in the backseat.

"That the kid you been lookin' for?" Vince asked with surprise.

"Yeah. Turns out he was clipped by a hit-and-run driver. No serious damage, but it dazed him. Being retarded, too, he's been wandering around in a fog."

"That's the biggest pile of shit I ever heard."

Doc looked hard at his old boss.

"Yeah? Try this one on. I found out who's responsible for all those disappearances, and when I talked to Sergeant Frank Pankraz about it earlier this evening he hung up on me. Does that sound more believable to you?"

"That asshole. Tell me what you got."

"Sorry, my information's outdated."

"Doc, don't jerk me around. You're not a cop anymore. You can't play vigilante."

"Now, Vince, how could I do that? I don't even remember where I put my gun."

Doc knew he had Vince. He'd bet his good eye that Vince hadn't told the guys or anyone else about slipping him the Beretta.

"Tell you what, Vince. If I find out anything more I think the department should know, I'll make sure you get it. You can decide what to do with it. Is that fair?"

Vince didn't say anything. Doc stood up and offered him his hand. After a moment's hesitation, Vince took it.

"I've got to be going," Doc said. "A pleasure as always, gentlemen."

"*Answer*, goddammit!"

Rudd Wetherby heard Doc Kildare's number ring for the tenth time. When he got no answer he jammed the phone hook down with his finger and called again.

He'd just finished several hours of negotiating with the U.S. Attorney for the Northern District of Illinois, who was representing the Attorney General. They'd agreed that the government would settle Doc's claim for nine million dollars, with certain provisions.

It made Rudd crazy that he couldn't reach Doc to tell him he was a millionaire. As he looked at the papers on his desk, it also made him anxious to get Doc to agree to the deal. A third of the settlement belonged to Rudd, and he didn't want Doc getting hit by a truck before he could sign the papers.

A sudden chill passed through the lawyer. He had just remembered that Armando Guzman was out there somewhere. Maybe Doc had more than traffic accidents to worry about.

"*Answer*, goddammit!" he shouted into the ringing phone.

75

Doc felt Jerry's shoulders tremble under his arm as the two of them entered the east side of Hardrock Park.

"We'll be together all the way," he said to the boy. "Just remember what I told you, and why we have to do it."

Harry waited for them in the car a block away. She hated what they were doing, and had told Doc she would curse his memory to her dying day if he got either Jerry or himself killed. Then she kissed him so hard Doc thought she chipped one of his teeth. If they weren't back in an hour, Harry would go tell Vince what had happened.

Hardrock Park was still officially referred to as "Harding Park." It was the site of one of the city's first housing projects, a sixteen-square-block area. After the projects had deteriorated into jungles, the federal government said, "Tear them down." The city obliged, just in time for a new administration to take over in Washington and slash the funding for low-income housing to zip. The city couldn't even get the money to cart away the rubble. Hardrock Park was born.

Doc and Jerry picked their way through the nightmare moon-scape of Hardrock's streets. The instructions Harry had given Doc said that he'd be picked up right in the middle of the wasteland.

That, of course, would be the best place to shoot someone, with nobody around to see or hear. Doc was counting on that.

Harry had wanted him to let Vince take care of Armando. But that was the problem. Vince, or any other cop, would want to take care of Armando first. Sure, they'd be concerned about Glenna. They wouldn't *want* anything to happen to her. But first and foremost they'd make sure Armando didn't get away again.

Doc, on the other hand, didn't give a rat's ass about the Colombian. Well, he would *like* to kill the sonofabitch. But if he got Glenna back safely, then he could live with Armando's getting away.

Sitting behind the wheel of the Mercedes, Fausto saw them first.

"There they are. Hey, that little one isn't a woman. Didn't *el jefe* say alone or with a woman?"

Eraldo nodded and took out his machine pistol. He got out of the backseat and pulled Hector out with him. Fausto flashed the headlights to signal their location to the cop and whoever he had with him. Fausto followed the others out of the car. He, too, had an Ingraham in his hands.

Doc and Jerry stopped fifty feet from the three men. Doc had one hand draped over Jerry's shoulders. The other hung at his side. Obviously he was unarmed. Fausto and Eraldo took note of this, and Doc saw them relax their grips on their weapons.

They weren't bothered by the boy. He was a ridiculous figure, filthy and battered, his hands in the laughably oversized jacket. He was so scared they could see him shaking. He was no worry.

"Here we are," Doc said.

Eraldo said something in Spanish to Hector. He

shook his head and replied in the same language. Fausto got into it and rebuked Hector.

"What do they want?" Doc asked.

Cousin Hector looked a lot less cocky than the last time Doc had seen him.

"Armando told them to bring only you," he said in English, "or you and a woman. They want to kill the boy here." Hector looked at Jerry for a moment. "Is this the imbecile? You found him?"

"This is Glenna's son."

"That's what I told them. I said it would do no harm to let the boy see his mother."

"That was my idea, too."

"I'm sorry, I could not persuade them. Please step aside."

Doc turned to the boy. "Jerry, those two men with the guns, they work for the man who has your mama. They want to kill you."

Then he tapped the boy on the shoulder. Jerry shot each gunman squarely between the eyes.

As the shots echoed in the night and the bodies fell beside him, Hector stood there gaping at the imbecile. The insides of the boy's jacket pockets had been cut away, and he held a smoking gun in each hand.

One was Vince's Beretta, one was Andy's Browning. Neither would ever be found.

Doc took the guns from Jerry and held the boy to him, comforting him with one arm around his shoulders. He used his free hand to point the Beretta more or less at Hector. He saw that Hector was stupefied, couldn't believe what he'd seen.

Doc explained.

"His mother taught him to shoot."

76

Armando saw Hector's Mercedes pull into the mouth of the *caleta's* dead-end street. It was right on time, but that was the last right thing about it. Instead of driving to the end of the block and everyone coming inside, the car parked crossways, shutting off the entrance to the street. A woman got out from behind the wheel on the far side of the car and walked around the corner and under the elevated structure of the expressway without looking back.

From where he watched, Armando thought he could make out two figures sitting in the back of the car. It was hard for him to be sure because of the car's tinted windows. He cursed. A grab that should have been easy had obviously been fucked up.

He couldn't understand what had gone wrong. He'd talked to both Fausto and Eraldo and had been satisfied that they were up to the job. At the very worst, he'd expected them to bring him a corpse and a suitable apology for not being able to carry out his wishes. But this situation, this he couldn't comprehend at all.

Other than the fact that his gunmen had to be the ones who had been killed.

Armando shifted his attention to Glenna. She lay unconscious on the floor. He considered killing her immediately, but then thought things through. A dead woman would be of no value at all. A live hostage would, especially in a situation he didn't understand.

He unknotted the bindings around her ankles and slapped her awake. When her eyelids fluttered he stepped back and pointed his Ingraham at her.

"Get up. We got to talk to your friend."

There was no doubt in his mind that was what the cop wanted. Armando intended to see if Kildare would shoot through the woman to get him. He certainly would to get the cop.

He wasn't about to take any unnecessary chances, though. He led the woman through the corridors of the *caleta*, his gun pressed constantly into her spine, until he came to a ground-floor room with a window that looked out on the front end of the Mercedes.

He could see things more clearly from here. The cop was sitting in the back with Hector, a gun pointed to Hector's head. Armando laughed softly. The fool. He thought he had his own hostage, when all he'd done was make it easy for Armando to kill both of them.

For something this good, Armando wanted to get up close. He pushed the woman out of the room, down some stairs, and into the street. He had his left hand around her throat while his right pressed the gun against her. She was tall enough to shield him against a quick shot.

The cop didn't shoot. He just held the gun on Hector, who still wore his idiotic hat. Armando couldn't see his cousin's face through the darkened glass but he'd bet Hector was crying, afraid for his precious life because he knew Armando would sooner shoot him than ransom him.

Armando yelled, "Hey, cop, you want to settle with me? An eye for an eye?" The Colombian laughed.

Armando thought he saw the cop's gun hand move. The Colombian was bringing his gun out from behind the woman to shoot the cop when the skinny bitch stamped on his foot and pulled free.

"Shoot him, Michael!" Glenna yelled, diving aside.

Armando ignored her; he had no time for an unarmed woman now. He ran at the car firing his weapon on full automatic. The tinted windshield exploded into a million fragments. The bodies in the back seat jerked and danced as the rounds slammed into them. When his gun clicked empty, Armando realized he'd been screaming, berserk with blood lust.

The adrenaline rush left him, and he stepped limply to the car to inspect his kills. He opened the back door and leaned inside. He saw the body dressed in Hector's clothes. The hat had been knocked off, and Armando saw a head covered by a plastic bag. The right hand of the second body was bound with wire to the neck of the plastic-covered head; a gun was taped into it. The left hand was manacled to the armrest of the back door. The feet were bound. The bloody head faced away from him, with a gag knotted at the back of it. Dark glasses hung from one ear. Unable to stop himself, Armando turned the head around.

Hector!

Armando recoiled in horror. Where was the cop?

Something moved under a blanket on the floor of the front seat. A hand appeared. Holding an eye! Armando's mouth dropped open. The cop came out from under the blanket, one eye empty, one eye piercing Armando.

Doc stuck his gun in the Colombian's open mouth.

From that range he needed only one eye.

The crowd gathered at Nat's Tap an hour before dawn. Ray was there. So were Tony Szell and Artie Fuentes and their wives. Ben Haskins, Monie Watkins, Sy Wasserman, and Ella Tolbert arrived as a group. Red Penwell stood behind the bar, with Nat's permission, and handed out a free drink to anyone who felt the need. The early hour didn't deter many. Nat manned the door, opening it for his neighbors and locking it again after each arrival.

Doc sat at a table with Harry, Glenna, and Jerry.

People smiled at Jerry, glad that he was alive and back with his mother, but none of them approached the table. It was plain to see that something *awful* had happened to the boy. He wouldn't meet anyone's eye. He kept his face buried against his mother's breast, and he was caked with grime and shaking. Glenna comforted him and whispered in his ear, but her face was badly bruised and she wouldn't look at anyone, either.

Doc would, but he wasn't wearing his sunglasses anymore and people were afraid to look at him. Harry offered sympathetic smiles, but one out of four wasn't good enough to make anyone step forward.

Nat let Bill Spengler in and locked the door behind him.

"That's it," he announced, "anybody else will have to find out from someone here."

The murmur of conversation died, and all eyes turned apprehensively to Doc. He let them wait a bit and gathered his thoughts.

"As you can see, Jerry's back. He almost didn't make it, but he came through. Glenna raised him strong enough and smart enough to survive. And to help his mother—and me—when our lives depended on it."

Jerry raised his head to look at Doc. He'd heard what Doc had said about him. A ghost of a smile crossed the boy's lips, a spark of pride shone from his eyes. Then he turned his face back into his mother's chest. Tears from Glenna's battered eyes washed her son's filthy hair.

Nat approached the table with his collection jar. He put it down in front of Glenna, nodded that it was hers, and stepped back without a word.

Doc continued.

"Jerry and Glenna went through hell this past week, but it hasn't been easy on any of us. Something terrible was going on in this neighborhood. Something that made me suspect that one of you might be . . ."

Doc didn't want to say it aloud.

"We know," Ray said. "We understand."

But only some of them understood. Others still resented. Resented him. Doc could see that.

"I'm sorry I had to pry into your personal lives. Believe me, I didn't want to."

More than a few of them were uneasy even to hear that subject mentioned.

"Is it over?" Red Penwell said. "That's what I want to know. Is . . . it . . . over?"

"Yes."

"We don't have to worry anymore?" Tony Szell asked.

"No."

"Who was it?" Red asked. "Who . . . was after Jerry?"

Doc stared at him for a moment, then let his gaze drift over the others.

"You really want to know? If you do, you can talk among yourselves and figure it out." Doc pushed himself to his feet. His body ached. He was exhausted.

"But if you want my advice, just be glad it's over. Forget about it as fast as you can."

77

That evening, Doc and Harry drank champagne in a VIP lounge at O'Hare. A ground hostess came by and told them their flight would be ready for boarding in fifteen minutes.

The first leg of their travel would be to a major U.S. hub airport. From there they had reservations in several names to other domestic hubs. From these, there were still more reservations, some to domestic destinations, some to foreign cities. To confuse any would-be pursuer further, berths on trains and ships had also been booked.

Doc didn't know if anyone actually intended to come after him, but with six million dollars to his name that had originated with Armando Guzman, he wasn't going to take *any* chances.

Rudd had told him, after complaining how hard he'd been to reach, that the cops and the feds had been more than a little embarrassed about Armando Guzman's escape and disappearance. The DEA's discomfort had been especially acute when they'd been reminded that the only justification for their share of the forfeited funds had been Armando's imprisonment. Neither the CPD nor the DEA wanted Rudd to beat them up in public any further.

Besides the money, the deal was that Doc couldn't speak to the media or reveal the nature or the amount of the settlement to any member of any law-enforcement agency.

Doc agreed to the dollar amount and the conditions.

He arranged to give the Handees a hundred thousand dollars, and for Rudd to sell his house and give those proceeds to them, too. That was the most he could persuade Glenna to accept. She and Jerry were already on their way back to West Virginia, but they weren't going back poor.

Harry actually seemed a little sad that Doc had put the house up for sale; not for herself, but for him. He told her it was all right. It was time to leave The Wedge. His stock there had fallen dramatically.

As for the arrangements she'd made, Harry was sure no one would be able to track them. Except for the ghosts. They would be with them for the long haul, and, in a way, that comforted her.

Harry looked at Doc over the rim of her champagne glass. She liked the way he felt comfortable enough not to wear dark glasses anymore.

"Doc?"

"Yeah?"

"How did they paint the marble to look so much like your real eye?"

He smiled. "I'll tell you on the plane."

His mind was on the envelope that lay on the table between them.

Harry said, "You don't have to do it, you know. You could let matters rest."

"I know," he said.

But he mailed it, anyway.

Then Doc and Harry caught their first plane.

Vince DiGiuseppe was wondering how to establish a spy network in the office of the new

Superintendent—who was no better than the old one—when the envelope landed on his desk. There was no return address, but he immediately suspected who had sent it.

Doc had dropped out of sight the same night Vince had seen him on the street in front of his house. No one had seen Armando or Hector Guzman after that, either. Even though a hell of a lot of people were still looking.

For a while Vince worried that those fucking Colombians had actually gotten his old friend, but when he called Doc's lawyer he was told that Doc was fine. He'd just gone into seclusion.

Seclusion! Cops, even ex-cops, didn't go into fucking *seclusion*. They went into *hiding*.

Then he'd heard a whisper that Doc's claim had been settled, and one of the terms of the deal was that Doc couldn't say a word about it. At that point, Vince thought he'd understood everything.

Now, after opening this fucking envelope, he wasn't so sure. There was an unsigned cover sheet and all it said was: *You decide.*

In back of this there were these two crazy diagrams stapled together. Vince looked at the first one. Boxes with names in them. What was this shit?

BAD DADDY. BAD TOMMY. BAD JACK. On and on down the page. What the hell was this?

He found out when he saw the names on the second page. BAD FRED. *Click.* Frederick Welles. And in a row all their own: BAD ANDY. BAD ARMANDO. BAD HECTOR.

Jesus. Doc had said he knew who'd grabbed all the kids off the street. Was this "Andy" him? Buried with the Guzmans?

And who the hell was MAMA?

There was a street address, written in block letters, at the bottom of the second page. He looked back at the cover page. *You decide.* Vince did. He put the whole works back in the envelope, got up from his desk, and walked down the hall.

The administrative officer saw him coming.

"Sorry, Lieutenant. Can't see the Captain now. He's busy."

"So am I," Vince said.

He dropped the envelope into the department's fancy paper shredder and watched the goddamn thing turn into confetti.